AS FAR AS THE I CAN SEE

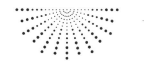

JULIE HEIFETZ

i thank you God
i thank You God for most this amazing
day; for the leaping greenly spirits of trees
and a blue true dream of sky, and for everything
which is natural which is infinite, which is yes.i who have
died am alive again today
E.E. Cummings

CHAPTER ONE

*T*he humid heat nearly took my breath away as I stepped out of the terminal of the airport into the parking lot to look for Victor, Molly's driver. I felt like I'd just returned from a trip to the moon and had finally landed: victorious and exhausted. This trip was different from all the vacations I'd taken to visit Molly. I now knew what paradise would look like. This time, I was not going for a vacation, but to live permanently on 600 acres of banana and coconut trees in the middle of the Yucatan jungle: a place that I had lusted after for so long that my heart was already there.

Victor spotted me and drove up to the front of the terminal. I smiled as he jumped out of the front seat and got out to open the rear door of the car for me.

"Hola, Senora."

"Hola, Victor. "

"Hace calor hoy."

"*Si.*"

The tar melting on the pavement of the parking lot in

the intense afternoon sunlight was a blessing compared to the February ice and cold I'd left behind in St. Louis. I would never have to wear a winter coat again. I sighed and settled into the seat of Molly's blue Lincoln as Victor started the engine, turned up the ranchero music on the radio, and pulled the car out of the parking lot. I tingled with excitement as we started down the shoulderless highway, preparing myself for the long ride past the endless rows of scruffy trees and billboards as we headed further south. Soon, the billboards would disappear and the jungle would stretch out like the sea on both sides of the road. The tension that had built up over the past two months as I extracted myself from a lifetime in St. Louis started to fall away; I could feel my shoulders start to relax.

The wind blew warm whispers through the car window as Victor drove. I'd never have to leave again. I was inspired by the tropical beauty and the stretches of time that were the Mexican commodity. A white stucco house with a mile and a half of isolated beach that bordered the property would be my permanent backyard. I closed my eyes, imagining walking through the front door of my house again: stepping into the entryway, looking up at the high-arched ceiling, down at the marble floors, and around at the curved wall of the living room to the Mexican tile in the kitchen. I was already anticipating the warmth of the architecture and the smell of the voluptuous garden just outside the dining room wall of windows. It was a dream house, one I could never have afforded in the States.

"Agua, Senora?" Victor asked, offering a cold bottle of water over the front seat of the car to me.

"No, gracias."

I would wait until I got home to have a long, quenching glass of water in my own kitchen. Home. How delicious. A place so remote and isolated that only those that had been told about it would know it was there, set back into the jungle a mile and a half down the road. It was a world of blue sky and the smell and sounds of the jungle and the sea.

"La musica es bien," I said to Victor, practicing one of the few phrases I had learned recently in Spanish. He nodded in agreement and turned up the volume. I was uncomfortable being chauffeured and wished Molly could have come to the airport for me herself, but I was grateful that she had sent Victor and spared me the expense of a cab. I was riding in a car on my way to remaking myself into the person I longed to be—free from the expectations of family and friends, far from my midwestern suburban roots. I couldn't wait to see Molly, to settle into a routine as her full time neighbor and employee. I wanted to become more like her over time: able to navigate in Spanish, preparing Mexican recipes that tasted as though I'd grown up cooking them, and reciting the stories of the native Mayans who lived on the ranch and came from little villages in the jungle. I was impatient to get started on the new iteration of my life.

I watched the scruffy trees scurry by as we travelled down the two-lane highway south of the airport, thinking that Molly and I had lived such different lives since we'd been neighbors in our early twenties. She had lived in the jungle for more than ten years, when nothing existed on her property but their house. I admired her for the risks she'd taken and the way she'd adapted to change. Now we'd be counting on each other. She would help me learn about Mexico, how to navigate the challenges of living in a foreign country. I would help by being her friend; she had felt so vulnerable after her husband's heart attack.

The silver bracelet on my wrist jangled as I shifted positions. I remembered making the purchase last minute at Cancun airport before going back to St. Louis on my last visit. I'd never taken it off since that day because it reminded me of the ranch and my visits there, a shiny promise of more to come.

Over the years I'd visited, I'd felt I was slowly becoming part of Molly and Luis Felipe's ranch, part of their story, especially once I'd bought my own house on the property a year and a half before. But owning a vacation home felt like riding on the link between cars of a train, straddling two worlds: the one I'd always known in St. Louis and the one that I longed for in Mexico. It was unbalanced and unsteady. Now, I could begin to take root and make the Yucatan my real home. I'd be like the palm trees that ran up and down the peninsula that had been brought from other islands in the Caribbean and transplanted to this coast by the ranchers. Like the palms that were foreigners, I, too, would flourish and grow in this soil and sun.

I closed my eyes, trying to relax until we got to the ranch, but my stomach churned from anticipation for the entire ride. Suddenly, Victor turned the wheel hard and our car crossed the highway, making a sharp U-turn. Barely visible from the road was the dirt path that led through the jungle. I sat forward in the seat to get a closer look, wondering what changes had been made to the property since my last visit several months before.

The car bumped onto the dirt path, and I felt a familiar thrill as we started the two-mile ride that would take us deeper into the tangle of trees. The stick hut that had once stood at the entrance to the property was gone, as was the gate manned by the flock of children who reached out their hands for beechnut gum or coins as payment for their help closing the gate behind the cars. The hut had been the home of the Mayan caretaker and his family, who'd lived on the property ever since Luis Felipe had bought it. I still saw the fragile house in my mind's eye as we drove down the hand-made road into the jungle, though it had had been cleared away long ago, along with the used tires, empty bottles and cans in the front yard, which the family collected to take home to their village on their yearly visits.

When Luis Felipe started to build a hotel on this property, the first thing he did was take away the stick house from the entrance—he didn't want that to be the first view guests would have of El Torbellino. He had his masons build a new two-story stucco house with indoor plumbing and kitchen for the caretaker's family, intending to move them down another smaller path far from the road, with their new house hidden among the trees. But when the caretaker's wife saw the new building designed for them, she looked up at the cement ceiling and proclaimed, "That will never work." She didn't trust cement, and she was convinced the ceiling would come tumbling down around them. She had lived in the jungle all her life under a thatched roof, not this new-fangled kind. So instead of moving the family into the new house with its fancy indoor kitchen and plumbing, she moved the turkeys into it. It took her two years to move the family.

I loved the caretaker's wife for standing her ground against "progress" until she was ready. I hoped she was satisfied now, but I missed seeing the wild turkeys that used to run around her family's yard and the smell of wood smoke rising from the open fire where she made tortillas for her family every morning. The rickety bamboo gate at the entrance had been replaced by a stucco guard house, which made me sad.

The uniformed guard recognized Molly's car and Victor

and waved us through. We crawled past the entrance into the belly of the ranch down the hand-carved road.

It was more path than road. Pot-holed after the rainy season, it wound its way surreptitiously into the jungle of the Yucatan. The dirt path, barely wide enough for one car at a time, was the one constant that remained over the years that I'd been visiting Molly and Luis Felipe's ranch, except for the sea itself that bordered the front of the property. Passing under the cool, dark, overhanging green leaves of the palms was like entering a chapel. A renewed sense of awe came over me.

I shut my eyes and moved my lips in a silent prayer. *Please God, let Luis Felipe be all right. Let me have done the right thing by making this move so suddenly, by promising to help Molly when I didn't know the first thing about working in a hotel, when I didn't even speak Spanish.* If it didn't work out, I could always go back to the States, though such a move felt unacceptable now that I had made it this far. I'd sold my car and my house and said goodbye to my lifelong friends and my mother. Goodbye to a harried life in middle America.

I rolled down the window of Molly's air-conditioned Lincoln and breathed deeply, inhaling the wet, rich earth outside. The air was still as a catacomb except for the occasional calling of an unseen bird. *Go,* it seemed to say. But I was not going to go. I felt a shudder of excitement and pride for having made the leap.

"A mi casa, por favor," I told Victor when we got to the fork in the path that led one way to Molly's house and the other to mine.

"Si, Señora."

My ochre-colored tile roof rose above the foliage of the

jungle like a mirage. The house had been abandoned and neglected for seven years before I bought it from Luis Felipe, but I'd had it renovated and now it was everything I had hoped it would be and more. Most beautiful of all was that it was mine.

The car pulled up to my front door and Victor waited as I climbed out of the back seat with my overnight suitcase in hand into the welcoming humidity and smell of the sea.

I stood facing the house, admiring the green lush lawn and the voluptuous red blossoms on the hibiscus tree near the door. The French doors off of the living room were wide open and the water in the blue tiled pool in front of the doors sparkled.

"I'm home," I said out loud to myself as I opened the front door and went inside. Every time I arrived I felt a surge of pride, greeted by the soaring arched ceiling and sense of calm and space that the stucco walls created. There were no sharp angles to the design, only round, feminine curves. The ceiling fan whirred softly overhead. The house smelled like it had just been cleaned.

The leaves of the large potted palms by the French doors still had beads of moisture from having been watered, the pink tile floors were spotless, and fresh flowers graced my kitchen table. A full jug of distilled water waited on the kitchen counter.

"Eliseo, Sebastiana?" I called, hoping the caretakers who worked for me might still be there, but no one answered.

I climbed the stairs to my second-floor bedroom, my favorite room in the house. It had rounded walls and floor-to-ceiling windows that opened to the jungle. Sleeping there was like sleeping in a tree house. The white cotton sheets had been ironed, and my new blue striped hand-woven blanket was folded at the foot of the bed. Clean towels hung in the blue tiled bathroom. I couldn't wait to thank Eliseo and Sebastiana for getting the house ready for me when I got here and to tell them that this time, I'd come to stay.

I glanced at my watch. Crap. It was already two-thirty and the employees' party had started two hours ago. Molly was expecting me, now that I'd be working with her in the office of the hotel they'd built and owned. I would be helping with sales, whatever that meant. I threw open my bamboo closet and rifled through my clothes to find some-thing to wear to an anniversary party celebrating the opening of the hotel. Nothing I owned seemed right, but I had to choose something.

The black and brown rayon maxi dress with a V-neck and capped sleeves would do. It wasn't too dressy or too casual or too low-cut, and I liked the way the skirt made my hips seem smaller. I had curves that attracted men and embarrassed my mother and made me feel the push-pull of self-criticism. At just over five-feet tall and a hundred and five pounds, I could look sexy or too heavy, depending on the outfit and the mirror. I often felt critical of the way I looked and had to remind myself that it was what was inside that counted. But I never really believed that.

I pulled off the slacks and t-shirt I'd worn on the plane, slipped the dress over my head and zipped it, found a pair of black patent sandals with kitten heels, some dangly earrings, and examined myself in the mirror. My shoulder-length brown hair curled softly at the ends framing my face. I smiled at myself just for practice, my lower lip slanting down not unpleasantly as it always did when I smiled fully. "It'll do," I said out loud as I hurried down the steps and out through the front door. My palms were beginning to sweat and I had that hungry emptiness in the pit of my stomach that came from nervousness, not from want of food. I was going to meet the employees of El Torbellino, the world-class hotel where I would be working. It was important to make a good first impression.

CHAPTER TWO

*I*took the path that led from my house through a
stand of trees, under overhanging branches and
walked until I came to a clearing. I stepped out into the
sunlight again into a cobblestone courtyard with a circular
driveway that meant I'd arrived. The warm air was still and
serene as peacocks pecked the ground for food and a lone
goose bathed lazily in a reflecting pond. There, beyond the
pond, El Torbellino, the world-class intimate hideaway for
the rich and famous, rose from the jungle like an ancient
Mayan temple.

I had never gotten over the wonder of it, how something
only six years old could look and feel so ancient. Large stone
steps led to a heavily carved wooden door, framed by
roughly-hewn, towering stone columns. It was hard to
remember a time when there had been no hotel, but I had
visited when there was only jungle.

There was no doorman in the small reception area. I
hurried through the small lobby to the grassy courtyard in
the middle of the two-story casitas that made up the collection of 36 guest rooms that lay like a string of pearls in front

of the ocean. All was quiet other than the twittering of a ruby-throated tanager and the gentle rolling of the surf. I hesitated, wondering where to go, until I heard the faint strains of Ranchero music coming from a different area of the hotel grounds. I followed the sounds until I saw blue and red balloons poking their heads through the treetops, which told me I was in the right place.

A throng of people were crowded on the patio and the grass eating and drinking, everyone wearing costumes. Actually, not costumes, but uniforms; each department differentiated by color and style. It looked like a scene from a circus, a profusion of color and music; red skirts with white, short-sleeved peasant blouses and blue cummerbunds; white cotton skirts trimmed in lace with matching white lacy blouses, black pants and white short-sleeved guayabera shirts, rainbow-colored cummerbunds. The swirl of color under the cerulean sky made my head spin. I looked down at my brown and black rayon dress feeling dull as a burlap sack when everyone else was in fine linen.

I waited under the leafy branches of the trees at the edge of the lawn feeling too self-conscious to join them. A strikingly beautiful group of people with blonde hair and Aryan features stood laughing and talking among themselves on the grass, stood apart from the other employees. They were dressed in beachwear, the men in white pants and shirts and an older woman with a mane of shoulder-length curly blonde hair wearing a sarong skirt tied at the waist and a crocheted bikini top, looking as though she'd been born to the sea. Her curly locks played with the breeze as she bent over to get a light for her cigarette from a beautiful, young, blonde, bare-chested man in cropped pants. The group fascinated me and I wondered who they were, but didn't want to stare too long.

If Mike, who'd been my lover for the past eight years, had been with me, I would have felt less insecure. He was tall and elegantly handsome and knowing I was his had made me feel younger and more attractive too. But when the relationship with him fizzled out, I felt like the scullery maid back in the kitchen. It had been more than a year since our separation, and I had to make my way through this crowd without him—I'd been hiding long enough. I had to step out and go find someone to talk to. Where the hell was Molly? I have never been good at big parties, and this one was overwhelming, a lawn full of strangers dressed in colorful costumes speaking Spanish in muted voices. Everyone looked to be a good twenty years younger than I and was beautiful. I felt like an extra surrounded by starlets and leading men.

A waiter in a tux, bow tie, and white shirt carried a steaming tray of food toward a long buffet table covered with white linen and crowded with chaffing dishes. I followed him to the table as though I were hungry, just because it gave me something to do. I focused on the silver dishes and moved down the row of selections: rice and beans, sauce-smothered chicken, rice and beef with vegetables, pork wrapped in banana leaves, and pyramids of roasted ears of corn were all arranged next to a tower of tortillas wrapped in white linen napkins to keep them from drying out. Bowls of guacamole and pico de Gallo and chips sat next to the tower of tortillas.

The waiter turned from the table with an empty chafing dish in hand, smiled at me and motioned to the stack of plates. I picked one up and helped myself to some guacamole, pico de gallo and chips. The waiter nodded, smiled again and hurried away to refill the dish. I nibbled slowly, all the while keeping my eyes out for Molly. The sun beat down on my shoulders and I wished I'd been wearing something cool like the women in their peasant blouses. A tall thin dark-haired woman appeared wearing a high-necked, buttoned-up collar, an ankle-length skirt tiered with ruffles and a flouncy matching hat. She twirled a yellow parasol that matched her outfit, like a character from *Sunday in the Park with George* who had wandered onto the wrong set. She looked as ridiculous to me as I felt, but that gave me no comfort.

The crowd shifted, like a curtain parting, and I spotted Molly and Luis Felipe. They were sitting together on a separate patio shaded by a palapa roof, apart from everyone else. Molly's brown hair was swept up on her head in a chignon, her face wrinkle free in spite of the fact that she'd turned fifty-one on her last birthday. Her expression was aloof and positively regal. I was stunned to see her looking like this when she'd sounded so shaky the last time we'd talked, just two weeks before. I was surprised to see how healthy Luis Felipe looked, considering he had had a heart attack just weeks earlier. At sixty, he was a paunchier version of the swarthy Casanova who had swooped Molly off her feet and changed her life sixteen years ago. I had never seen him in anything but a short-sleeved print shirt and pajama style pants, but this day, he and Molly wore matching cream-colored outfits and silver pendant jewelry. Only a crown and scepter were missing.

Was this the same Molly I'd met thirty-two years ago when we were young neighbors in St. Louis? She had been so quiet and shy, she would barely say a word all evening and wouldn't leave the house without her first husband. When she divorced and moved to New York, she blossomed. A few years later she took a spur-of-the-minute junket to Cancun for a week with a friend from work.

When she got back to New York, she called, and I thought she'd jump right through the phone wire she was so excited. Luis Felipe, a Mexican entrepreneur she'd met at his bar in Cancun, had proposed to her. They'd only known each other for a week, but she wasn't dismissing the possibility. I thought she was out of her mind. Three months later she'd given up everything: condo, job, friends, family, independence, everything except for her cat, and moved to Cancun. I was afraid I might never hear from her again. A year later she called to say that Luis Felipe was having a house built for them on his property in the jungle and they'd be moving soon, so I should come visit when they were settled.

Her look was serene but in charge as she stared out over the heads of her subjects gathered before her. I was floored. How could she, who had seemed agoraphobic when I knew her in St. Louis, look so confident here in this foreign land? I was the one who traveled around the country in tours of my one-person shows, first *Voices and Echoes,* then on to several others, including *Sarah's Song,* which had been nominated for a regional Emmy. I was the poet, the writer who had fallen in love with a musician ten years younger than myself. I was the risk-taker, not Molly. And yet I felt so unsure of myself, so lacking the confidence which she projected from where she sat next to Luis Felipe; it was difficult to think she'd known any other life than the one they had forged together in the Yucatan. She was not just a friend I'd visited, a comfortable expat padding around her kitchen in a pair of shorts and sandals making the morning coffee, she was the fully-evolved Molly, transformed into the role of Patrona, the wife of the owner of a world-class hotel, with a husband who was able to make it all happen. She had held paradise in the palm of her hand until Luis Felipe's heart attack threatened to take it all away from her, which is when she had called and offered me a job working for them at the hotel. I reminded myself that she needed me, that I was there to come to her rescue.

If Molly could reinvent herself so successfully, I intended to do the same. I'd be free of St. Louis, where I'd lived all of my adult life within two miles of the place where I'd been born. I'd be free of the people and places that reminded me of my failed marriage and my failed love affair that had shaken me to my core and destroyed my confidence. I'd be free of the six calls a day from my mother who had criticized me all of my life for not being the kind of daughter who would be her carbon copy. None of that had a hold on me here. At fifty-three, I could start my life over and help Molly at the same time.

A woman in a white lacy uniform moved across the dais to stand behind Luis Felipe. The bosom of her white blouse pressed against the back of his shoulder. She leaned down and whispered in his ear, and he smiled. Molly didn't seem to notice, but the intimacy made me squirm. That's when Molly saw me. She smiled and waved and walked over to give me a hug. I hoped the woman in white noticed.

"Oh, Julie! I've been wondering when you'd get here."

"This is quite the celebration!"

"It's kind of a combined Valentine's Day and anniversary party for the hotel at the same time."

"I didn't realize how many people work here. There must be more than a hundred for a hotel with only thirty six rooms!"

"This is just the morning shift."

That meant a whole army of people I'd have to get to know. Just then, a tanned, barefoot grey-haired man wearing sloppy shorts and an unbuttoned shirt elbowed his way over to Molly and me, with a burning cigarette in hand.

He was over six feet tall, his face lined, his skinny chest wrinkled. He grabbed Molly with his free hand and kissed her exuberantly on each cheek, European-style. His tower of ashes teetered over Molly's shoulder.

"Hola Molly! You look beautiful!" he effused with a French accent. "I'm so glad you are home. Luis Felipe, he really worried me. I was so depressed when he was in the hospital, but now he is looking fine. He needed to be back here. You were too long in Miami."

"Hi Gaspard," Molly said, backing away from his grasp. "We're glad to be home. I want you to meet our friend, Julie." She turned to introduce me. "Julie owns the house closest to the Carillos. She's going to work in the hotel."

"Hello, Julie," he said, barely looking at me before turning back to her. "Now, Molly, when will you and Luis Felipe come for dinner? I can cook for you, now that Luis Felipe gave me my own house."

"We'll have to see when he's feeling up to it, Gaspard."

He frowned, clearly worried. "He's well now, yes?" he asked, looking over the heads of the people standing in front of him to size up Luis Felipe.

"He's better. He just needs to take it easy for a while."

"I will go invite him myself." Flicking his cigarette butt onto the patio, Gaspard padded over to Luis Felipe who was having a conversation with the young woman in white. The elastic neckline of her uniform was pulled down seductively low off her shoulders. I didn't need to meet her to dislike her instantly.

"Gaspard can be really annoying, but Luis Felipe likes having him around."

"And you, what do you think of him?"

"I can't stand him," she scowled. "He's Luis Felipe's friend, not mine. He came for a visit while we were building

16

the hotel and he's never left. He calls himself a painter, and he says he's going to make a painting for each room in exchange for free room and board. Honestly, I don't like his paintings either, but Luis Felipe says his work's getting better."

"It's good he's in staying in his own house, not in yours then."

"Maybe, but he's over at ours all the time anyway. He comes in whenever he feels like it, even when we're not home, and helps himself to the liquor we keep in the cabinet. One day, when I came home from shopping, I found him standing over the bird cage on the patio with his pants unzipped. He was peeing on one of our parrots. He looked up when he saw me and said, "I hate zees damned birds!"

"Oh my God, Molly! What an ass! Who would even think of pissing on someone's pets? How come he's still here?"

"Luis Felipe finds him amusing."

"Amusing?"

The woman with the parasol and the eighteenth-century costume waved to Molly from the other side of the lawn. Molly turned her back away from her.

"Don't look over there. That's Alexis. If she thinks we see her she'll come over. I don't want to have to talk to her now."

"Who is she?"

"She runs the gift shop. She's a talented fashion designer, but Luis Felipe says her books are always wrong, so they're fighting. He won't talk to her anymore, so she talks my ear off instead. You know her husband, Charles. He's the one who took you to see your house for the first time."

"Of course I remember Charles, but I didn't know he had a wife."

"She's the one who made his leopard shorts and shirt to match his marguay."

"His *what?*"

"His marguay, his little leopard. You've never seen him? Charles found him in the jungle when he was just a baby, and he took him home and is raising him as his pet The guests love seeing them together when they walk around the grounds of the hotel."

"A leopard on the hotel grounds?" Just then, a chorus of laughter burst from the group of beautiful people at the back of the patio. Molly looked over at them.

"That's the French Canadian family, the Lemottes."

Lemotte was the one name I knew already. How could I forget? I stared hard at the group again. I'd been wanting to see what they looked like. While my house was being renovated, the younger Lemotte and her boyfriend were living in my it without my permission like squatters. In the middle of the construction, their baby girl was born in my built-in bed in my bedroom. I was horrified when Molly told me. I'd hired Eliseo and Sebastian after that to watch over the house until it was finished and I moved in. But seeing them in person, they didn't look like criminals, as I'd imagined. They were just hippies like the rest of their family, as foreign to me as ancient mariners.

"Those Lemottes, they're the most natural thieves I've ever met." Luis Felipe laughed as he walked over to Molly and me.

"You mean living in my house without asking permission?"

"No, not that. François Lemotte, the older barefoot one with the hair that looks like yellow seaweed, the one in the center? He runs the waterfront. The hotel's supposed to collect half of the money he brings in, but we never see it. We give him the vouchers, he turns them back, but we know he makes more. We can't figure out how he gets away with it. Maybe you'll figure it out when you work here."

"Not if you can't. But why don't you fire them if you can't trust them?"

"They're very clever those people. They moved into a house on the property meant for employees. I didn't know about it for seven years, but when I found out, it was too late to do anything. Squatters have legal rights in Mexico if they're in a place long enough. I'd have to take them to court to get them out, and that would cost me a lot. Anyone who sues has to pay."

I'd never heard of squatters' rights. I only knew that in the US most of the time the one who starts out with the most money is the one who wins in court. I was getting a headache thinking about all of these crazy people that worked and lived on the property: Bertrand, Charles and his wife, the family of Lemottes. I felt so conservative, so normal compared to everyone else around me. What was I doing here? I'd heard enough stories about the strangers for one afternoon.

The woman in the white uniform motioned to Luis Felipe.

"Carla wants us to come to the patio. They're waiting for me. Come, Molly."

"Excuse us for a minute, Julie." Molly followed him to her seat on the dais as Luis Felipe took the microphone.

"Buenos tardes a todos." A hush fell over the crowd as though the Pope himself were addressing them. They had hung around long after they'd finished eating, waiting for this yearly address. I tried to understand what he was saying and every now and then a word or phrase that I knew jumped out at me, but I lost concentration after a while and the words were a river of sound. I could have kicked myself for not having studied Spanish before I left St. Louis, but I was always traveling then from one city to the next for a performance or a consulting job and there wasn't time. Someday, I'd told myself. But now I was standing there feeling like an idiot, comprehending only that the voice was strong and Luis Felipe was in charge.

It hit me like the news that someone I loved had died realizing that I had, in fact, given up a great deal by moving so far from home. I had wanted to escape my midwestern bland existence and dive into adventure. But I'd lived my entire life in the suburbs of St. Louis, where my grandparents and parents had been raised, and I had felt safe and sought-after. I had graduated from the same high-school my father had gone to and my sons after me. I had life-long friendships there and a consulting business I'd worked hard to create, creating my experience as a psychotherapist, teacher, writer and public speaker. Everywhere I went in St. Louis, people knew who I was. I'd had two books published, *Oral History and the Holocaust* and *Too Young to Remember*. I'd performed my own one-woman show and had written and performed musicals with my lover and creative partner. I'd interviewed for the Steven Spielberg Shoah film project. Here in this gathering of employees, none of that mattered, not where I came from, or my parents, or my children, or my past accomplishments. I didn't know the first thing about sales or working in a hotel. I only knew I was Molly's friend, and that would not be enough.

It was a shock when I heard my name come through the

loud speaker. Luis Felipe had switched to English and was looking at me. "Welcome to the Torbellino Family, Julie."

He motioned me to the mic. I wanted to pretend it wasn't me he was talking to, but now the crowd was staring in my direction. They parted to let me through. Oh God, what could I say in baby Spanish that would be meaningful I thought as I walked up to take the microphone. I wanted to sound genuine, to tell them how grateful I was to be coming to work here. I wanted them to know that I wanted to get to know them and that I was a good person. But I couldn't fucking speak Spanish, and I struggled to say anything.

It was the height of irony. I had made my living by giving speeches at corporate meetings, by teaching adults and children, by acting in my own one-woman shows. I knew how much words matter. Luis Felipe and Molly would expect more of me than this stuttering silence, but I was mute, stupid and humorless. I could feel dark circles of sweat under my arms. My rayon skirt clung to my hips and legs like a shroud.

Take your time, Dooliebug, you can have the King of Siam if you want him, my grandfather used to tell me. But I was out of time. Luis Felipe was waiting.

"Gracias," I said into the mic. "Muchas gracias." And then I was silent. With a sideward glance Luis Felipe took back the microphone and handed it to Carla, who turned the volume higher on the Ranchero music that came through the speakers overhead as he and Molly were swallowed up by the worshipping crowd.

CHAPTER THREE

*M*olly found me before I made my get-away from the employees' party.

"Come over this evening for a glass of wine." She didn't mention my poor performance at the mic, which was a relief. A few hours later, we were sitting together in comfortable silence in their outdoor living room under a sparkling sky and a forgiving moon. The cats curled up on the cool tile floor in the middle of the room, their eyes at half-mast. Lulu, the little furry white dog, was stretched out next to my chair, her paws twitching with pleasant dreams as she slept. The slight breeze crossed the open-air room and stirred the leaves of the palms in the corner.

"I think Luis Felipe just came in," she said suddenly. "We ought to go downstairs. He wants to talk with you." He and I had never had a conversation just between the two of us before, and I knew it was about my job. I needed direction. I didn't know shit from shinola about sales.

He was in the outdoor dining room, sitting under its soaring palapa roof at a marble dining table, slowly feeding crackers one by one to Samantha, his Weimaraner who was perched under the table. As soon as he saw me, he pulled out the chair next to him and waved his hand, commanding me to sit.

I felt uncomfortable in the room alone with Luis Felipe. His voice was too quiet, too controlled, and made me feel unsure of myself. Sitting side by side was more awkward than face to face.

"So, you're gonna work for us now. You gonna help with sales," he said, taking a cracker from the package for himself.

"That's what Molly says. I'll help her in the office... write the newsletter, that kind of thing...which is fine with me, but the rest of it...I don't know anything about sales. I've done a lot of things in my career, but I've never worked at a hotel before."

He chuckled. "Our sales manager quit two weeks ago so she can't help, but you're smart. You'll figure everything out like Molly and me. We didn't ever work in hotels either, but we made El Torbellino because we had a dream. We knew what we wanted. We would make a hotel different from other places. Not like Cancun, those big monster buildings all crowded together up and down the tourist zone. They pack in as many tourists as they can. No, El Torbellino is our home. Special guests come to get much attention, people who have traveled many other places. They can afford to go wherever they want, but they come to us because there is a special magic that happens here. You have felt it yourself. It is something spiritual, an aura."

"Yes, that's why I wanted to live here, to work with you."

He turned in his chair and looked at me as though seeing me through a magnifying glass, every pore, every flaw revealed. "So tell me. What words do you think of when you think El Torbellino?"

"Intimate...earthy...remote."

"These are good. You will use these in sales. You know our style. You know the food we love. You know the restaurant. It is the heart of the hotel. You have been there as a guest. It is theater. The food, lighting, music, the service of the waiters, they all play a part."

I was beginning to feel impatient. I knew El Torbellino. I wanted to know what actually I was going to do, what would be required of me.

"Are there some procedures I should follow when I start work? A job description for Sales?" He scowled, annoyed by my directness.

"We are not so corporate. This is not the USA. We make something different here. We call it hand-made hospitality," he said proudly.

"Yes, I know. I understand," I pressed. "But...I don't even speak Spanish."

He smiled, amused by my frustration. "The heads of the departments speak English. Spanish won't be your problem." He took a cracker out of the package and passed it under the table to Samantha.

"If Spanish won't be a problem, what will be?"

He smiled. "You're a woman."

I was stunned. This was 1998. I was used to working with men as a consultant for Monsanto, Barnes Hospital and Einstein Healthcare Network. I was about to say just that when one of the masons who worked for him came into the room and Luis Felipe stood up.

"Excuse me," he muttered. "This is my head mason. He needs to talk with me." With that, he grabbed his walking stick and followed his workman outside, with Samantha trailing close behind.

I looked around the room while I waited, remembering with longing the last time I was a guest at a party at their house. The party started at three o'clock on the patio for cocktails and appetizers and a swim in the ocean. By eight, we moved into the dining room, gathering under the soaring palapa roof around the massive mahogany and marble table; French, Germans, Canadians, Americans, plus Luis Felipe and Molly speaking multiple languages. Bougainvillea vines grew through the glass skylight and romantic Spanish guitar music played softly through the speakers on the wall. Molly effortlessly served a feast, which included two fish dishes, one of meat, plus two kinds of vegetables, rice, and Luis Felipe's favorite chocolate cake for dessert. Everyone stayed until after midnight and left tipsy from the wine and conversation. I thought that this is the way to live.

But so much had changed since that night. The room looked disheveled now, a ghost of what it once had been. Gaspard's crude paintings were propped up against the stucco walls, left to dry between stacks of boxes that had never been opened. Fabric samples lay in piles on two of the chairs. The once gracious dining room that had buzzed with life had turned into a storage room since Luis Felipe's heart attack. Molly was too stressed and worried to put it right again.

I sat for a long time waiting for him before I realized my meeting with Luis Felipe hadn't been interrupted, it was over. I'd learned nothing about my job from our talk. I'd have to wait for Molly to tell me more. I was tired anyway. It had been a long, emotional day for me, starting with the flight from St. Louis, then the employees' party, and the meeting with Luis Felipe. It was late, and I had to get up early for my first day of work. I set down my wine glass and called upstairs.

"Molly I'm leaving. I'll see you in the morning at nine."

She came to the top of the stairs in her nightgown with a book in her hand. "Do you need help getting home?"

"No, I'll be fine. Can I borrow a flashlight?"

"Sure. There's one on the kitchen counter."

"Good. Can you give me directions to your office? I've never been there."

"It's just on the other side of the employee parking lot. It's a low white stucco building."

"OK, see you tomorrow."

I switched on the flashlight. Outside, the sense of failure I'd experienced at the party and the dissatisfaction with my conversation with Luis Felipe felt insignificant compared to the pleasure I found listening to sounds around me. Nature made up for all that had gone wrong. The night was alive with the din of frogs. High-pitched chirping, barking, and grunting like grumpy old men, they kept up their choral concert as I made my way home. So many species making music together. Stars twinkled overhead as I walked slowly down the path. There was so much to learn, so much to appreciate living here. Tomorrow would come soon enough, and Molly would show me what to do.

When I got home and into bed, my mind was still racing. Even the perfume of Plumeria blossoms from the tree just outside my window didn't help me relax. It would be hours before dawn. In the moonlight flooding my room, I thought how blessed I was to have my own dream house, remembering the years it had taken to get there.

One spring years ago, while I was still married, my husband and sons and I came to visit Molly and Luis Felipe.

It was a perfect week-long vacation. The boys loved everything about the trip; everything seemed wild and exotic: the jungle, the deserted beach, exploring little nearby villages, the parasailing. At the end of the week, Luis Felipe offered to build a little bungalow on the beach for us. My husband wouldn't even consider it. He made the big bucks, I didn't. So we said no to the bungalow, but it was an offer I never forgot.

After our divorce, I vowed to become both my husband and me. I'd be practical and earn enough money to support myself, but I wouldn't give up my dreams to do it. My first year on my own I wouldn't spend money on a new pair of shoes for myself. I worried I'd turn out to be a bag lady, but little by little I relaxed as my consulting work and success as a writer/performer grew, along with my savings. Visiting Molly became my yearly retreat, and every year I'd talk with Molly about my dream of owning a vacation house on their property, a place where I could eventually retire when I could afford to stop work.

At a dinner party at Molly's house one night after the hotel had been built, somebody mentioned an abandoned house on the property that was for sale.

"Really? I want to go see it," I said eagerly to Luis Felipe.

"The house is a mess."

"That's OK, I want to see it anyway."

I was already dreaming about owning it, sight unseen; my own home in the jungle down the dirt path from Molly's, with the sea at my doorstep. It would be a place to hold writing workshops and have romantic getaways with my lover. It would be my sanctuary, my bungalow on the beach that no man would stop me from buying. Owning it would be a victory.

Luis Felipe's friend Charles took me to see the house the next day. It was ten minutes from Molly.

"Initially, the house wasn't built as a house. It was a place to store the generator for the windmill that brought electricity to the ranch."

"That was when Molly and Luis Felipe first lived here."

"Yeah, I wasn't here then, but I hear that didn't last long. A storm blew the blades into the jungle and Luis Felipe put in electricity, and this guy came along who wanted to buy a house on the ranch, so Luis Felipe had his masons turn the storage place into a house."

I was already intrigued hearing the history of the place, when a towering, three story, stucco, free-form structure rose up from the tangle of weeds in front of us like a mirage against the clear blue sky; two large rectangles joined together in a geometric design under an orange ceramic tile roof. It took my breath away; this was no bungalow.

But as we got closer, the ravages of time and neglect became obvious. Black streaks ran like rivers of tears down one wall, the stucco was dark and faded, the small swimming pool in front was cracked, with filthy rain water in the bottom heaped with the dead carcasses of hundreds of mud crabs from the jungle. I cringed remembering. Some had been still alive, crawling with a last gasp of energy over the backs of others to escape from their cement grave.

"This is the garage," Charles said as we walked to the side of the house. "The guy who owned the place left all these recreational vehicles and never came back for them. That was seven years ago. Look, there's an old beat-up Volkswagen and a sunfish, all kinds of stuff. It's all rusted out and worthless now."

"Why did that guy just leave everything here?"

"I don't know. He was kind of a weird guy. You'll have to ask Luis Felipe."

He opened the wooden front door. Inside, the house reeked. Hardened animal scat lay in the middle of the entryway on the pink marble floors. A winding marble staircase led to the second and third floors.

"This is disgusting," I said to Charles, stepping around the dried shit, holding my breath.

The kitchen was a wreck, and so was the dining room, with rotting wood window frames, but I was seeing past all of that. With a lot of work and enough money, the house could be spectacular.

"There are three bedrooms upstairs," Charles said.

"That's OK, I've seen enough."

That night at dinner, I asked Luis Felipe how much he thought, ballpark, it would cost to buy and renovate the place.

"A lot less than in the States," he said. "You don't have to worry about heating or air-conditioning or water. I own the land, and since there are no sidewalks, there are no taxes."

In the morning, Luis Felipe came down to breakfast with a scrap of paper in his hand. During the night he'd made free-hand sketches of three different designs for renovations.

"Which one you like?" he asked

I pointed to the one with the master bedroom on the second level, the one w wall of windows.

"That one, I think we can do it for a hundred seventy thousand dollars American."

"A hundred seventy thousand." Reality hit me in the stomach like a sudden virus. It would take most of my savings to come up with that amount of money. I already had a mortgage on a house in the suburbs of St. Louis that I was going to keep. Thinking about buying a vacation house made me feel selfish and privileged and spoiled.

"I know it would be beautiful." Reluctantly, I handed back the sketches. "Let me think about it." But I was stalling. The house and the opportunities it offered me and my children and friends had me by the back of the neck and wouldn't let go. I'd dreamt of owning it for so long.

At breakfast with Molly the next day, I could hardly sit still until Luis Felipe joined us. "I'm going to do it," I announced. "I'm going to be your new neighbor."

"Good, if you think you can afford it," he said, looking at me over his mug of coffee.

"Oh, I can't afford it," I laughed. "But I'm going to do it anyway."

"There is one more thing, one little problem maybe for you. You need a Mexican partner. Only Mexicans are allowed to own property so close to the beach," Luis Felipe said, setting down his cup on the rainbow-colored woven placemat.

"A partner?"

"Yes. It's Mexican law. You could use a Mexican bank, or you could have me be your partner. I would own the land, and you would own the house. That's how it goes."

"I need some time to think that over."

"Of course."

When I got back to St. Louis, I called the lawyer who had handled my divorce. He told me he'd talk with his partner who knew more about international laws and real estate than he did and he'd look into it for me. A week later, his partner called and said Luis Felipe was right. To buy a house in a restricted zone in Mexico, any land next to a beach or on either of the borders, I needed a Mexican partner.

"How risky an investment do you think this would be for me?"

"It all depends if the guy who's your partner turns out to be a good guy. If he isn't, you could lose everything."

"I'm not worried about Luis Felipe," I assured him. "He's a good guy. He and his wife have been my friends for years."

"Well, good luck then. I'd like to have a beach property in Mexico myself. Let me know if there's anything else I can do for you."

He didn't say go ahead and buy it, which was what I wanted to hear, even though I knew he never would. But the longer I waffled, the more certain I became that passing up the house was more of a risk than it would be to lose the money. Besides, how much of a risk was that? I wanted to be the kind of woman who was willing to take one. I'd worked to earn that right.

I called Molly to tell her I wanted Luis Felipe to be my partner.

"That's great. I'll tell him. He said it'll be ready in five months."

"Only five months?"

"Give him nine," Molly laughed. "He's always too optimistic."

I came back once a few months later to see how the construction was going. The mason measured my height to construct the countertop as I stood in the middle of what would eventually be the kitchen. Molly and I shopped for furniture and bedding in the old section of Cancun City, which was a confusing tangle of buildings without addresses on unnamed streets. I would never have found any store without Molly. By the time we got back to the ranch, having bought a couch and a chaise lounge and a small piece of sculpture, I was elated and so excited thinking about the move that I could hardly sleep for the entire ten months it took for the house to be built.

By then I had hired Eliseo and Sebastiana to work for me. When I walked into the finished renovation, the house was every inch the dream I'd imagined and more. Molly had left a lovely large ceramic bowl on the kitchen counter with a note.

"Bienvenido a Casa Julie." My eyes filled with tears. I was home.

A glimmer of light came in through the window and the pink polished marble floor glowed brighter. While I'd been in bed, remembering my history with my house, night had given way to day. I threw the covers off the bed and got up to get dressed. I had to meet Molly at nine at her office, and I didn't know the way.

CHAPTER FOUR

I heard the splash of water hitting the plants under my window, a sign that Eliseo was there already watering, the two of us up at sunrise. He liked to start work early so we'd have time for his English lesson, a routine we'd started almost as soon as I hired him. We both looked forward to the lessons and the easy camaraderie between us as we talked, filling in with pantomime to communicate. He was desperate to learn English, and I enjoyed teaching him just as much. He lapped up vocabulary and grammar like a thirsty cat, never fully sated. He was a dream of a student, quick and bright, and sort of flirty, without crossing the line of what was appropriate between us. He was handsome, in his early twenties, the age of my oldest son, although Eliseo was already a father three times over and my son a newlywed immersed in establishing his career. In spite of the age difference between us, there was a physical attraction that made me wonder what might have happened between us if I weren't careful. I wasn't looking forward to telling him this morning that I wouldn't be able to teach him as often now that I was going to work.

"Hola, Eliseo," I waved from the window.

"Good morning, Señora Julie," he called softly up to me.

"You're earlier today," I said. It was just after six.

."I know you are here. I see light." He pointed up to my bedroom window. "Is OK?"

"It's fine."

He smiled. His perfect, white row of teeth shined like mother-of-pearl shells against his golden brown skin. No one smiles like Eliseo. He was barefoot and bare chested, wearing red swim trunks.

He was alone in the mornings when he worked outside, but later in the day Sebastiana, his wife, would come to clean the house. I was amazed when I found out she was the mother of school-aged children; she was so small and slight she looked like a child herself. They had come to work for me as a package deal, splitting one salary between them. Molly said I should only offer the going rate of four dollars a day. If I paid more I'd piss off the two other home-owners. It was an outrageously cheap price, so I gave them five a day, in spite of Molly's warnings. Sebastiana spoke only Nahuatl, the Mayan language of her people, and had no interest in trying to learn English or Spanish. Eliseo said she didn't have enough confidence to try. Neither of them had gone past third grade in Valladolid, where they came from. I wished I could have talked with her, but we made do as best we could.

I walked downstairs, made myself a cup of coffee, and took it outside to the garden to talk with him.

"My house looked beautiful when I came home yesterday, thanks to you and Sebastiana."

Eliseo turned off the garden hose and picked up a long-handled net to clean the pool.

"No cangrejos esta mañana," he said jokingly. No crabs

like the ones I'd found stacked on the bottom of the empty pool the first time I'd laid eyes on the house. With Eliseo to manage it, every day the water was clean and clear. He whistled as he made his way around the pool dragging the net to make sure no debris was left.

"Eliseo?" I waited for him to stop cleaning and look at me. "I'm sorry. No lesson today," I said apologetically.

"No leccion hoy?" The smile disappeared behind a cloud of disappointment.

"No. I am going to work today."

"To work?" He looked confused, although he knew the word.

"Yes. I'm going to work at the hotel." I thought he'd be pleased to know.

"No," he said emphatically shaking his head. "No hotel."

Now I was the one who was confused. Maybe he meant he wanted me to stay at home to have time to teach, to be the woman of leisure he'd come to expect. But something else was troubling him.

He frowned. "Muchas problemas en el hotel."

I remembered that long before Luis Felipe had gotten sick, Molly had mentioned that the employees didn't get along, that somebody was always complaining to Luis Felipe about someone else. I dismissed it all as petty jealousies, but whatever the employees' problems were at Torbellino, it would be different for me.

"It will be OK. Luis Felipe is my friend."

"No," he shook his head sadly. "Señor Luis Felipe no es tu amigo. *Señora Molly* es tu amiga," he said emphatically.

"Qué?" Luis Felipe wasn't my friend, only Molly was? What did he mean by that? He launched into an explanation, forgetting to speak slowly, but I caught the gist of it,

something about the man who owned my house before me...
Luis Felipe had cut off the water to the house...the guards
wouldn't let him back onto the property. The part I understood was unsettling to hear, but surely there had to be some
explanation that Eliseo wasn't aware of, or maybe he was
just repeating a rumor he had heard and there was no truth
to the story.

"Thanks, but don't worry. I'll be fine," I said, trying to
reassure him. At the same time the image came back to me
of the first time I saw my abandoned house and all the
expensive recreational equipment the owner had left in the
garage, and how creepy I thought that was at the time. Did
something happen to make him leave so abruptly? Did Luis
Felipe prevent him from coming back to his own house? My
skin prickled as though I'd stepped into a deep shadow and
was instantly cold, but the feeling only lasted long enough
for me to remind myself that I knew Luis Felipe and Molly
better than Eliseo did.

He nodded and turned back to cleaning the pool. I
thought he might have been mad at me, but maybe he was
just worried. I was nervous enough about starting my first
day on the job, and the conversation with Eliseo hadn't
helped. It was eight-thirty. I was supposed to meet Molly at
nine. "It's down the limestone path to the left of the circular
drive at the entryway. When you get to the employee
parking lot you'll see two adobe buildings. My office is one
of those." It sounded so simple the night before when Molly
gave me directions, but I'm the kind of person who could
turn around three times outside her own house and get lost,
even in St. Louis where I'd lived all of my fifty three years
before, so I gave myself half an hour to find it even though
the office wasn't more than a fifteen-minute walk from my
house. I wanted to be sure to be there on time.

"Hasta mañana, Eliseo," I called, pulling the front door closed behind me.

"Sí, Señora."

I walked down the path where the masons had long been at work. There was no harsh rat-a-tat tat of machinery, no heavy equipment. The sounds they made were gentle and pleasing. The buildings grew quickly by hand, brick by brick, from hardened sand that the masons laid squarely one on top of another, the excess smoothed away by their trowels. The sound of slap, scrape was as rhythmic and as soothing as the ticking of a grandfather clock.

"Buenos dias, Señora," one of the masons called cheerily as he stopped in mid-motion over his wheelbarrow, poised to scoop up more cement. I recognized the man's face, but I wished I knew his name. He'd worked for Luis Felipe for so many years he didn't need an architect's blueprint, he just created the drawing Luis Felipe made with his walking stick in the sand. That's how well he knew his style.

I waved back and stopped to watch the crew. I was proud to be going to work for Luis Felipe too.

A romantic ballad, "Te Lo Pido Por Favor," was playing on the mason's radio. "Wherever you are today, forever I want to be with you." I felt a sharp sudden pain in my stomach like I'd been drop kicked, which was the way I felt whenever I heard a love song after Mike left me, even though that was nine months ago. I hurried past the construction site. Mike was history, and I was half-way to my future; a new job, a new country, a new me.

The air was moist and fresh; the dew sparkling. Eventually, the path narrowed and dipped into a grove of trees where the air was cool in their shade. This was the way to the hotel, through a buffer zone between the residential section of the ranch and El Torbellino; two completely separate worlds. I had walked this way before with Molly when I was her guest at the restaurant, and I'd passed through the grove the day of the anniversary party, but I hadn't had time to stop. I looked around expectantly. Wouldn't it be amazing to find a ceiba tree growing there this day? I'd never seen one, and it would be a good omen just to happen on one. The ancient Mayan myth said the Earth began where a giant ceiba tree grew; its roots reach down into the underworld where demons dwell. The trunk, where we humans live, holds up the thirteen layers of heaven, where the gods rule. But there was no ceiba tree anywhere in the grove that I could see, only scrubby young trees and low growing palms.

After walking for five more minutes, the trees came to an abrupt end, and I stepped out of the shade onto a circular cobblestone driveway. El Torbellino rose up in the clearing like an ancient Mayan temple that had withstood the ravages of time and survived unchanged and filled me with awe. Chipped statues of the deities Chaac and Huracan were crouched next to the towering stone pillars that seemed to have been carved centuries ago. I imagined ancient worshippers climbing the massive stone steps to the heavily carved wooden door at the top of the staircase bringing offerings to the gods.

On the other side of the driveway, Manuel, the head gardener, was watering a new bed of flowers. I recognized Manuel from the work he'd done at my house, turning my tangle of weeds and overgrowth into a lush garden. He cared for the flowers and plants of the hotel as though they were his children, while his actual wife and nine kids lived back on the farm he owned in Veracruz. Every payday he sent home a portion of the twenty-eight dollars he earned for a week's work. I admired him enormously, not only for his skill, but for his devotion and felt terrible that he was paid so little in return. Luis Felipe said that he was paid the going rate and Manuel was grateful for the work. That was the way things were here.

"Hola, Manuel," I called.

"Buenos dias, Señora." He smiled, took off his straw hat, and placed it over his heart. His characteristic gesture was so deferential it embarrassed me. As much as Manuel knew about gardening, that's how little I knew about working at a hotel. I could only hope one day I'd be as valuable an employee as Manuel was.

"La oficina de Molly?" I asked.

"Ve por este camino, Señora." He pointed to a narrow stone path at the far end of the drive that led through a hedge of palms.

"Gracias, Manuel."

I mentally made a list of the questions I needed to ask Molly. What went into the newsletter? How often did they send it? What else would I be doing in the office? And tell me please, what is the difference between marketing, reservations and sales? And what about communication? How did the hotel function without telephone land lines? When Molly called and I lived in St. Louis, the phone would go dead because it was too windy or a storm would come up on the ranch, and it would take days to get service again. Forget about letters; they'd take two or three weeks to get to the States, if they ever did. Even FedEx delivery was unreliable. So how did they run a business without modern technology?

I followed the broad smooth stones of the narrow, winding path through the hedge where it ended at a large barren dirt parking area. A dilapidated van was unloading a group of workmen and waiters who were just arriving for their shift. Beyond the lot were several small, nondescript one-story stucco buildings clustered together.

"L'oficina de Señora Molly?" I asked the men.

"No se," they shook their heads apologetically, and walked off in the direction of the main courtyard of the hotel.

Just then, a pleasant voice behind me offered, "I can show you. It's this way, Ma'am."

CHAPTER FIVE

he voice offering to show me the way belonged to a man wearing a weathered Stetson hat, khaki pants, and shirt like an African safari guide. He spoke English without the trace of an accent. I had noticed the hat at the party the night before, but I hadn't seen the face until he spoke to me this day. He was middle-aged and nice-looking. The acne scars on his face added to his rugged appeal; he was a guy's guy with a devilish grin and a slight paunch.

"I'm Jimmy," he said, reaching up to tip his hat without actually removing it. "I'm in charge of maintenance here. But really, I'm Luis Felipe's friend. We've known each other from way back. Come with me. I'll show you Molly's office."

"Thanks, I'm Julie, by the way"

"I remember. Luis Felipe introduced you last night."

"Right. That was some party," I felt the color rise in my cheeks remembering how I'd screwed up the chance to make a good impression with the staff. "I have an appointment with Molly at nine."

He led the way.

"That's it," he said when we got to the front door of one

of the buildings. It was so plain I was surprised that it was hers. It had none of the architectural detail of the guests' casitas.

"Thanks for your help," I said, turning the handle. But the door was locked.

"Here, I've got the key. I can let you in. You don't want to wait out in the sun for Molly, it's a beast out here already this morning. That's the advantage of being in charge of maintenance. I've got the master."

He took a bandana out of his back pocket to wipe the sweat off his face before pulling out a ring of keys and unlocking the door.

"After you," he said with a gentlemanly sweep of his hand.

A blast of frigid air from an air-conditioner turned up high enough to freeze helium took my breath away as soon as I stepped into the room. I hate air-conditioning, even in the middle of St. Louis summers, which was why I was excited about moving to a climate so hot I could sweat in the middle of February.

"It's freezing in here, Jimmy. Even my goosebumps have goosebumps. Can you do something about the temperature?"

"I'm afraid I can't touch the thermostat. The boss wants it like this. He's a nut about air-conditioning, says it kills the germs if you keep it really cold." I wondered how Molly felt about that since she was the one who worked there.

The room was barren and was furnished with one chair; a small, scratched-up round wood table; a low ceiling; and bare white walls. Molly was the owner's wife and the one who had designed all of the guest rooms, but there was no care given here to details.

"This is the reception area where guests come to pay

when they check out. It doesn't look like much right now, but my guys haven't finished moving everything in yet. Luis Felipe wanted some changes made for you. I'll show you where you'll work." Through the door was another office with the usual desk, chair, and bookshelf, plus a large dented metal file cabinet, and a couch built into the wall. Molly and her first husband had a couch just like that in their apartment in St. Louis.

"The masons just finished fixing this place up. My guys will bring Sylvie's files over for you. I guess you know she was the sales manager before you got here? We'll get you a different table and chairs too from Luis Felipe's factory."

I was only half-listening. I was wondering about the black pair of men's loafers and a belt that were lying on the top of the desk and some papers. Some man had recently been working there and I wondered who he was.

"Mind if I have a seat?" Jimmy asked, bending to put his hat down on the couch.

"No, that's fine until Molly gets here." I didn't know whether to sit behind the desk or next to him on the couch, and it felt important. This wasn't a social visit, it was my first meeting with a colleague in my office. He was relaxed and friendly and I didn't want to be rude, so I sat down next to him with his hat between us. I had twenty minutes to kill until Molly showed up and I might as well spend it getting to know someone who worked there.

"Might be a while before she comes." He draped his arm across the back of the couch, slouching into the cushion comfortably.

"Why is that?" I asked.

"Just sayin.' I've been around them both for a long time, Luis Felipe and Molly. Since before I started working here, and I can tell you they don't live by the clock those two. They set their own hours."

"I've known them a long time too. Molly and I have been friends for thirty-four years. How did you meet them?"

"Me and the wife used to own a little restaurant down the road, and they used to eat there all the time. Luis Felipe says I make the best chilaquiles he's ever tasted. We did everything ourselves, you know. No short cuts."

"You're a chef? That's a pretty big leap from being a chef to being in charge of maintenance."

"Yeah. We had a kid after a couple of years and it got too much for Maria, having a restaurant and taking care of a kid too. We closed the place and I had to find other things to do. I started working different jobs for different bosses. I'd see Luis Felipe around town, and I'd invite him over for dinner. Sometimes on a Sunday he'd show up, just him, not Molly. He'd eat with us, whatever we were having. He ate meat back then, especially pork. That was his favorite, a big, smoked pork roast."

"He doesn't eat meat or pork at all anymore."

"He's changed a lot since those days. He used to stay at our house late after dinner, like, till two in the morning, drinking and smoking cigars with me out front, while Maria and Consuela were in the bedroom sleeping."

"And Molly?"

"Nope, she wasn't with him. Guess she didn't worry about him much. That's the way Maria is with me. I might go on a bender for a few days, or at least I used to back in the day, but she knew I'd always come home to her."

"She must be a very tolerant woman." I didn't say, "*And a doormat*," but that's what I was thinking.

"A smart woman," he said with a grin. "She knows better than to try to pin me down. Me and Luis Felipe, we're a lot alike that way. Anyway, when he started building the hotel I helped him out here and there, doing different stuff. One day, he came to the house and asked if I'd go to work for him full-time, be in charge of maintenance here at Torbellino."

"Had you done that kind of work before?"

"Never. Didn't know the first thing about it: hot water heaters, plumbing, and painting, all the stuff that needs doin' here. But I figured I owed Luis Felipe...for a couple of favors...And that's what he said he needed, so here I am."

I wondered what kind of favors, but I didn't ask. I didn't want to know. I glanced at my watch. Five minutes to nine.

"Our reasons for being here are the same for being here. Molly said they needed me, so here I am. I'm taking over Sylvie's job in the sales department. Did you know Sylvie?"

"Yeah. Sylvie, sure, I knew her. We started together when the hotel first opened. She was good at first, but she changed here lately. I think it was the young cat she was married to. More than once she showed up to work with a black eye. She started missing a lot of days and then she just quit comin' at all. She still has Molly's old van."

"That's so strange."

"I'm supposed to get it back from her next week. Probably Luis Felipe will let you use it next."

"That would be great." I said, surprised by the idea. I hadn't thought about getting a car, and I'd need one for doing errands and getting time away from the property on my days off.

"Molly has a nice new Lincoln now. None of us here can use her old van. She brought it from the States when she moved to Mexico and it's against the law for any Mexican to drive an American-made vehicle."

"Really? That's lucky for me."

45

"Yeah. I've had my share of luck in my life too. You gotta grab hold of it when it comes your way."

"I know. I feel lucky just living here, having a job at the hotel."

"Let me tell you, it wasn't always like this, rubbin' two sticks together to make a living. I used to make more money on the streets than Luis Felipe does now. I wore the fancy suits, had a gold Rolex watch, drove a Cadillac. There was a picture of me in the Dallas paper standing with these two gorgeous gals in front of this expensive restaurant," he shrugged. "But that was a long time ago. I was just a young punk then."

I wished he hadn't told me that. I liked bad boys when I was in grade school, the kind who got into trouble and had their desks in the principal's office, but I'd steered clear of any guy who spelled trouble when I got older. Maybe Jimmy went to jail for dealing drugs, maybe for something worse. Luis Felipe hired him to work at Torbellino anyway. Whatever he'd been in his past, he seemed to have turned his life around. I'd learned enough about him in our time together to know I'd be friendly to him because we worked together, but I'd be careful.

He went on, telling me about his move from Cuba to the US as a kid, but I was getting antsy. I checked my watch. It was almost nine-thirty. Where the hell was Molly? Weren't we supposed to meet at the office?

I stood up and interrupted Jimmy's story. "I think I'll go to Molly's house to see if she's waiting for me there," I said, getting up from the couch.

"Okay, ma'am," He stood and put on his hat, adjusting the brim at an angle over one eye. "But if you need anything, remember, I'm your guy. These other executives, the heads of the departments, well, let's just say they're going to tell you a bunch of crap. I'll tell it to you straight, whatever you want to know. My office is right behind the guest rooms, down the path from the kitchen. If you don't find me there, I'm somewhere on the property. Ask one of the gardeners, they'll know where I am."

"I appreciate that."

It was a relief to get out of the air-conditioning and back into the heat and humidity. I started back down the path on my way to Molly's house, but when I got to the parking area, Molly's blue Lincoln Continental pulled up suddenly and jerked to a stop. The door flew open and she jumped out. Her shirt was half-untucked, her pants were wrinkled, her hair was frizzy and uncombed. The look in her eyes was wild, like a beast from the jungle was closing in on her. With one hand she held onto the roof of the car to steady her as she stood.

"What's wrong?!"

"It's Luis Felipe. He's had another heart attack," she said, her lips quivering.

I felt as though my legs went numb. "A heart attack? No!" How could this have happened so soon? He'd only been home from the Heart Institute for ten days and he seemed to be doing so well. And I had just gotten there.

"It happened this morning, about an hour ago. I only have a minute."

"You're going back to Miami?" I said in a voice an octave higher than my own. I could hardly believe what she was saying. They were leaving and I'd just gotten there. I felt like I was on a tilt-a-whirl, going too fast.

"I knew we came back home too soon, but he wouldn't listen."

I felt her panic course through my body. I didn't know anything about working in sales, but I knew how to be a reassuring presence, to be her friend. That was in my bones.

"What can I do for you while you're gone?" I touched her lightly on her shoulder.

"Come see about the dogs when you can. Victor will feed them and let them out, but they're used to having me around."

"Of course. What else?"

"Luis Felipe's worried about the hotel. He says you're to be our eyes and ears. Keep an eye on Carla. She always causes trouble."

Carla. How could I forget the woman in white who hung all over Luis Felipe at the party?

"I'll do my best."

She stood up straight and let go of the roof of the car, patting her hair into place, seeming more together. "Please tell the staff we've gone back to Miami. Maria Elena, Luis Felipe's personal secretary, has his cell phone number, and that's it. We don't want anyone else calling. If any of the managers at the hotel needs to tell us something, they're to tell you the information and you can pass it on to us when I call you. You're the Coordinator while we're away."

"All right, the Coordinator...but what about my sales job?" I was too dumbfounded to feel. It was as though she were speaking in tongues.

"You'll be sales manager, taking Sylvie's place. They're bringing her files to your office so you can look through them to see what she did."

"Sales *manager*?" I could feel the color drain from my face. "How can I be a manager, Molly? I don't know the first thing about sales. And I just got here. "

"It's just a title. There's no one else in the department."

"But you were going to show me..."

"I know. There are brochures in the cabinet files that are coming to your office, and copies of magazine articles. Start by putting them together to make PR packets...and get one of the anfitrionas to organize the guest list and type it up for you."

"Anfitrionas?"

"The women in the guest services department. Carla's their boss. They have all the names of every guest who's been here since the hotel's been opened in these guest books, but they've never been alphabetized."

"OK, PR packets and guest list." At least she was telling me something specific I knew how to do.

"Oh, and one more thing. Luis Felipe would like you in the restaurant during dinner hours. He says you'll do well with the guests. We have this new manager, William, who's supposed to be in charge of the restaurant and the hotel, but he's useless."

"A manager? I've never met him."

"We gave him a three-month contract, and he kept trying to see Luis Felipe about extending it, but we're not going to. Only, Luis Felipe didn't feel up to dealing with him yet so he's still here."

"Coordinator, sales manager, go to the restaurant at dinner..." My voice came now from a hollow place inside me.

"You'll be fine."

I said nothing more. I was too busy trying to remember everything she was saying to argue; my breath was trying to catch up to my mind.

"I'm so worried about Luis Felipe." Her lip was trembling, and her eyes welled with tears. She needed reassuring more than I did.

"The doctors in Miami helped him before. I'm sure they can help him now. It's going to be OK, Molly"

"I hope you're right. I'll call you from Miami, but I have to go now." She opened the car door. "You know, Torbellino is our baby."

I did know how much they'd been through to make the hotel happen in the first place. It had been like a giant wind swept through their dreams. Right after they dug the foundation, the Mexican economy crashed and Luis Felipe's financial partners disappeared. Construction came to a standstill. Molly confessed then to me how worried she was about her husband; he was so depressed he was sick, gaining weight, and popping antacids to settle his stomach as he traveled from country to country for two years to try to find investors. He was beginning to feel desperate and had almost run out of options. But suddenly, without explanation as to where the money came from, the hotel was built and up and running, getting rave reviews from clients and press alike, but the process of getting there had changed him. He was more emotionally removed, more consumed by meetings. Fittingly, he had named the hotel El Torbellino, "the whirlwind". And now this. I wasn't surprised he'd had a heart attack. I was surprised it had taken this long. He'd paid a price for his success, and I hoped it didn't kill him or me for that matter, left to fend for myself in its wake.

Molly climbed into the driver's seat of her Lincoln, slammed the door shut, and started the engine. I raised my hand to shield my eyes from the sun and watched as she turned the car around and headed down the path and through the trees, leaving me in the empty employees' parking lot, alone in the blinding light.

CHAPTER SIX

I came to Torbellino imagining I'd have time after work to write; to find the freedom in words to explore the beauty and newness around me. I'd imagined that a book, a play, or a collection of poetry would be born as a result. But now that idea was being sucked out from under me due to the surge of new responsibilities that Molly had dumped on me. I didn't know if I'd have time to breathe, much less write.

My legs moved me in the direction of my office, but my heart stayed dumped in the dirt of the parking lot. I felt as vulnerable as a squawking newborn. I had depended on Molly and Luis Felipe to teach me how to navigate. *Just breathe,* I thought. *You can do this. Take one step at a time.*

Be the eyes and ears of Torbellino, what was that supposed to mean? I was one giant question mark with no time now to wallow in self-pity. I'd learn the sales job, whatever it took; it couldn't be that hard. I'd ask the other managers for help. They'd want me to succeed, to keep the hotel running smoothly until Luis Felipe recovered and was home.

But there was this gnawing anxiety in the pit of my stomach that felt like it was going to swallow me whole and made me want to pack my things and catch the next plane out of Cancun. If I hadn't just sold my house in St. Louis and made such a big deal about telling my friends goodbye, bragging about going off to live in this amazing place in the Yucatan jungle, I might have just gone right back, but something else was making me stay. I had dreamed about living on the ranch for ten years. I'd come to work for Molly and Luis Felipe to make that possible, and now they needed me. I couldn't just walk away. I'd feel like a shit if I did.

Three maintenance men elbowed their way into the office lugging an armful of leather-bound notebooks and a large, dented file cabinet with them.

"Senora?" one of them asked, wanting instructions as to where to put everything.

"Aqui," I said. "Todo aqui." I pointed to one empty wall and watched as they set the cabinet into place, stacking the notebooks on top and on the floor, since the bookshelves were already taken up by cookbooks. I assumed the books belonged to the man Molly said they'd recently hired as manager. The shoes and belt must have been his too, and this had been his office before I came. I hoped Luis Felipe had told him before his heart attack that it would be mine from now on.

The maintenance men disappeared, leaving me alone in the austere office with the air-conditioner spewing out stale frigid air. Jimmy had said not to mess with the temperature gauge, but I couldn't concentrate when I was freezing. I tried fiddling with it, but it wouldn't budge. Defeated by the cold, I sat at my desk and stared at the blank walls thinking this is it, everything is up to me now. *Just suck it up and get to work.* I hoped the rusty file cabinet would hold the keys to the kingdom for me, give me forms to follow, hints as to what a sales manager is supposed to do.

The air-conditioner droned on. I paced back and forth around the room before walking over to face the cabinet. I felt as afraid as if it were a rabid dog. The drawer was so rusty I had to yank twice before it opened, spewing forth its pitiful contents; a few dog-eared manila folders half-filled with notes written by hand in tiny, faded lettering. I carried the stacks of folders over to my desk and sat down to read through them, but no matter how I held the pages, I couldn't make out the handwriting. I held one page closer to the light and tried focusing again. Suddenly, I realized that the problem wasn't the handwriting or the faded print. The notes weren't written in English. Sylvie's signature was at the bottom of each page. It dawned on me: *Sylvie is a French name; the notes must be in French.* They were totally useless. I knew as much French as I knew Spanish. I snapped the folders shut, shoved them back into the rusty drawer, and slammed it closed. I was *furious.*

Breathe, just breathe. Keep your ass in the chair and figure out what to do next. Don't just sit staring at the walls; accomplish something, anything.

But what? I had no education or experience in sales. I had an advanced degree in counseling and had attended the graduate writers' program at Washington University. I had put those two educational backgrounds together to interview survivors of the Holocaust and had written a book and a one woman show that I gave based on those interviews. I'd then combined the two disciplines to design and deliver a program for hospitals to help humanize the environment. Working in an office doing paperwork seemed the antithesis of who I was. And now the paperwork was in a language I couldn't read. I was like a trout flopping on the office floor, trying to catch my last breath.

Molly had said there were guest records that needed to be alphabetized. They must be in the leather-bound books the maintenance men had brought. There were eight in all, with records starting in 1995 when the hotel opened. Alphabetizing the names and entering the rest of the information would take me several days. I just needed to find a damned computer.

I looked everywhere in the office, but there was only an old electric typewriter with Spanish symbols on the keys. I couldn't turn it on no matter what keys I pushed. While I was still fiddling with it, a slender man I'd never seen before burst through the doorway into the office. His greasy black hair hung in fringed bangs over his forehead, his black mustache looked as though it had been plastered on. A large ring of keys dangled from a loop in the waistband of his khaki pants. When he spotted me he screeched to a stop like the Roadrunner in a Loony Tunes cartoon. I knew it had to be William, the man they'd hired as manager but planned to get rid of. I felt guilty for taking over his space.

"Hello," I said, standing to greet him. "Can I help you?"

"Help me? I'm William. I'm the Innkeeper, the Food and Beverage Manager. What are you doing here? That's my desk."

Oh God. He hadn't been told.

" I'm sorry. There must be some confusion. I guess Luis Felipe didn't tell you, I'm supposed to use this office now. I'm Julie, the new sales manager." I put out my hand to shake his, but he looked at it with such contempt, I might as well have had leprosy.

"Oh yeah? And where am I supposed to go, to that shit-hole they put me in at the back of the bakery?" He spit out the words like they were rancid pork. I didn't want a confrontation, so I tried making nice.

"I don't know. The maintenance men just brought over the things from Sylvie's old office, because I'm the new sales manager."

"Great. That's great. Luis Felipe could have told me that himself, but I shouldn't be surprised. He never has time to talk to me."

"I don't know anything about that." The more upset William seemed, the calmer I tried to sound.

He glared at me, running his fingers through his thin black bangs, shifting nervously from one foot to the other. I wouldn't look away, no matter how hostile he sounded, but I was glad to hear the workers outside my window. They would hear me if I needed help.

William ran his hand over his cheek to wipe away the tiny beads of perspiration running down to his collar.

"It's not your fault," he said. "It's just that I haven't been paid in six weeks and I haven't had a day off in three."

"Six weeks is a long time," I said, relieved that he wasn't blaming me anymore for his problems. He looked as forlorn and pathetic as I felt. "You must be exhausted. Would you like to sit down?"

He hesitated, eyeing the couch as though it might be a trap before taking me up on my invitation.

"I need to talk to Luis Felipe about extending my contract. "

"He's been sick. I'm sure he's had a lot to do since he's been home."

"I know, but he's been here long enough. He could fit me in if he wanted to. What am I supposed to do, just keep on working without getting paid? For how long?"

"You sound very frustrated. I wonder why you don't just quit."

"I guess...because I keep thinking it'll all work out. I love this place. Who wouldn't? I mean the *physical* place, not the people who work here. Torbellino's a madhouse. Just wait, you'll see. I'm supposed to be the manager, but no one listens to me. Especially Carla."

There was that name again. The woman Molly told me not to trust. I wanted to hear what William had to say about her.

"Whatever I say to do, she does the opposite. She's so sweet and smiley to all the guests, but I'm telling you, she's evil. The women who work in guest services are terrified of her."

I thought if I listened as long as he wanted to talk he'd eventually calm down. If he felt I understood him, he might see me as an ally. Thank God for my counseling background. I'd rely on that to work with William.

"It's too bad that Carla's so difficult to work with. I can see why you'd want to stay, in spite of the problems. It's an extraordinary place. It always was, even before they built El Torbellino."

His eyes narrowed as he said warily, "You mean you knew Luis Felipe and Molly before they built the hotel?"

"Yes. Molly's been my friend for more than thirty years, and I started coming to visit after they'd lived on the ranch for only a year." I had dropped the counseling approach, which I shouldn't have done. My pride in my relationship with Molly and my long history with the ranch caused a door to slam between us.

."Oh, they're your *friends*. That explains it," he said caustically.

"That explains what?"

"Why the office is yours, not mine. It was *Molly's* decision." He stood up and reached over the desk to grab his belt. "The shoes over there are mine, and the books too."

"Sure. You can take them with you now or come back for them later, whatever's better for you."

"I'll need the typewriter, too. Unless, of course, Molly said the typewriter would be yours too."

"That's OK. You can have it. Actually, I was looking for a computer."

"Hah! A computer?" He scoffed. "How do you expect computers to work without a cable line through the jungle?"

"I forgot about that."

"I'll be back for my things later." He stormed out of the office, the door slamming shut behind him. I couldn't believe what was happening. Not only had Molly and Luis Felipe left, but there was a madman who was the manager of the hotel, and he already hated me.

When the door opened again, I stiffened, thinking William was back, but it was Jimmy.

"'Scuse me, ma'am, but I wanted to tell you there's an executive meeting at nine-thirty this morning. I'm headed that way if you want me to show you where it is," Jimmy said from the doorway. I was more than ready to get out of there. I felt as at home in my office as an artic hare would feel in Florida.

CHAPTER SEVEN

"Thanks for coming to get me, Jimmy." I was more grateful for his company than he realized as I walked with him into the sunlight and down the dusty path. He may have had a questionable history, but it would be better to have him in my corner than no one.

"I wouldn't have known to show up if you hadn't told me about this. How often is there a meeting?"

"It's supposed to be every Monday. Sometimes we start at nine-thirty, sometimes ten, you never know. Whenever William gets around to having it."

"That must make it hard to plan."

He shrugged. "It doesn't matter if we skip it. We don't get anything done anyway. There's always somebody mad at somebody else, and we spend the whole time on it. Carla, she gets pissed off at William. Or William, he gets a feather up his ass about Gerardo and all of 'em get on me about something, and then everybody's fighting, and that's how the meeting ends."

I would soon have a chance to witness the tension for

myself before I broke the news to them about Luis Felipe. I was excited to have something so important to tell them, and I would wait until the time was right to deliver the bombshell. Until then, I'd just listen and learn. Jimmy looked at his watch and picked up the pace until we reached the front of a two-story stucco building set between two leafy trees.

"Anyway, here we are. This is the gift shop, and the Bambucco Bar is over it, up these stairs, that's where we meet."

We climbed a winding concrete stairway to a round room with waist-high walls, the top half of which were open to the ceiling. Wood chairs were scattered randomly around the room. At one side of the room was a bar with a bamboo counter and shelves behind it filled with empty liquor bottles and glasses. It was as desolate and welcoming as a bomb shelter.

"It doesn't look like this on Saturday nights. You'll see. After dinner, the waiters bring up cafe tables and chairs, and there's music and drinks. People love it when it's not too hot a night. But it's a good thing I got here early today. Look at this mess! I told my guys to clean it up, but they probably forgot. Those suckers can't keep anything in their heads for more than a minute. Most of 'em didn't go to school long enough to learn to read, so there's no sense writing it down."

I looked around the room at the random chairs.

"Just take a chair for yourself and have a seat anywhere. The others should be here soon." He grabbed a broom from a closet behind the counter and started to sweep the dust toward the stairs.

Suddenly, there was a blood-curdling scream, followed by another. It sounded like a woman being tortured somewhere close by. I froze, thinking Jimmy would jump to see what the trouble was, but he acted as though he had heard nothing. She screamed again and this time Jimmy put down his broom, sauntered nonchalantly over to the half-wall, and leaned over the side.

"Damn peacocks! Shoo! Git! Go on!"

With a thundering of wings, a bird I would have thought was too heavy to lift its enormous body rose from the roof, hovered briefly, and disappeared over the edge of the wall.

"I've never heard a peacock scream before."

"No peacocks where you come from, huh?" Jimmy brushed some scat from the wall with his hand. "There must be a nest up top. Look at the crap it left. My guys will give it a good cleaning as soon as we finish our meeting. At least we've got enough chairs for today. The other executives will be here in a bit."

The other executives. I was part of the management team, but the word 'executive' made me squirm. Calling myself an executive would feel like a stone in my mouth. Call me a therapist, a teacher, a consultant, a writer, an actor, a mentor, all of those applied, but not an executive. I had always been happy to leave that role to someone else and do my work with front-line employees. I cared more about the lives of people than I did about the bottom line of businesses, which was why I preferred working for non-profit organizations.

"How many will be here today?"

"Seven, counting you, me, Carla, Gerardo, William, Alejandro in accounting, who's Carla's brother, and Carlos."

Faceless names of people I'd never met meant nothing to me.

"Carlos is Luis Felipe's nephew. He's the money guy, the one who signs all the checks."

I stood up and moved seven of the random chairs strewn around the room into a circle for the meeting. The click of high heeled shoes on the stone steps let me know that I was about to meet Carla, even before I saw her. She carried a leather-bound day planner that she held close to her chest, paused briefly as she glanced around the room and crossed the floor brusquely. Her body was perfectly erect and her eyes were fixed stone cold ahead of her as though she'd been trained to walk with books balanced on her head. Her white cotton anfitriona's uniform was immaculately laundered and pressed, the elasticized neckline of her peasant blouse pulled low down her arms to reveal her pale, smooth shoulders and accentuate her youthful, perky breasts. Her black curly hair had been slicked back with pomade and gathered into a mother-of-pearl barrette at the nape of her neck, the curls hanging past her shoulders. Her hair looked still wet from a shower. Arched, penciled eyebrows; curled, mascaraed lashes; bronzed cheeks; and pouty red lips had been artfully tended by the hand of a perfectionist. She looked to be in her early twenties and arrogant as only a young woman sure of her looks can be.

"Good morning, Julie," she said, bobbing her head in my direction without really looking at me.

"Hi, Carla." There was the distinct scent of jasmine as she passed by to take the seat farthest from me.

A mustachioed, partially bald man wearing a pair of white pants and a white short-sleeved guayabera shirt followed closely behind her. "Good morning," he smiled. "I'm Gerardo."

According to Molly, Gerardo was married to a woman who lived in Cancun, but during the week shacked up at

Torbellino with Carla. He looked older than her by more than twenty years and trailed closely behind her like a fancy toy poodle on an invisible leash; he took the chair closest to her.

"Hey," Jimmy said.

"Jimmy," Carla nodded officiously. She turned to Gerardo and the two talked quietly together, ignoring both Jimmy and me. With the manicured fingers of one hand, Carla opened her planner and with the other hand took out a pen from the tab along its inside binding. I wished I had brought a pen and paper, if only to have something to do with my hands while we waited for the others to show up. I was eager to get started until it suddenly occurred to me that I wouldn't understand anything they had to say if the meeting was in Spanish. Then what?

Carla whispered something to Gerardo that made him laugh, a sniggering laugh that felt unkind, the way two middle-school kids can sound. I just knew she was going to be pissed off when she heard that I was the one Luis Felipe wanted to call, not her. I sat quietly, like a newly pregnant woman holding onto my news until it was the right time to share it, when everyone was together.

My mind wandered. By now, the helicopter had come for Luis Felipe and Molly and they had left for Miami. I imagined him on a stretcher, lifted from gurney to plane to a waiting ambulance, sirens screaming as it rushed him out of the airport parking lot onto city streets, barreling through traffic to get to the hospital. Only when he was surrounded by doctors under the sterile bright white lights of an examining room would Molly breathe normally.

My thoughts were interrupted by a tall, powerfully built young man with a shaved head; a pleasant, cleanly scrubbed face; and a neatly trimmed goatee who had just stepped into the Bambucco Bar. I had never seen him before. He looked immaculate in his white shirt and freshly pressed black pants; solid and dependable. When he saw me he paused, waiting for me to say something.

"Hola. I'm Julie Heifetz, the new Sales Manager," I smiled.

"I'm Carlos, I'm in charge of finances," he nodded seriously. Jimmy had said Luis Felipe's nephew worked at Torbellino, but they looked nothing alike. Luis Felipe was darker, with heavy features, shorter, and more squat; Carlos' features were more open. He sat down, leaving two empty seats between himself and Gerardo, as though he didn't want to associate with him. Just then, a thin young man came bounding up the stairs, two at a time, and burst into the room. He smiled politely at me and sat on the other side of Carla from her lover. I assumed this was her brother; there was a definite family resemblance, but I was shocked seeing how young he looked—like a kid in his first job after college, not the head of an accounting department at an elite resort.

Carla and Gerardo continued whispering to each other as the rest of us waited for William to show up. I felt awkward not speaking with anyone, not knowing where to look. I kept thinking that everyone in the room was Mexican but me, except for Jimmy, who was born in Cuba and also spoke Spanish as his first language. The meeting would probably be in Spanish and then I'd be toast.

Just then, William hurried into the room, a ring of keys jangling from his belt loop as he took the last chair. He had cleaned up since our awkward meeting in the office. His hair was neatly combed, he had changed clothes, and his expression was almost serene. He seemed like a different person. I was relieved that he had calmed down, but there was something unsettling about the change in him in so short a time.

"OK," he said. Today's meeting will be in English so Julie can understand."

"Thanks, William, thanks everyone," I said, gratefully. No one else responded.

"It's time for weekly reports. Jimmy, you first," William said, getting right down to it.

"Nah, I got nothin.' Oh, except to say the executive dining room's taking more time than we thought to fix it up. The wiring for the fan's slowing us down. And we're short a couple of hands for painting. But the room should be ready by the end of the week, and remember, that's where we're supposed to eat. None of this bullshit about eating in the guests' dining room anymore."

"Tell that to the Lemottes," Carla sneered. The Lemottes, the family of thieves breaking employees' rules? I wasn't surprised to hear it.

"Yeah, well, everyone needs to remind them of the rules, but I'll talk to them again." William said.

"They need more than talking to." Carla said in an authoritative voice. "You tell us we're not supposed to eat in the guests' dining room, so why should the Lemottes be allowed to eat there? Every morning they have breakfast in the restaurant. The waiters say they resent having to serve them, but they'd never tell the Lemottes to their faces. And fixing up the executive dining room isn't going to help. It's a useless idea," Carla scoffed.

"It was my idea to fix up the executive dining room. Do you have a better one?" William bristled, flipping the keys in his belt loop like worry beads.

"Well, it's not going to work, I can tell you that."

William's face contorted suddenly like a dog that's just

been kicked, his nostrils flaring. "Luis Felipe hired him. Let him deal with him and his whole fucking family," he snapped. "But you will all eat in the new dining room, you understand?" His voice shook and went up an octave.

Uh oh, I thought. Here he is, the William I'd met a couple of hours earlier, a man clinging to control by his fingernails, and Carla wasn't going to let it alone.

Now Gerardo jumped in. "You let the Lemottes do whatever they want to do. They get away with everything. They're not supposed to make personal calls from the hotel phones, but they call France every day. But what about your department, William? The restaurant's your responsibility, and you need to hire a new head waiter if Amador's not coming back."

I was trying to keep up. Amador was the head waiter I'd met at the restaurant of the hotel and now he'd quit? Amador had worked at the restaurant since it had opened. What had happened to him? He was Luis Felipe's shining light, the best head waiter in the whole Cancun corridor, according to Luis Felipe. "He's sexy. All the women like him and that's very important," he had said.

"He may think he's coming back to work here, but I say he's not, he's done!" William snarled.

"We hear he quit because of you, William." Gerardo challenged.

"Well that's a lot of crap. I tried to call him, but he didn't answer his phone. The trouble is, he thinks he can take off whenever he wants a vacation, without asking permission. He's pulled this stunt before, and he's not that special."

"Tell that to Luis Felipe. Amador's his Golden Boy, you know. The Boss won't be happy when he hears he's gone." Jimmy warned.

"Call the boss's secretary if you want to know anything about Amador. She'll know where he is and when he's planning to come back. Maria Elena and Amador are friends; well, *friends* is what they call it. They used to be more than that, before Ricardo came to work here. Now Maria Elena's his woman. She makes the rounds of all the waiters," Gerardo snickered.

"I'm not asking Marie Elena about Amador. I won't talk to that bitch about anything," William snarled back at him. "She's a pain in the ass. She comes to the restaurant to sit at the bar and have a drink and flirt with the waiters while they're working. She's supposed to stick to the corporate office and stay away from the hotel."

"Talk to Marie Elena or don't, but find us a head waiter," Gerardo said.

The room was still and the heat outside was getting more intense. The other executives who had said not a word during the meeting so far shifted in their chairs. William cleared his throat. "What else is going on in the other departments? Alejandro? Carlos? Does anybody have anything to report this week?"

"No."

"Nothing."

I had been waiting for my opening and this was it. "Actually, if no one else has anything more to say, I have something I need to tell everyone." The group looked at me as though they'd forgotten I was there. I surprised myself; my voice was calm and self-assured, while the rest of me felt like I was climbing out on a sliver of a limb three stories up in a wind storm. "Earlier today, Luis Felipe had another heart attack. He's okay, but he's on his way with Molly back to the hospital in Miami. They wanted me to tell you that they'd left."

No one spoke or moved. The silence hung over the Bambucco Bar as the group sat wooden-faced, absorbing the news. I waited for someone to say something, anything; to sound worried about Luis Felipe or the future of the hotel or their jobs, but whatever they felt, they kept it hidden. I blithered on, filling the silence like a novice teacher who doesn't allow enough time for students to think after asking a question.

"Molly said to tell you they're sorry but they can't take any calls from anyone for a while. Of course you understand they need their privacy now while Luis Felipe is in the hospital. She says she'd call me and she'll let me know how he's doing. I'll tell you what she says as soon as there's any more news."

Carla blinked once, her face expressionless.

"And what's your position here now?" William demanded.

"Coordinator. That's the title Luis Felipe gave me before he left."

"Coordinator? Hah. That's a new one," Gerardo said to Carla.

"Yes," I said weakly. "I'll relay Luis Felipe's messages to you and pass yours to them if you need something. What's important here is that we keep things running while they're gone."

"We know what we're supposed to do," Carla said testily. "This isn't the first time he's been gone."

Her brother, the young accountant, leaned over and started whispering to her, and soon the room erupted into rivulets of conversations running in rapid-fire Spanish. They had shut me out as easily as if they had flipped a switch. I tried to pick out familiar words, but they were speaking too quickly and I gave up trying to understand.

My moment of significance had combusted into the atmosphere. I had become invisible, sitting alone while their conversations swirled around me. Without Spanish, I was a blind person alone on an unfamiliar street, and I was terrified, a feeling that rarely subsided during the next ten months.

CHAPTER EIGHT

I went back to my office and sat at my desk, shuffling purposelessly through stationary and office supplies, not knowing what else to do. The executives' meeting had not gone well. After a while, I got up and walked around the grounds of the hotel, trying to look purposeful before going back to my desk again. The clock slowly ticked off the minutes before my first interminable day would end and I could retreat inside my house again. Guests here would think I was so lucky to live at Torbellino with its immaculate powder white beach, the verdant jungle under an azure blue sky, and days that ran like honey from the hives of the sun gods. Just a few days before I would have agreed with them. I thought I had moved to paradise.

Molly had said I should go to the restaurant in the evening to greet the guests, but most reservations weren't until seven-thirty or eight, and I couldn't stay at the hotel that long, having started my day so early in the morning. I was emotionally drained. I made one round of the hotel grounds to say hello to guests on their way back from the beach to their casitas to get ready for dinner, but I didn't go inside the restaurant. I took the path back to my house. As I got closer, I could hear Eliseo and his family outside in their yard next door; three-year-old Alonzo's sing-song, high-pitched voice bubbled with the sheer joy of being alive.

Sitting at my dining room table with a glass of wine, I stared through the open curtainless floor-to-ceiling window, trying not to obsess about the hotel. If Mike had been there with me, everything would have felt different. I ached for his arms around me as I sat there long enough for the light to fade to dusk and then turn to night. The moon wouldn't have looked so lonely or as cold as it did this night if he were there. I imagined his long fingers strumming his guitar, his tenor voice singing lyrics I'd written. They fit so perfectly together, my lyrics and his melodies—it was like making effortless love. What I missed most, even more than the sex or the companionship, was the work we did together. Now that he was gone, I felt impotent, out of ideas for songs or plays, unable to create without him. Mike was my phantom limb after an amputation.

Too tired to be hungry, and after one more glass of wine, I dragged myself to bed. Sometime before dawn, just as the frogs were settling down, I dozed off for a couple of hours. When I woke up I was sure this day would be better. Mornings were such hopeful times. Nothing had gone wrong yet. I was determined to figure out whatever I needed to know for Molly and Luis Felipe's sake. I couldn't let them down.

Too restless to do anything else, I got dressed quickly and was at the hotel by six-thirty. The waiters for the morning shift were already in the restaurant. I ducked in to pour myself a cup of coffee to take back to the office and say good morning to the staff who were delivering coffee service and baskets of pan dulce to the patios of the guests' casitas. The head waiter, a cheery, lovely man about my size, looked surprised to see me so early and asked if there was anything he could get for me.

"No, pero gracias por el cafe."

"No hay problema, de nada."

I appreciated that brief exchange, which was friendlier than any reception I had recieved from the managers. With coffee in hand, I went to my office and spent the next couple of hours looking through the brochures and magazine articles about El Torbellino that were in the file cabinets to see what I might use to put together a presentation notebook.

I kept checking to see when the customer services department in the building next door would open. I'd already been at work for more than two hours and I expected everyone else would have been too. I wanted to ask Carla what she knew about the sales office, hoping she'd be willing to help. Finally, by mid-morning, a young woman in white walked past my window headed toward the anfitrionas' office. It wasn't Carla, but a woman who worked for her. I got up and followed her into her office.

"I'm Julie Heifetz." I said, slowly, smiling. "I'm the new sales manager. And you are?"

"Eliza."

"Eliza, I'm just trying to understand the difference between the sales office and guest services and reservations. Do people who want reservations call my department?"

"No, there's a reservation department. If they want to book a group event, then they call the sales department." She seemed hesitant to be talking with me. "If you have other questions you should wait to talk with Carla. She usually comes to work by ten-thirty."

Ten-thirty? By then, I would have been at work for four

hours, which made my North American work habits seem even more absurd and at odds with my new culture.

"Thank you, I will. You've been very helpful." The distinctions between reservations and the sales department now was obvious. That meant I would be responsible for clients booking the hotel for parties or meetings or weddings. Molly and Luis Felipe had a friend who did advertising and marketing, so that wasn't my territory, but it was up to me to recruit new prospects; but how? I took out a pad of paper and wrote *Ideas For Attracting Groups* across the top, but nothing came to me. The air-conditioner droned on, spewing dead air into the uninspiring office. I couldn't sit still, I couldn't think; the room was too cold, the chair too uncomfortable. Feeling guilty about abandoning the blank page of ideas, I hurried through the courtyard of the hotel, my eyes fixed straight ahead, my lips pursed as though I was on my way to meet someone important, but I was headed to the beach.

It was windy and the ocean was restless under dark clouds, like the first day of the writers' retreat in Mexico that I had organized for some women I knew. It was our first day together, and I wanted everything to be perfect. I remember showing them around the hotel and to their rooms. When we got to the beach, the ocean was restless under threatening dark skies. I was so worried that the weather would be lousy all week and ruin everything, but by the next morning, the sun was shining. The warm Yucatecan sun and sea, together with the special brand of what Luis Felipe called the "handmade hospitality" of El Torbellino, inspired the women's creativity, and they all went home pleased with the retreat and the progress they had made on their writing.

Standing looking out at the troubled water, I realized

that a writers' workshop had worked for those women, and it could do the same for other writers that I didn't know. I only needed to figure out how to attract them. And then it came to me. We could offer free room and meals for a well-known author, and she could reach out to her contacts to get participants. It was a natural way to increase group sales.

With a new idea in mind, I could hardly wait to get back to the office. I was flooded with ideas of other possible groups to contact: birders, naturalists, photographers, lepidopterists, writers, artists. El Torbellino would be perfect for them. I was imagining evening performances of guest authors reading from their works in the Bambucco Bar, musicians giving recitals in the restaurant after dinner. El Torbellino would be enhanced by the artistic guests who would come to us. If only they could afford our prices. I'd have to figure out how low we could go for group rates and still make it profitable. I would start by gathering information about group rates that the high-end hotels in Cancun offered.

Just as I was getting ready to call the Ritz, the heavens opened up, and a torrent of driving rain and high winds beat down on the roof of the office, rattling the windows. I picked up the phone, but there was no connection. I couldn't call out and no one could call in, and the storm could last for days. Living in the middle of the jungle without a way to communicate to the outside world in the midst of a possible hurricane like those that had hit this area before wasn't romantic, it just added to the cavernous hole in the bottom of my stomach.

The outer door of the office opened and slammed shut. I hoped it wasn't William. I couldn't imagine who would have braved going outside at this point. From my desk, I could see two maintenance men making their way through the door, struggling under the weight of a fax machine. A young woman from guest services stood shaking water from her umbrella. Her white uniform and long black hair were soaked, but even so, there was no mistaking that she was beautiful.

With the machine in place and connected, the men disappeared back outside into the downpour. The woman from guest services put a stack of papers she had brought with her onto the machine and started copying them. When she finished, she peered into my office hesitantly.

"Hi, I'm Julie," I said.

"Hola, Señora, I'm Dulce." She spoke with no trace of an accent.

"I didn't know we were getting a fax machine in this office."

"That's where Luis Felipe wants it. Guests used to check out in the guest services office, but they'll come here now. Carla's not happy about the changes. May I ask you a question, Señora? It's not about the office. I was wondering if you could help us," she said, hesitantly lowering her voice. "You're a woman. I think you will understand. We have a problem, some of the other anfitrionas and me. We live together in a room on the property, near some of the managers' apartments. Someone was looking in our window, watching us get dressed in the morning. It's very upsetting."

"You mean you've seen a peeping Tom?"

"A peeping Tom? What is this?"

"Someone like the man you're describing who looks at people through their windows."

She nodded. "It's one of the men from maintenance. I don't know his name, but I saw his face before he ran away yesterday morning and I recognized him. We don't know what we should do to stop him from spying on us."

"I'd say you should put up curtains right away."

She shook her head. "Carla says Luis Felipe doesn't want curtains on any of the buildings on the ranch. He is very strong about that. He says curtains would distract from the way the buildings look."

Now that she mentioned it, there were no curtains on the guest room windows of the hotel or on the windows at my house or Molly's. Until Dulce told me about the peeping Tom, the design plan hadn't worried me.

"You should tell Carla about this. She's your boss."

"Carla doesn't care. She gets mad if we complain about anything."

"I'll tell Jimmy to put up curtains for you." I was pleased she felt she could come to me for help, and I was sure it would be all right with Luis Felipe when I explained the problem. He couldn't leave young women so unprotected.

"Would you really talk to Jimmy for us?" Her eyes widened with amazement.

"Of course, I'll tell him to get to it right away."

She sighed. "Thank you, Julie. My friends and I will be very grateful."

"You can thank Jimmy when the curtains are up."

Jimmy's office smelled like my first boyfriend after he'd been working in his garage on his Austin Healey. Jimmy was leaning back in a chair balanced on two legs with his feet on the desk. A greasy motor part and an ashtray overflowing with cigarettes were parked next to them. When he saw me, he put his feet down and rubbed out his cigarette with the toe of his shoe. "Jimmy, can you give me a minute?"

"Sure, ma'am. Have a seat." He gestured to a chair next to his desk.

"Thanks, but I just came to ask if you could take care of something for me. Dulce just told me that some guy's been hanging around the room where she and two other anfitrionas live. There are no curtains on their windows and she's seen him watching when she and her roommates get dressed. Could you hang some curtains for them?"

"Sure, but Carla won't like it. The anfitrionas, that's her department."

"Just tell Carla the curtains were my idea." She couldn't object to such a simple solution, and if she did, I would welcome a confrontation with her about it. She'd been cold and unwelcoming ever since I'd arrived, and from what Dulce was saying, her lack of caring carried over to the women in her department.

"Tell the girls nobody's going to bother them anymore, or that sucker will have to answer to me."

"Thanks, Jimmy."

He checked his watch. "It's twelve o'clock already. The other executives don't eat lunch until three, but I eat now. You must be hungry too. Wanna walk over with me?"

"Sure." I hadn't had anything but coffee for breakfast. I had never seen the employee cafeteria before. He put on his hat and led the way down a path to the side of the parking lot. I felt like a hot house plant reaching for the light and heat, drinking in as much as possible.

"I saw you got to work early this morning," Jimmy said, coyly.

"How do you know that?" I was suddenly on guard. I hadn't noticed anyone around when I got to the hotel in the morning.

. "I have my spies," he winked. "I know everything that

happens here. Like I know the anfitrionas don't clock in until nine-thirty or ten, sometimes later, and Carla and Gerardo leave the property most nights around ten. It's all in the log."

I shivered hearing I had been watched unseen, knowing that I would be again. The walls had eyes and ears. We kept walking until we got to a stone wall surrounding a courtyard shaded by leafy trees full of green berries.

"Here's the cafeteria. They give us breakfast and lunch, and I can tell you, our chef's better than the one at the restaurant, hands down. C'mon, I'll introduce you."

I didn't want to think about unseen eyes knowing when I got to work or went home. I didn't want to think about peeping Toms harassing the anfitrionas. I was just happy to be in the warmth and peace of the courtyard for lunch with the one person of all the managers who was willing to be helpful.

"Don't brush up against that tree," Jimmy cautioned, motioning me to go ahead of him. "If you're sensitive to mangoes the sap from those trees will drive you crazy. Lots of Gringos are allergic to them."

"Gringos? You mean people like you and me?"

"I'm no Gringo. I was born in Cuba."

I recoiled at being called a Gringo, being labeled and set apart, but I followed him to the back of the cafeteria to get our lunch. A large man in a white butcher apron and chef's cap stood over a large pot with a ladle in hand. He and Jimmy greeted each other like old friends while I stood inhaling the sweet comforting scent of chicken soup. I hadn't realized how hungry I was until then. I started salivating like a Pavlovian dog.

Jimmy turned to introduce me. "Jorge, el jefe, Señora Julie," Wait. He called me chief. Or did I misunderstand

and he said chef, not chief? No, I was sure I heard correctly: el jefe, Senora Julie. Jorge smiled broadly, took a bowl of soup that had already been filled, and added an extra ladle-full. Then he slapped a slab of meat doused in a sea of mushroom sauce onto a plate and a mound of potatoes next to it and put it on a tray with the soup. I could never have eaten all of that at one lunchtime, even before he added a slice of iced lemon cake big enough for Paul Bunyan. I'm five-feet one and a hundred and three pounds. I looked at the gardener's tray in front of mine. He'd been served only half the size of my portions of everything, and with jello, not cake, for dessert. I was embarrassed to be getting special privileges when I'd done nothing to earn them, but I didn't say anything. I didn't want to offend the chef, and like the polite Midwestern woman I'd been raised to be, I took my tray and smiled.

"Delicioso," I said. "Gracias." The chef beamed proudly, and I turned to see where Jimmy wanted to sit, but once he had his food, he walked to one of the stone tables where two workmen were eating, without saying a word to me or even looking my way. I made my way to an empty table, resigned to eating alone. I was the only woman in the courtyard, and the only North American. I felt like an intruder who had happened into a working men's club.

The unspoken message in the cafeteria was clear; I was management and belonged with the other managers and the women from guest services. Jimmy was the exception because he was maintenance, and didn't seem to count with the other managers. I wasn't going to wait until three o'clock to eat when they did, and having lunch with Carla and her posse would be no picnic. I'd rather make myself a salad at home. This would be the last time I'd eat in the employee lunchroom.

The chef was busy at the stove and Jimmy and his men were talking. I got up and scraped my left-over food into the trash bin, returning my tray, ashamed at how much food had been wasted on me. Every hour that passed made me feel more isolated, desperate to hear from Molly.

CHAPTER NINE

I'd been working at the hotel for more than two weeks, trying to establish a routine for myself. Every morning at six-thirty, I'd head for the restaurant to pour myself a cup of coffee and watch the waiters prepare trays with thermoses of coffee or tea and baskets of freshly baked pan dulce to deliver to guests' casitas. The first time one of the waiters called in sick, I offered to help deliver the trays, but they said thank you but no, I should just sit and enjoy my coffee. They were uncomfortable with the idea of having me pitch in and couldn't understand that for me it would have been a pleasure to feel I was making some small contribution. After my second cup of coffee and a few friendly exchanges with the waiters, I'd head over to my office where I wasted time sitting at my desk distractedly waiting for a phone call from Molly.

Every day I was disappointed when I didn't hear from her. She could have at least called to say they were all right, at least that. But I tried to be patient and see it from their perspective. It must have been a nightmare for them thrown into the foreign world of hospitals and medical interventions. I could understand that Molly would be too busy during the day meeting with doctors and helping Luis Felipe to be able to call and too exhausted at night to have the energy to talk. Maybe there was no diagnosis or treatment plan yet. I would hear from her when she had something definitive to report, but it was getting harder to wait as the days went by. I knew from my training as a counselor and my work in hospitals how draining it was for patients and their families going through a major medical crisis. I tried to put Molly and Luis Felipe out of my mind and focus on my work.

The storm had passed and the sea had returned to its usual calm, a stretch of lilting waves gently lapping onto the shore. The sky was a spectacular blue and the temperature was high, around eighty degrees Fahrenheit, with a constant light breeze. This was the weather I'd moved here for. At the office, my research about group package rates was coming along nicely. I'd work all morning and then take a break after lunch to walk on the beach before going back to the office for the rest of the afternoon. The first time I'd visited the ranch, there had been nothing but cool white sand without buildings or people, except for Luis Felipe and Molly. Even now that the hotel was there, with so few guests rooms and El Torbellino the only hotel on the cove, the beach remained a protected unbroken empty landscape with few people to interrupt the view. I never lost sight of how singular a privilege it was to breathe in that solitude, and it calmed me, despite feeling as shaky as I felt most of the time.

But this day, farther up from my house and out of sight of the hotel, some of the workers who had finished their morning shift were playing a ferocious game of soccer. I stopped to watch, enjoying the breeze and the playful shouting as the young men dove with lustful energy after the ball. Their exuberance reminded me of how I felt when I was in love. I liked men from a distance these days, watching their athletic bodies twist and bend, seeing their camaraderie. But Mike had sort of done me in as far as another relationship went. I'd been too badly burned not to want to steer clear of a hot stove.

A close woman friend was all I longed for now. If Molly were home we'd be taking our walks together, like the days when I was her guest, with Lulu and Samantha leading the way, darting after each other in and out of the waves. But Molly and Luis Felipe had been gone for more than a month, and I hadn't seen Lulu, Molly's little furry white pup, in days. I'd stop by the house now and again to check on her, but Victor clearly didn't want me hovering. Lulu went crazy when she saw me, jumping up, trying to get on my lap and lick my face. My Midwestern accent must have reminded her of Molly. Of the two dogs, she was my favorite, and I missed her. Samantha was Luis Felipe's and kind of a loose cannon. If a stranger ran past us while we were walking on the beach, Samantha might chase after him and nip him in the butt, which was not exactly a habit that endeared her to me.

I kept walking past the soccer game and past the back patio of Molly's house. I'd had a productive morning and I needed a break. The tangerine fabric of my skirt rose and fell in waves at my ankles. With my shoes off, I dug my toes into the sand, grateful for the warmth. My hair blew wildly in the wind like the wings of Monarch butterflies over-wintering in Mexico. I raised my hand to protect my eyes from the blazing sun and scanned the shore. As far as I could see, the beach was bare; only nature stretched out her welcoming arms. I breathed in the fresh salty air and bathed in the sunshine, feeling truly blessed. No matter what else happened, there would always be this.

I felt greedy. Usually my walks were quick, but this day I decided to keep going. In a quarter of a mile, I'd get to the place we called the Point: the piece of land that jutted out from the shore, where jungle took over and the walkable beach ended. Then, I'd turn around. I hadn't been all the way to the Point since I'd come to work at the hotel.

I was watching the dip and dive of a frigate bird, not where I was going, when I stepped on something sharp and looked down to see if I was bleeding. A broken piece of glass stuck out of the pad of my foot, daring me to pull it out. The glass hadn't gone in too deep and came out easily. I'd wash the cut thoroughly later, but it wasn't serious enough to abort my walk. I tucked the shard into the pocket of my dress. A few feet away, I saw a plastic bottle lying half buried in the sand, and I pocketed that too. The farther I walked, the more debris I could see. Now, it wasn't a discarded bottle here and there, the beach was covered with trash: shoes, toothbrushes, soda cans caught in fishing nets and seaweed piled up all the way to the Point. The debris made it impossible to walk.

I was furious. The cruise ships and their passengers dumped their trash overboard, and the tide did the rest of the dirty work carrying it here to our shore. How could it look like this? Torbellino's beach was one of its greatest selling points. There were so few beaches left in the world as isolated and pristine as ours that offered luxury accommodations. The hotel and beach were ranked number one in all of Mexico by Conde Nast Travel Magazine. No-one would believe it deserved that ranking this day. Guests might blame the Mayans for ruining the beach, and they would certainly hold the hotel at fault for not cleaning it up.

The beach in front of the hotel itself was immaculate. Every day a crew hand-raked the sand, but there wasn't enough time or manpower to clean past El Torbellino's property line, which ended after half a mile on either side of the hotel. But guests who liked to walk often went past that, strolling all the way to the Point. I remembered Molly telling me that after a particularly difficult rainy season one year, they had organized a volunteer beach clean-up at the hotel. The staff plus some of the guests participated, and everyone had a great time being part of it. *Why couldn't I do that now?* I thought. A beach clean-up would be a perfect team-building exercise, a great way for me to start getting to know the staff, with everyone pulling together to work toward a common goal. Besides, it would give me a legitimate excuse to be out of the office. The condition of the beach had an impact on sales, so I should be the one to initiate a project to clean it, I rationalized. I'd tell William and Jimmy about it and ask them to get the staff to help. Carla's guest services department could put up notices, so everyone would know about it.

I picked up the pace and ran back to the hotel excited about my great idea, full of energy, and impatient to start planning. The research on group packages would have to wait. We'd schedule two days for the clean-up, starting early morning, before it got too beastly hot; we could stop in time for breakfast and reconvene the next day to finish the job. Volunteers could agree to help on either one or both days.

When I got back to my office, my phone was ringing. Still full of thoughts about the clean-up, I distractedly picked up the receiver.

"Hi, Julie, it's Molly." I was stunned to hear her voice. It was the first time I'd heard from her. I'd been waiting for weeks, but now hearing her voice was jarring, something out of the past, like a shade talking to me from the underworld, familiar but distant.

"Molly, I'm so glad you called. How are you? How's Luis Felipe?"

"He's okay. We're still in Miami. The doctors have been great."

"What do they say?"

"They say it's good we got here right away, before there was more damage to his heart." I could hear Luis Felipe mumbling in the background but couldn't make out the words.

"It looks like we're going to be here for a while."

"A while?" My enthusiasm about her call crumbled. I was hoping she'd say they'd be back next week. Hospitals in the US discharge patients almost before they finish sewing them up, even after brain surgery. I thought they'd be home in another week, anyway. But I couldn't object. It wasn't my husband who was critically ill.

"Yes, tell the staff so they don't expect us. And no phone calls yet. Is everything OK there?"

"Oh, everything's fine," I lied. "The storm's over here, but the beach looks like shit. I was thinking maybe I'd organize a hotel clean up, like the one you had a few years ago. What do you think about that?"

"Nice idea," she said, but I could hear Luis Felipe's voice grumbling in the background.

"Necessitamos ir, Molly," he said impatiently.

"Si, si, en un minuto I'm sorry, I have to get off the phone Julie. Luis Felipe's waiting to have lunch now. He slept through breakfast and he should eat. I just wanted to let you know we're here. I'll call you when I can talk longer."

And then, before I realized it, the conversation was

85

over. I didn't have time to ask if Luis Felipe was still in the hospital or to find out where she was staying until he got out. He didn't want her staying on the phone, and she probably didn't feel free to talk with him standing next to her anyway. At least I knew they were ok, and she'd approved the cleanup. I hung up feeling buoyed by the fact that she'd called, and armed with her long-distance support, I walked to the hotel kitchen to find William's office. He was thumbing through a worn Mexican cookbook with food stains on the open page when I walked into the claustrophobic space behind the pastry kitchen. I could see why he felt like it was a demotion to be moved here from his old office.

"Just looking for some recipes," he said, closing the book as though I'd caught him doing something forbidden.

"I want to ask you something. It's about the beach. Have you been to the Point lately?"

"No," he smirked. "I haven't had time for walks on the beach. I didn't get to bed until two o'clock last night."

Ignoring the sarcasm, I told him my idea for the cleanup, and that Molly had approved. Then I asked if he'd help recruit volunteers. I really wasn't expecting much interest, but his answer surprised me. "Sure, we can do that. Do you want a special breakfast for volunteers after they finish at the beach? Pan dulce, omelets and steak might be good."

I was delighted; maybe I'd judged him too quickly. It had been a shock finding out that I was taking over his space, and now he was willing to help.

From William's office, I went straight to Jimmy's. He agreed to put up signs about the clean-up in all the offices, with sign-up sheets for volunteers. The morning of the clean-up, he'd bring garbage bags and a truck to haul away the trash when we finished. He assured me the guys in his department would be there on Thursday morning at six-thirty. Everything was arranged, and I could hardly wait for clean-up day the next week.

On Thursday morning at six-fifteen, Jimmy and I waited at the blue and white lounge chairs on the beach to meet the other volunteers. I wondered who would show up. Francois and his family? They were in charge of the water-front and should have been interested in participating. We waited until after six-thirty when a small band of gardeners and maintenance men, two waiters, plus Dulce and Erika from guest services joined us, but that was the entire turnout. This was it, this measly handful? I tried to hide my disappointment and reminded myself to be grateful for the ones who were there rather than worrying about the ones who weren't.

"Gracias a todos. Thank you all for coming. We've got a big job ahead of us and it's not too hot yet, so let's get started."

The men from Jimmy's department couldn't under-stand a word that I was saying. I put on the gloves Jimmy had left for us and picked up one of the trash bags deposited on the beach to show the group that I was going to be working with them. The trash bag was long and heavy as a punching bag. Even though it was empty, it fought against me, the wind blowing it against my legs as I tried to drag it behind me on the sand like the train of an inglorious black wedding dress. I lumbered over to the nearest pile of kelp and trash, but there was so much litter even this far from the Point that collecting all of it was more than our motley crew would be able to manage. Jimmy's truck engine started up as he called out the window, and I felt a brief minute of panic. This was more than I'd bargained for.

"I'll be back in the afternoon to pick up the bags," and

the truck pulled away. The volunteers from his department moved with their sacks far from the rest of us down the beach.

Bend, gather the swill, stuff it into the bag, then bend, gather, stuff again, over and over. I pivoted without straightening up to clear a patch of sand about as big as a cat's eye, compared to the size of the beach that remained. *Crap*, I thought. *Some bright idea this was.* I'd always hated yard work. What made me think this would be any different? I stood upright and stretched. My back was already hurting and the sun was beating down, the sweat running in rivulets down my cheek, dripping off my chin, and I didn't have a handkerchief. There was no conversation to break the monotony of the work, no one was singing. We were spread out across the beach, far from each other, the guys from the maintenance department working as far away from me as possible. I was management, no matter how I saw myself. I paused to wipe the sweat with the back of my hand. A frigate bird screeched high up in the sky, like a pirate circling overhead, planning its attack on some unsuspecting fool feeding just below the surface of the waves. Lucky bird catching the wind.

It was nine-thirty and we'd been at it for hours. The maintenance men had disappeared into the jungle. My stomach growled, and I was sure everyone else was thinking about breakfast too. I called to Dulce to tell her I was going to the executive dining room and that she should bring everyone there in half an hour. William would have everything ready by then. I wondered if he would have put out tablecloths, or if there would be music. That would be a nice touch.

When I got to the executive dining room, no one was there. We hadn't talked about where breakfast would be served, I had just assumed he had meant the executive dining room. Seeing it empty, I hoped I'd been mistaken and that he must have meant the employee cafeteria, so I hurried there next. But William wasn't anywhere to be found, and there was no special breakfast waiting; no pan dulce, omelets, or eggs for the volunteers, only the usual toast, oatmeal, and coffee waiting on the counter, just like any other day.

I was shaking I was so angry. I'd promised that breakfast would be the reward for all the hours the group had put in without getting extra pay, but William had never intended to do anything extra for them. He had set me up to look a fool, and it would seem to all of the staff that I'd gone back on my word. I couldn't blame them if they didn't trust me from here on out.

I should have gone to meet with the team to apologize, but I was too mortified to face them. Instead, I charged over to William's office to confront him. It was no surprise that he hadn't come in to work yet when I got there, but I waited. As soon as he walked in the door, I let loose.

"What happened to the special breakfast for the volunteers?" I demanded, my voice shaking.

He brushed by me without saying a word and threw his keys on the desk casually and sat down, as though he couldn't tell from looking at me that I wanted to rip him a new asshole.

"Nobody went hungry. If you spoil those guys, they'll just take advantage of you."

"Then you should have told me that instead of promising to help!" My voice was an octave higher than it should have been and I fought to get it under control. "I believed you. This was not a good way for us to start working together, William."

89

"I don't know about that," he said coolly. "The clean-up turned out all right. "

"For whom?"

"For the hotel and for you. One of the guests at breakfast said she saw a woman and a few other people helping her clean up the beach. She asked if the woman was the owner's wife. She sounded impressed."

"And you're telling me that because?"

"I just thought you'd like that, having someone mistake you for Molly."

I swallowed hard and gave him one long hate stare, wishing on him all the shame that I felt before I walked away. Fool me once, but not again. I wouldn't waste my breath trying to win him over a second time. He could do his work in the kitchen and the restaurant, and I'd do mine.

I'd been at Torbellino for nearly a month. I was beginning to make headway knowing what I was doing in the sales department, but I was getting nowhere with the person who called himself the manager of the hotel.

I slammed out of the kitchen and nearly crashed into Dulce in the hallway. I was embarrassed that I hadn't come to find her earlier, but I was glad to have the chance to talk to her now. "I'm sorry you didn't get any special breakfast after the beach clean-up. I thought there would be. Please apologize to the others for me."

"No problem," she said. "We all had to get to work right away anyway." I was glad I'd been able to help solve her problem, and now, she was forgiving for mine.

Later that morning, no one mentioned the beach clean-up at the managers' meeting. It was as though I had imagined the whole thing. On the second day of the scheduled clean-up, the same motley crew was there. We did as much as we could for the next few hours, and by the time we broke for breakfast, bags full of trash were dumped like turds trailing over the sand, almost as far off as the Point. I waved good-bye and called thanks, knowing we really needed another couple of days to finish the job, but two days was all I had asked for. I was grateful that the volunteers had willingly come back for a second morning, this time expecting no special reward.

I walked back to the hotel by myself, sweaty and grubby from the work at the beach. Gerardo, Carla's boyfriend, appeared on the patio looking like a hospital orderly in his white housekeeping uniform. He rushed down to meet me.

"There you are. I've been waiting for you."

"I've been a little busy," I said sarcastically. He knew about the cleanup that morning because the notices asking for volunteers had been posted in all the employees' areas. Not only hadn't he volunteered, he hadn't sent anyone from his department. Now that the work was done, here he was like a genie out of the bottle, magically appearing too late to help.

"Carla and I are going to a club at the Marriott in Cancun tonight after work. We'd like to invite you to go with us." He smiled confidently. That's so odd, I thought. Is this an apology for not having volunteered? Why else would he have asked me to join them? Carla had been so unwelcoming and cold ever since I came to Torbellino. She could barely say hello when we passed each other at work. Why this sudden change of heart? After the incident with William, I wasn't exactly feeling trusting of anyone, especially of Carla and Gerardo. Luis Felipe had said they didn't trust her either.

"It's a good floor show," Gerardo said when I hesitated. "And we like to get away from the ranch for a while in the evenings after work. You should, too. Why don't you come with us?"

A flashy floor show was the last thing I felt like seeing. I would have been interested in going to a more authentic performance, and I didn't relish the thought of spending time with him and Carla, but I didn't want to be rude. There was also the unlikely possibility that they were being truly friendly and wanted a chance to get to know me better. I shouldn't judge them so quickly. Maybe I was wrong about them, and besides, a night out would be a good break from the hotel. I was too tired to resist.

"OK, yes, thank you. I'd like to go," I lied, pretending enthusiasm.

"Good. Meet us at the entrance at ten o'clock. That'll give us time to change clothes after work."

I half-expected them to be no shows, after my experience with William and his promise. But a few minutes past ten, I heard the click of stiletto heels on cobblestone and Carla and Gerardo appeared at the circle driveway in front of the hotel. She had changed out of her white uniform into a tight-fitting sheath dress, the color of a fiery red-orange sunset. She was just this side of plump, delectable as a ripe persimmon. She nodded a perfunctory hello to me, and moved closer to Gerardo, to remind me that he was hers. He had changed into khaki-colored pants and a print short-sleeved shirt, with a thick gold chain hanging down onto his chest bared by his unbuttoned shirt. He looked less like a hospital orderly now, and more like a consiglieri.

"All set? My car's this way." He motioned to his Volkswagen beetle idling at the front curb. With a backward glance to make sure I was following, he put an arm around Carla, steered her to the front door of his car, and waited while I climbed in the back.

"That's a beautiful dress, Carla," I tried.

"Thank you. My mother had made it. She makes all my clothes," she sniffed haughtily, brushing off my compliment.

"That must be really nice not to have to go shopping."

She didn't answer but stared stiffly ahead, even though it was too dark to see out the window. I was already kicking myself for accepting Gerardo's invitation as we rode in awkward silence down the highway to the Marriott in Cancun's hotel zone.

The show was just starting when we got to our seats. The dancers were as I had imagined: flashy, sexy, heavily made-up, wearing sequined, revealing costumes with elaborate feather headdresses. Their eyes barely blinked as they moved gingerly across the stage under the weight of their headpieces to the beat of loud electronic music. As one number ended and the next started, only the costumes and the colors of headdresses changed, and I was bored.

Then, the lights dimmed, the stage cleared, and a half-naked man in a loin cloth and hair almost waist-length entered slowly holding a tortoise shell drum. The air filled with misty smoke and incense and flute sounds as the man started to beat his lonely drum. It was supposed to be an ancient Mayan ritual, and even though the staging and costume were contrived, the music was earthy and haunting, the rhythm hypnotic.

I closed my eyes, imagining the village where Eliseo and Sebastiana had been born, where their family still lived. The rhythm of the solo drum was soothing and the auditorium was warm from so many people crowded in together. My head dropped to my chest as I nodded off for I don't know how long, but by the time I jerked awake, the sultry women in skimpy costumes were on stage again. I glanced sheepishly at Gerardo or Carla to see if they had caught me sleeping, but they were too entranced by the show girls to have noticed me.

It was after two in the morning when we got back to the entrance of Torbellino.

"Thanks for taking me," I said as I waved goodbye and walked home to the accompaniment of barking frogs.

The evening had done nothing to further a friendship with Gerardo and Carla, but one thing was certain, Jimmy would know we'd had a date together and stayed out late, and it wouldn't take long for everyone else on the ranch to hear about it too. Gossip spread around the ranch faster than beach seaweed and was twice as difficult to get rid of. People would assume the three of us we were getting to be friends, which couldn't have been further from the way things turned out. Carla and I avoided any open conflict under the guise of masked mutual indifference, but the tension between us was building.

CHAPTER TEN

Two weeks later, angry voices pierced the hush of the slow late afternoon. As I rounded the corner of the restaurant, there on the walkway of the lawn that separated the white guest bungalows from each other, William and Carla stood, their noses inches apart. William was raging at her, and Carla's back was ram-rod straight as she stared back at him. I couldn't catch his words, only his threatening tone and her silence that seemed to enrage him all the more the longer it lasted. He raised a clenched fist toward her face that stopped me dead in my tracks. I wanted to scream, but I didn't want the guests to hear. We were in the middle of the courtyard of the hotel, where any guest could happen by and see the ugliness unfolding.

"William, stop!" I called harshly.

His arm hovered in mid-air over her, like the wing of a wounded bird, suspended in flight.

"William," I hissed again. He glared at Carla, breathing hard like a mad dog. Slowly, reluctantly, his fist opened and landed at his side, but his eyes never lost their grip on the woman in front of him. Carla didn't move or utter a sound.

Her chin was raised in stony defiance against his menacing stare.

"I don't know what's going on between you, but whatever it is, let's go into my office and talk about it," I pleaded. Even though I had sworn to myself that I wouldn't waste another single breath on William after the beach-clean up incident, I couldn't walk away from this situation. I had to deal with him. He wasn't a big guy, but his voice shook with rage as he turned to me.

"I'm not talking to you either. Just leave me alone. I'm out of here. I'm taking a week off. Let Carla run things since that's what she wants."

He looked as though he hadn't slept in days, and he was sweating profusely. I thought he must have been on something, speed or cocaine; drugs were easy enough to come by in Playa and Cancun. I wasn't Carla. I was afraid of him, and I felt my fear on display for any passerby to see. He seemed so out of control. If he was on drugs there was no telling what he might do. He reached into his pants' pocket and pulled out something that he held tight in his hand. The sunlight caught a flash of silver. A knife? A gun? I couldn't tell. My legs turned to cement and I couldn't move out of his way. He darted toward me on the path. As he came closer, I could see his dilated pupils and the way his one free hand trembled, his face contorted in anger. He reminded me of patients in the psych wards where I had consulted.

I felt like a moving train was heading straight for me, gathering steam. My eyes were fixated on the hand that held something in it. I would duck if he lunged. But suddenly, William stopped in the middle of the path feet from me. He looked at me as though seeing me for the first time and something changed. He seemed surprised to find himself there in the middle of the courtyard, standing bare in his fury. He opened his fingers that had been wrapped around the silver object from his pocket like a magician demonstrating some slight of hand trick and revealed what it was; it was no knife, but his set of keys, flashing silver in the bright sunlight. William stood stock still and looked around, nervously flipping the keys back and forth over his knuckles like a tic. I was so relieved to see those keys and hear them jingle, I almost laughed.

He stormed past me like the eye of a hurricane under a clear blue sky and I moved closer to Carla.

"It doesn't matter if he stays or leaves," she said coolly watching him hurry away. "We don't need William. He calls himself innkeeper, or manager, of El Torbellino, but we just ignore him. You can see why."

The threat had passed, but the weakness in my legs had not. Carla seemed unfazed. "What happened to make him so mad today?" I asked.

"I just talked with the chef about a special birthday dinner for one of the guests, and when William found out, he started yelling at me that special dinners weren't up to me to plan."

"That was all?"

She nodded.

"That doesn't seem like the kind of thing to make someone so furious." I was wondering what she had done to piss him off that she wasn't saying.

"Something's wrong with that man." She ran her hands over the front of her white skirt, straightening the waist. The confrontation had been no more disturbing to her than a fly landing on her shoulder. But she was right about William. Something was wrong with him that really worried me. What if he had actually hit her? Or someone else? He seemed like a crazy person, drug-induced or from another cause.

William wouldn't have been the first manager to go crazy at El Torbellino. I'd heard the story from Molly. The first manager they hired when the hotel opened was also the chef and in charge of the restaurant. He was a talented German, but he had a terrible temper that got more out of control the longer he worked at El Torbellino. One night, he got in a fight with his wife and stabbed her with a kitchen knife, and Luis Felipe had to call an ambulance for his wife and the police to get the chef off the property. She had showed me the knife marks in the kitchen wall. And now there was William coming unhinged. Was there something about El Torbellino that drove people crazy?

I had never worried about violence before, even though it seems absurd to say that now. Violence to me was something that happened in other communities, not where I lived in my protected suburb of Clayton, Missouri. College in Boston only furthered my belief that the world was a welcoming one.

I knew intellectually that there was an undercurrent of violence in Mexico that was statistically higher than in the US. I'd read about the gang wars and murders and the high rate of domestic abuse, but I had always trusted my own experience over generalizations that I read. In none of my previous trips had I felt afraid. I felt I was in the protected environment of the ranch, and Molly and Luis Felipe were always close by. But William was no generalization about violence. He was a bomb that could detonate at any time, a threat to the very peace I thought would be mine when I moved from the States.

I didn't see William around the hotel for the next two days after the confrontation between him and Carla. I wished he'd left for good, though I guessed we probably wouldn't be that lucky. In the meantime, I wanted to find out whatever I could about his background, if he'd left a history of trouble at his other jobs, and so I asked Jimmy what he knew about him.

"Not much. He says he was trained at some fancy cooking school in the US."

"So he's not Mexican?"

"Oh no, he's Mexican. I hear his mother lives in a shack near Puerto Morelos and he lived with her before Luis Felipe put him up in a room at the hotel."

"Well, he must have a resume and references."

"I wouldn't know about that." He took off his hat and wiped his forehead with his handkerchief. "Corporate would have the paperwork. Ask Maria Elena, she's Luis Felipe's secretary."

I was still obsessing about what to do about William when the phone rang. It was Molly again, and the connection was clear for a change.

"I'm so glad to hear from you, Molly!" It was a gift every time she called. Her voice was up-beat this day, and since I'd talked to her only the week before, I thought she was probably calling to tell me good news, that they'd be coming home soon. But that wasn't it at all.

"We hear from Maria Elena that Amador hasn't shown up for his evening shift for a few weeks, and that he's looking for another job. We need him in the restaurant. All the women love him, and he's such a draw. Farrah Fawcett's been to El Torbellino maybe six times, and the last time she tried to get him to go back to California to work for her. Luis Felipe wants you to call him. Maria Elena has his number."

"I'll try to talk with him. But meanwhile, we have a big

problem on our hands here. It's William. He's a scary guy, Molly. He came close to hitting Carla and..."

"I know. Luis Felipe didn't have the energy to deal with him when we were home. Tell Carla to try not to provoke him.

"But..."

"And call Amador."

"William won't let him come back to the restaurant, no matter what."

"This decision's not up to William. He doesn't know what's good for Torbellino. Luis Felipe says to get Amador back. You'll be able to work with him. Get his number from Maria Elena and give him a call."

I promised I'd talk to Amador, but I didn't call to get his number from Luis Felipe's secretary that day. I wasn't ready to talk to him yet. I had to think about what I'd say to him. I had no authority at the hotel, and as Molly and Luis Felipe's guest at the restaurant, I'd only met Amador a few times. Besides, the weather was good, with no wind, which meant the phones were working well and I needed to return a message from an ad agency in France. They wanted to bring some models and a photographer for a photo shoot at the hotel. I was excited about the possibility and needed to know when they'd be coming, how long they'd be staying, and how many rooms they needed. Tracking down Amador would have to wait.

Just as I was getting ready to return the call to the ad agency, I heard he outer door to the office open and close. A small dark-skinned woman with curly greasy black hair, wearing a too-short skirt and stiletto heels, rushed into my office and over to my desk.

"Hello, Señora Julie. I'm Maria Elena, Luis Felipe Helu's personal secretary," she said, with an air of self-importance. I'd heard about Maria Elena from the other managers. At the last executive meeting, William had complained about her and everyone agreed that she was a pain in the ass. They said she'd come to the restaurant all the time to sit at the bar, drink wine and talk with the waiters during their shift, even though the restaurant was supposed to be off-limits for her. But Luis Felipe relied on her, and everyone who worked at the hotel knew it, so there were never any consequences when she showed up and took a seat at the bar.

"Come with me, please, Señora, Amador is here. He wants to talk with you." She winked, as though we shared a secret. I followed her tight black skirt all the way to the corporate office on the other side of the hotel grounds. I was going to meet with Amador, whether or not I was ready.

The corporate office was an imposing building on the opposite side of the hotel from the other departments' offices. It was so cold inside that I could have ice-skated in the toilet bowl of the rest room. Two young Mayan men sat at two chairs in front of a desk guarding the front door. One of the men was Victor, the driver who'd picked me up many times from the airport to bring me to the ranch. I didn't know he worked at the corporate office, or why two guards were necessary, but he must have recognized me.

"Hola, Victor," I smiled. He nodded and gazed solemnly ahead, as though cracking a smile would be contrary to his job description.

Maria Elena led us to a long, concrete, winding staircase. At the top was a high-ceilinged, massive executive office. An enormous wood desk and padded leather swivel chair dominated the room. Amador was waiting for us, standing up, leaning against the desk. He was wearing grey slacks, a black and grey silk, open-collared shirt and black loafers. He looked like a businessman, not like a waiter. He smiled confidently at me, revealing his signature gold front tooth.

Maria Elena held out the desk chair and gestured for me to sit, but the chair was too big, too imposing, and too masculine for me. I would have felt dwarfed, like Lily Tomlin's character, Edith Ann from *Laugh-In* sitting in it, a little girl pretending to be someone I wasn't. I motioned to the two smaller chairs next to each other on the opposite side of the desk; one for me, the other for Amador. With a tug at the hem of her skirt, Maria Elena closed the wooden heavy office door behind her, leaving me alone with Amador.

"Hola, Senora," he said, settling into his chair. "Thank you for meeting me."

"Hola, Amador. I'm glad you came. I've been wanting to talk with you. I hear you haven't been at work for weeks. I need to understand why you disappeared without saying a word to anyone. You're our head waiter. I expected more from you than that."

"I have been on vacation."

"On vacation? William said you didn't talk to him about getting your vacation approved, you just stopped coming to work. He said he called you but couldn't get in touch with you, and you've never called here once since you've been off to tell him your plans. What's up?"

"Señora, I love Torbellino. I love being head waiter. And I love Señor Helu. When he met me, I was just a mason. He say, me, I will make good waiter. The chef then, he was manager also and he hired me, he trained me. He was very, very tough, but he made me excellent waiter. Last year, Torbellino sent me to a competition with all the hotels' waiters from everywhere. We had to set the table, explain the menu, the wines, and serve the guests. I won second place for all of Cancun."

"That's wonderful. Torbellino must have been so proud of you."

"Next time I'm gonna win, I'm pretty sure. But now... it's...Señor William. He don't know anything. He don't know about table service. He don't know about food."

"You mean he doesn't appreciate you?"

"He don't listen. He talks to me like I'm...iguana."

"Without respect?"

He nodded emphatically. "Without respect. Señor William respect nobody. Guests sometimes, now, they complain about Señor William's menus...I don't want to see Torbellino fall down."

"I appreciate your standards, but you can't help get back the quality of the restaurant if you don't show up. Promise me you'll be here every day you're scheduled, that's how you can prove that you care."

"But Señor William? He don't want me here."

"But Luis Felipe does. If you come back to work and William gives you any problems, come talk to me. I can help if I know what's going on. I can count on you to tell me?"

He looked down at his feet. Something else was troubling him.

"Last week I had interview with the Ritz hotel in Cancun for waiter's job. They don't need head waiter...but waiter's pay is better at the Ritz than here."

"I see." I appreciated his honesty. Luis Felipe wouldn't like losing him to our biggest competitor.

"The Ritz is a fine hotel, but it's very different from Torbellino. It's very corporate, very big. I think you would miss our style of handmade hospitality. You would miss Señor Helu and this very special place that gave you a chance to improve yourself. But the money's important too. If you get an offer from the Ritz, think carefully, and then let me know what you decide to do."

"Si, Señora Julie. Gracias. Muchas gracias."

The meeting was over. Amador followed me down the concrete steps to Maria Elena sitting at her desk. She looked up quizzically, but didn't ask what happened. I knew Amador would fill her in later and would have good things to say about me. I felt great and had a hunch that in the end, deciding between the Ritz and Torbellino, he'd choose to come back to us.

I was worried about what William would do when he found out. He was so volatile, and bringing Amador back would be a personal defeat for him so it might just set him off. The longer I thought about William, the more I worried. I kept seeing this image of him with his fist raised at Carla. We couldn't afford to have an incident like that between him and Amador. The next one might not end as well.

I picked up the phone and called the corporate office to ask Maria Elena if she knew where William's employment files were. She said she had them, and within minutes she was in my office with a yellow folder with William's name.

"This is what we have; a resume, and an ID card from the Mexican army."

."Thanks for bringing it, Maria Elena."

"Don't trust that ID card in the file. Anybody can get a fake one made." It was easy to see that the sloppily put-together resume was a sham. No one with a college degree would present a resume like that. He claimed to have graduated from Dartmouth College, with a certificate from the Culinary Institute of America, but I was sure that was false. I called information for the phone numbers of both schools and then called each one and asked for the student record departments. They said William had never been enrolled in either school. I knew it! My heart was thumping as I tried calling his references. Not one was a working number.

He was an out and out imposter. Maybe he'd had experience working in a restaurant before or maybe he hadn't had any, but Luis Felipe had hired him out of desperation when he was sick and needed a manager and William just happened along. He didn't know William was a fire keg waiting to explode, but I did. And knowing that made me feel less afraid of him. I called William's extension and told him I needed to see him, not thinking past taking that step.

When he got to the office, he fixated on the folder lying on my desk.

"You have my file?" He asked, trying to sound casual. His eyes darted away and down, avoiding mine. He shifted nervously from foot to foot.

"Dartmouth's never heard of you, William. Neither has the Culinary Institute."

I had been right to look into his background, but I was the one who felt like a fraud for doing it. I was not the manager and had never claimed to be, but I was acting as though I were. I had no authority to hire or fire anyone, but the last thing Molly had said to me before she left was, "Take care of our baby," and that was what I intended to do, whatever that meant.

"There's no passport or green card in your file either. You must have a social security number from the US, if you have lived there most of your life as you've said. Please bring it to me so we can keep it for our records. All employees have to have IDs on file."

"Okay, sure, I'll get it to you. No problem." He turned to leave.

"When, William?" I demanded.

"Wednesday, after my next day off. I'll need time to go to my mother's house to look for it. I haven't seen my social security card since I moved back to Mexico from the States. Besides, you have my Mexican ID from the army, if you need identification." The anger in his voice was like an acetylene torch being lit. The angrier he sounded, the stronger the truth burned. He had frightened me before, but he wouldn't stop me.

"I want your social security number anyway."

I hardly recognized myself. It was an out-of-body experience assuming the authority of someone in charge. I felt elated. Nothing awful had happened. I was protecting the hotel, the guests, the staff by confronting a potential danger. When the door slammed behind William, I wondered if we'd ever see him again.

I couldn't sleep until this situation was behind me. He wasn't at the hotel on Wednesday, but on Thursday morning, I saw him crossing the hotel courtyard; he was whistling and casually flipping his keys, on his way to the kitchen. How long would it take for him to come to talk to me? I would wait. By three o'clock Friday, when his shift ended and he hadn't come to see me, I knew he wasn't going to show up. I called his extension and said I was waiting for him.

I should have asked someone to be with me in my office when he came, but I hadn't thought about that until he was standing in front of me.

"Did you bring your card?" I demanded. My palms were sweating, though William looked surprisingly calm.

"No, I couldn't find it."

I hadn't thought about my next step. I didn't know the rules. Should I give him a warning and put it in his file? How many warnings before he was let go? I was at a loss for what to do, but William didn't know that. He couldn't see the sweat on my palms or how my legs felt like collapsing. Silence permeated the space between us like thick smoke. What if there were a standoff and he refused to leave? None of the other managers knew what was happening between us. My breath was shallow and quick as I held onto the desk for support.

Out of the silence his voice came to me like a hand to the cheek slapping me awake. "Look, if you're going to do a background check I'll just quit. I don't want any trouble," he said clearly.

It took a minute to sink in. He was giving in. I mean, that was all there was to it. I had only needed to tell him that I was going to check him out further, and whatever his past had been, he didn't want me to stir it up. I didn't need to fire him, there wasn't going to be an angry argument. He was just going to leave quietly and without resistance. It was hard to believe, so anti-climactic I was almost disappointed, but William looked relieved.

Suddenly, Carlos, the chief financial officer, came through the door as though he'd been summoned. I had no idea why he showed up at that moment. He'd never stepped foot in my office before, but I was so glad to see him at that moment I could have kissed him.

"So I guess that's it," I said regaining the strength in my voice. I turned to Carlos and explained that William was going to resign. He somehow knew that already. As I've said, the walls at Torbellino had eyes and ears. Carlos nodded and told William to go with him to sign some resignation papers and to get his last paycheck.

"There's one more thing, Julie," William said.

"Yes?"

"I want to know if you're going to make it impossible for me to get a job anywhere else in the area."

I hesitated a minute before answering. We were going to be foisting off our employee problem on some other restaurant or hotel, but it wasn't up to me to warn them. I'd taken on more than enough responsibility already.

"No, I'm not going to do anything like that, William. What you do from now on is your business."

When the door closed behind them, I was still trembling from the aftershock. The whole experience felt surreal. William would be gone. There would be no manager of El Torbellino. The hotel was a mirage, an extended optical hallucination of beauty and serenity that hovered at the edge of my consciousness, in spite of what I'd just experienced. And I wanted to preserve that illusion of paradise for the guests and for me. I thought now that William was gone peace would reign over the kingdom. And it would be thanks to me.

I gave myself a few minutes before calling the other managers to ask them to meet me at the Bambucco Bar, feeling like the Good Witch of the North, ready to tell the villagers the evil witch had been defeated and they were free. William had been a thorn under their nails for a long time.

I thought the news would make a difference in my relationship with the other managers. They would know that I'd been responsible for William's leaving, and even if they didn't say they were grateful to me for engineering that, I'd feel more accepted. I called an emergency meeting, and when everyone was together, I made my big announcement, just as I had when I first told them that Luis Felipe and Molly had left for Miami.

Carla blinked once and then sniffed disdainfully. "We

can handle things without a Director, or an Innkeeper, or whatever William called himself." I was foolish to have expected more from any of them, even Jimmy. They would never let me in on how they were feeling. Keep your emotions under wraps. Don't wear them on your sleeves like North Americans.

I can't say that having them shut me out didn't continue to bother me as the days wore on. My friends in St. Louis would have celebrated with me, applauded me for what I'd done. I could have turned to them for help as they would have turned to me. I missed all the little things; hearing them complain about the weather, their stories about their children, all the myriad tiresome and wonderful details of their lives. I longed for the everyday togetherness more than I had ever realized I would, and I felt guilty for having taken them for granted. I was beyond lonely. It was more palpable than the humidity.

But I was glad to be rid of William, no matter what the others felt, and I was a lot more comfortable knowing I wouldn't bump into him when I walked around the property. The danger of his emotional volatility had passed.

Molly called now and then to ask me to relay some message to one of the managers, but it was never a satisfying conversation. I told myself that it couldn't be much longer and she'd be home and immersed myself in my daily schedule, which had finally settled into a routine. Mornings started optimistically enough, with a conversation with Eliseo who came to the house to take care of the gardens and pool. He was practicing his English at night with the tapes I'd brought him. He'd ask me to go over the workbook pages he'd completed and correct the errors. We avoided talking about the hotel the way new dinner party guests avoid talking politics and religion. It was easy to keep the conversation light and breezy, since we knew so little of each other's language, but I felt reassured starting off the day with his smiling face.

By six-thirty I was at the hotel to check in on the waiters. After hanging around the restaurant for weeks drinking coffee every morning, finally, if someone hadn't shown up for work that day, they'd let me help carry the thermoses of coffee and cups and baskets of pan dulce to the guests' patios. It felt special to walk from the restaurant to the bungalows in the grey light of dawn, leaving a gift behind for the sleeping guests like Santa Claus.

After dropping off the trays I'd stop on my way back to the restaurant to watch the sun burst free of the horizon and rise innocently into the sky. The beach stretched like virgin snow in each direction as far as my eye could see. Wrapped in the beauty of early morning, it was the one time it felt glorious to be alone.

By nine o'clock, reluctantly, I went to the sales office. After two months on the job, I realized I didn't have to worry so much about drumming up new business for the hotel. Calls would come to me through ads and articles in high-end travel magazines, through Luis Felipe's personal connections with the Mexican tourist industry, and through clients from his real estate company in Cancun. All I had to do was pick up the phone and give the information the caller wanted or schedule a tour with clients who were in the area.

I'd return calls and work on promotional ideas for group sales until noon, take a lunch break, work again until three or four, take a longer break for dinner, and go back to the restaurant to talk to the guests in the evening as Luis Felipe had requested. The ad agency brought its crew and took photographs all over the hotel. Without William breathing down my neck, it was a pleasant way to end the day.

Although I had hated going to large parties in St. Louis and didn't think I knew how to make small talk, at Torbellino, circulating among the guests was my job. The people I met came to us from all over the globe, and I loved listening to their stories. Besides, nothing unpleasant ever happened in the elegant dining room, where diners spoke softly under the arched ceiling of the sparkling white adobe room, not wanting to interfere with the flavors of an expertly prepared dinner. The intoxicating ocean air wafted through the accordioned floor to ceiling windows. Torbellino was a favorite hide-away for princes and presidents, writers, artists, and actors like Danny De Vito and Leonardo DiCaprio. I had seen their names in the guest registry, but most of the famous guests rented one of the residences on the property that came with its own chef and wait staff. Most celebrities didn't come to the dining room for meals, except for Farah Fawcett, who signed into the hotel under the name Peter Pan, although all the guests from the US who saw her recognized her. With Amador's constant attention, she was deliriously happy.

She and William were like pawns on a chess board with no hand moving them to check mate.

There were no celebrities present, but the dark-haired woman with olive skin at table one might have passed for one. It was the night after William resigned when I was making my rounds of the dining room. She wore a lovely blue silk sari trimmed in gold; her companion, a distinguished-looking gentleman in a white jacket, radiated kindness. When she noticed me standing at the entrance to the room, she smiled warmly.

"Hello, I'm Julie Heifetz, the Sales Manager for El Torbellino. Are you enjoying your stay with us?"

She lay down her fork to talk, the diamonds in her wedding ring set flashed in the soft light of the dining room.

"It's heaven here! Everything about El Torbellino is perfection, and we have the best room in the hotel. Last year, we stayed in the garden room because the Junior Suites were all booked. It was nice, but the suite is so wonderful. We're from Bombay, and we have amazing hotels there too. We've traveled all over the world and stayed in some extraordinary places; palaces, castles, a resort villa on Pemba Island in Zanzibar. But of them all, I can tell you, El Torbellino is a most special place. There's a magic here, an aura that draws us back again and again." She looked over the room with something close to reverence.

"That's what the owner says. There's a magic here in this cove. He felt it when he first bought the property and built Torbellino. It's an extension of his home and you're his welcome guests," I said proudly.

She nodded. "There is good karma here."

If she only knew, I thought.

."When we die, if we've been very good, maybe we'll come back here when we're re-born," her husband said with a half-smile.

"Do you live here at Torbellino?" she asked.

"I do. My house is on another part of the property."

"That must be wonderful."

"It certainly is beautiful."

We chatted for a few more minutes before I moved on to the next table, glad that there would be no check presented to them, no room numbers to give to make them feel this was anything other than a visit at a friend's home. Reality would hit soon enough when their stay ended and they checked out. How the servers kept the charges straight until then was a mystery to me, but few people complained about their bills when they left.

The Scandinavian-looking guest at the next table had a long thick blonde braid that ran down the middle of her back, as sturdy as steel. She was beautiful, like a statue you could use for a column to hold up a building. Since she was just finishing her meal and looked like she was getting ready to leave, I told her my name, that I was the sales manager, and that I hoped she enjoyed her dinner; I intended to move straight on, but she stopped me.

"Great meal," she said, wiping her mouth and putting her napkin down on the table. "You know my parents owned a hotel and that's where I grew up. I've lived in hotels ever since."

"Really? That must have been an interesting childhood."

"It was. I loved every place we lived. Sometimes we'd stay in the same hotel for years at a time, so I know hotels. I appreciate what you've created at Torbellino. You're lucky to live here."

"It's interesting."

"When I was a kid, I felt sorry for people who had to live in houses. It seemed so boring. Hotels are so convenient, and there's a great vibe at this one," she said. "If my boyfriend weren't expecting me to meet him tomorrow in Merida, I'd stay a lot longer. I'm a filmmaker, and I love the setting."

"You could make a good film here."

"Right now I'm working on one about my boyfriend's dead father. Listen to this."

She leaned forward excitedly as she told me more. "The movie opens with a slow zoom in and then a close up of a cadaver. The cadaver is his actual father. Before they took the body away, I had this idea for the film and asked my boyfriend if it was OK to use him like that. I was kinda nervous to ask, but he said yes right away. They had kind of a weird relationship."

"I'd say that's a bit strange. But I guess anything for art. He's not with you at Torbellino? Your boyfriend, I mean, not the cadaver?"

She laughed. "No, he's meeting me in Merida tomorrow, but he stayed on the sailboat where we live until then. It's been two years since I slept on land. I just needed a break."

"From sailing?"

"Mostly from my boyfriend."

"That's a lot of togetherness. Unless it's a really big boat."

"It's big enough for my piano anyway. I said I had to bring it with me."

"That's amazing."

"Now, we've been on the boat so long it's out of tune so it sounds awful. At first I kept having it fixed, but finally I gave up. There's too much humidity. I don't care though, I play it anyway. I remember what it's supposed to sound like."

She hadn't even told me her name, but she was so unusual I could have listened to her talk forever. I was sorry she'd be leaving in the morning, but that was the way it was. Guests came and went like exotic butterflies that landed on my shoulder for a brief moment to hover and refuel and then were gone. Getting too close to anyone would just mean another personal loss when she left and make me miss Molly all the more.

CHAPTER ELEVEN

*a*fter three months and little to no information from Molly about when they'd be coming home, I was feeling really angry and impatient. I'd done whatever they'd asked of me, and a lot of it I did feeling utterly inadequate and lost. I thought that getting rid of William would make life easier, but other problems popped up to blindside me. One morning when I got to the restaurant, Paulo, the head waiter for the breakfast shift, met me at the door. Usually he was smiling and cheery, but this day his generous smile was gone.

"Much silver flatware is not here," he confided. "The waiters for late shift say they count silver and put it back before they go home, but I see how much we lose. Every day, a fork, a knife, something."

"Oh, no! You don't think it just gets broken or thrown away by mistake?"

"No, Señora."

"You think someone is taking it?"

He nodded. "And come with me. I show you something." I followed him outside to the yard behind the kitchen. He pointed to the ground, where a whole carcass of a lobster was rotting next to the back fence.

"A lot of food from our freezer, they take it too."

"But doesn't anyone see them carrying it out?"

"They throw it over the fence. Someone waits on the other side. Look."

It had rained the night before, which made it easy to see the deep ruts left in the ground from a truck's tires. I knew that theft was a problem in the restaurant industry, but I didn't expect it here. I felt comfortable with the waiters at Torbellino, and I liked them, especially the ones who worked the morning shift. It felt like whoever was doing this was stealing from me personally.

"Who do you think's taking the silver?"

He shrugged. "I don't know who, but I'm sure it's nobody from the morning shift," Paulo swore. "The evening waiters put it away. Ask them about it."

I didn't want my questions to stir up a blame game between the two shifts; we needed a solution, not finger pointing. I told Jimmy about the missing silverware.

"Oh crap. Don't worry. We'll stop those *cabrones*," he said. "I have an idea."

I thought maybe he'd bring a metal safe for the flatware, but he had something more elaborate in mind. Two days later, he came to my office to present me with a beautiful, lacquered mahogany box that his men had made with an elegant silver lock on the front. I knew when I saw it that this was never going to work. Two days after that someone broke the lock. Our supply was running low.

Paulo brought me a catalogue of flatware. "Please, Señora, you choose. You buy for us." I wasn't sure that buying more silver pieces wouldn't just contribute to a never-ending cycle of stealing, but there didn't seem to be any other choice. It would be a temporary fix, but when a replacement for William was hired, then it would be up to him to deal with the problem. I had no idea when that would be, and I hadn't heard a word from Amador since our meeting, or from Molly.

I was operating on four hours of sleep, waking in the middle of the night worried about the hotel and my own inability to make things right. I couldn't excuse Luis Felipe and Molly anymore for staying away, for not calling more, for not being straight with me as to what was going on with them. I felt this unease about them that I couldn't talk myself out of. What was going on with them, really?

Maybe Luis Felipe had never had a second heart attack at all. Maybe there was some other reason that they were staying away that Molly hadn't admitted to me, something underhanded, illegal. I felt terrible for thinking that. Molly had been my friend for thirty-two years, and I didn't know the culture I was living well enough to stand in judgment of it or Luis Felipe. Maybe the loneliness and the isolation were making me imagine things.

The next time Molly called, I told her about William.

"He was impossible, Molly. He came close to hitting Carla. I saw the whole argument, and I was afraid next time he got mad he was going to end up hurting someone. So I looked into his file and he had forged his resume and references. Who knows about his background? Anyway, I confronted him about his resume and asked for his social security number or some legal I.D. He said if I was going to look further into his paperwork he was going to quit."

She didn't say anything to make me feel I'd done the right thing before relaying the news to Luis Felipe.

"He wants to know if you signed any of the final paperwork."

"No. Carlos took care of it."

"Luis Felipe says then that's OK. Just don't put your name on anything."

"I won't."

"Now, what we were calling for is to talk with you about Charles."

"Charles?" She couldn't possibly be asking me to do more than I was already doing. "I see him sometimes at the restaurant, but we don't talk then."

"He's supposed to be the maître d', but we hear the anfitrionas are complaining that he falls asleep in front of the restaurant during his shift."

I was surprised that she'd been talking with other people from the hotel. When they left, they said they didn't want to talk to anyone but me, but I didn't question her about this. I didn't want to sound jealous of their relationships with other managers. But Carla—she must have been the one to tell them.

"Sometimes I see him sitting in the chair at the front door and he's nodding off."

"Well get him to do something for a change. Work when it's his shift."

I bristled. It felt like she was implying it was my fault that Charles wasn't doing his job.

"Molly, I met with Amador like you asked, and I haven't even heard from him since. Now you want me to do something about Charles? I don't know if that'll do any good to talk with him. I'm sure people have already tried. Why doesn't Luis Felipe talk to him? Charles is his friend."

"Yes, but he's not up to that yet."

"What's happening with him, Molly? You've been gone a long time."

"He just walked into the other room, so I can talk for a

minute. Physically, he's better, but he's really depressed. He's not sleeping and he doesn't want to see anyone. Our friend Rick Israel wanted to visit from New York, but Luis Felipe told him not to come. That's so unlike him."

"What do you think it is?"

"Something really upset him the night he had his heart attack. I don't know what happened, but it was something with his nephew who works for him. They got into a big fight, and I could hear them shouting at each other downstairs. I'd never heard Luis Felipe lose his temper like that. Right after his nephew left, Luis Felipe had his attack."

"I figured something must have happened to trigger it. And now he doesn't wants to come home to have to deal with his nephew?"

"Yes. I'm so worried. I don't know anything about his business. I can't help. If anything happens to him..."

"What do you mean?"

"Like, he has all these lawyers that come around the hotel all the time. You may have seen them. We have to wait until Luis Felipe's strong enough to deal with them too."

"Of course. That's a lot of pressure on both of you."

At least she was talking to me like a friend. I felt close to her again and more understanding, less impatient for her to get home. I felt guilty about wanting to tell her my troubles when she was so worried about her husband.

"Tell Luis Felipe I'll try talking to Charles and see if I can get him to stop sleeping on the job. Meanwhile, you take care of yourself and of him."

I was on board again, planning to do everything I could to help while they were away. I felt like a marshmallow with no solid center, vacillating between feeling like I had no backbone to demand more from her and feeling I was doing the right thing by just doing what they asked of me. I reminded myself of all her kindness as my host over the years: her help decorating my house and the Spanish words she'd put on objects all over my house when I first moved in to help me learn the language. She had helped me accomplish my dream. Because of her I owned my house and had a job so I could afford to live there. I owed her my loyalty, even as my questions about Luis Felipe were growing.

Dealing with Charles would be better than sitting still with my free-floating anxiety, and I was always hopeful that this time there was something I could do to help. I thought about how to approach him and asked Dulce, the evening hostess in the dining room, about how Charles was for her to work with.

"Señor Charles is a very nice guy, but he's lazy. He doesn't really help in the restaurant. William tried talking with him when he worked here, and so did Amador, but nothing ever changed."

As Dulce predicted, I found Charles sitting in the leather sling-back chair outside the dining room door that evening.

"Hey, Charles, I haven't seen you in a while. How's it going? How's that little margay of yours?"

"Leo's okay, but he's gotten too aggressive to take him out. I can't even go into his room to feed him. I just throw the meat in and shut the door before he gets loose."

"That's scary. How about letting him go back to the jungle?"

"He'd never make it in the jungle. He's lived with me too long and he wouldn't know how to hunt for his own food, so I can't just let him go."

Now he'd given me something to grab hold of. If I could help Charles figure out a solution for Leo, I might have more leverage getting him to do his job. I remembered seeing a billboard not far down the highway, with an advertisement for Croco Cun Zoo. I'd never been there, and I'd always been curious about it. A zoo would know how to take care of Leo, if they were willing to take him. I thought it was a brilliant idea, but I wasn't sure how Charles would react to it. The next time I ran into him crossing the courtyard I brought it up.

"The Croco Cun Zoo's only about a twenty-minute drive from us."

"Oh yeah. I've been there before. It's a cool place."

"What about taking Leo there? They could take care of him and you could visit whenever you wanted."

Charles told me the next day that he'd thought it over and decided to take Leo to the zoo. In fact, he'd already made an appointment to meet the director, and he asked if I'd like to go along to check out the place.

While Charles went to talk with the director, I took a self-guided tour around the zoo. I was surprised how tiny it was; a dusty narrow path led in a circle through a patch of scruffy

vegetation and past a pile of crocodiles. The repulsive beasts were slammed on top of each other, penned up in a muddy enclosure. I walked on to another pen with a couple of monkeys, another with some snakes, and the final pen for two parrots. I caught a glimpse of a white-tailed deer as it ambled through the trees, but that was all there was to the place. I wasn't impressed, but what was important was how Charles felt about it.

"So, what do you think?" I asked when he finished his meeting with the director.

"He says he'll come pick up Leo tomorrow. The guy's also the vet for the zoo. He says it'd be good to have him." He was matter-of-fact and didn't say any more about Leo, but chattered the whole way back to the hotel about the ice-cream he and Alexa had made and were planning to sell. I felt so relieved knowing we'd found a place for Leo. I'd worried ever since I'd known about a wild animal on the hotel grounds, even if Charles wasn't letting him out anymore. I felt the sweet victory of success already, even before my conversation with Charles about his work.

He was on his way to the hotel when I ran into him again a few days later.

"How's Leo?" I asked, casually.

"Oh, Leo died," he said. I was stunned

I stared at Charles in disbelief.

"Yeah, he died." He shrugged.

"What?"

"The director called me."

"But, Leo was only there for a few days."

"They put him in a cage with a male leopard; they didn't have any place else to put him. Leo didn't stand a chance when he got attacked."

"I'm so sorry, Charles," I stammered. I felt sick. I'd come up with the idea to take him there. It was my fault the little leopard was dead. Charles must have felt as guilty as I did, but he didn't let on. Maybe he was just relieved not to have to worry about him anymore. I shouldn't have felt so responsible. It had been Charles' decision to take him, but if I hadn't interfered and proposed my great plan, Leo would still be alive.

The longer I stayed at El Torbellino, the worse I felt about trying to help when every plan turned out to be futile. I felt like I was going crazy, just like William, just like the chef who'd left the knife marks in the kitchen wall.

That evening when I found Charles asleep outside the

dining room, I didn't bother to wake him. Let Luis Felipe deal with him when he got home.

I'd failed at everything I'd tried to do at El Torbellino: the beach clean-up, the talk with Amador. How much of the problem was the hotel and how much of it was me? I wasn't going to get Charles to change. I felt like my whole life had been a failure. The books that had been published, the awards I'd won, the good press I'd gotten for my performances, the patients and students who said they'd found their voices by working with me, I discounted all of it. Even as a mother, I knew only too well the ways in which I'd been so much less than I should have been. I'd made so many mistakes. My life in St. Louis when I was married had been so safe, so predictable, but I had wanted more. I'd left behind a wake of lovers and a husband I'd discarded, friends who had counted on me, and now the dream I had of paradise and reinventing myself to be more like Molly had turned to dust.

After beating myself up for most of the night, I finally fell asleep. A strange noise came from the bedroom next to mine that startled me awake. I lay in bed frozen, watching as something darted across my doorway. Or had I imagined it? I jumped up and ran to the door in time to catch sight of a small black animal scampering down the steps. I flipped on the hall light, thinking at first that it may have been a wild animal that had gotten into the house somehow from the jungle, but when it hit the living room floor and stood still for a second I could see it was no wild animal. It was a dog: Francois's mangy-looking black mutt. I recognized him immediately because of his stubby tail. He dashed across the living room floor, hell bent on finding his way out of the house, and then he was gone.

By the time I got downstairs, the mutt had disappeared

through the living room windows, which is how he must have gotten in. I hoped François hadn't been lurking around the house with him. Later that morning, after delivering the coffee service, Francois was in my office sending his faxes to his friends in Europe, his mangy dog with him.

"François, your dog came into my house in the middle of the night and scared the bejeebers out of me."

"That was not my dog," he said defiantly. "He was in the house with me, so I know you are wrong. He doesn't need a leash. He must be free, like I am free."

I was pissed. I knew the dog I'd seen was his, but I couldn't prove it.

"Oh, and Julie, you think Luis Felipe will be back to Torbellino soon? You will never see him again." François laughed. "He's gone for good, poor man."

"What do you mean we won't see him again?" I challenged.

"He is in trouble with the Federales. A lot of things he did, and that's why he doesn't come back to Mexico. He's too afraid."

"Afraid of what?"

"You know, that house they were building on the land around the cove? Luis Felipe sold the land to Rick Israel, but he sold that same land to another man too. Two deeds for the same property. No, Luis Felipe won't be back. They are looking for him."

"That's not true. He's in Miami because he's recovering from a heart attack." I had my own suspicions, but I wasn't going to believe rumors spready by François.

"You will see. It is in the papers in Cancun. They are after him," he said, whistling happily as he walked away to the beach with the dog.

Nothing made sense. There was so much I admired

about Mexican culture and wanted to become part of: the color, the warmth, loyalty to family, the slower pace, appreciation of the arts. But here at El Torbellino, everything was rumor, gossip, or straight out lies. There was a constant swirly of *Chisme* as the Mexicans call it, a game of telling a story about someone in order to bring him down. Truth didn't figure into it, they gossiped out of boredom, or habit that was mean-spirited, and I didn't know how to deal with it. I was having enough doubts about Luis Felipe and I didn't need more stories from gossips. Was he the hero some thought him to be or was he a crook who made his money with shady deals? I tried to shake off François' story about Luis Felipe, but the story stuck and played over and over in my mind; it made me worry about the truth of this seductive world he'd built at Torbellino.

Eliseo had warned me when I first went to work for the hotel that Luis Felipe was not my friend. If what François said about him was true, his business deals couldn't be trusted. He owned half my house. Could he take it away from me suddenly just because he didn't want me there or if a better deal came along? I'd invested too much money and too much love to walk away from my investment, and besides, I loved the house itself and didn't want to give it up. But clearly, I hadn't understood what else I had been buying.

I took a deep breath and told myself not to let François bother me. I owed Luis Felipe and myself the benefit of a doubt. If I waited until he and Molly came home, everything would work out in the end. Besides, I'd shut the door on my life in St. Louis, and I didn't want to go back.

When it was early morning and a bird sang to me from the branch outside my window and the sunlight streamed in, my worries disappeared and I felt optimistic again. It's amazing what a little sunlight and warmth will do to help restore one's faith. I would do what I'd always done. Eventually I would figure things out.

When I got to my office, Ricardo, one of the waiters from the night shift, was waiting for me. He was a broad-shouldered, ruggedly handsome young man with perfectly slicked-back hair, except for the one front curl that fell to his forehead like a comma. He was wearing his waiter's uniform, but with the collar of his white shirt open since his shift wouldn't start until three.

"Hola, Señora," he said stiffly. I imagined he was there to ask if Amador was coming back to work.

"Hola, Ricardo. Hay algo que haga para ti?"

"Si, Señora. Quiero ser jefe de camareros." He drew himself up to stand at his full proud six feet in front of me. He wanted to be the evening head waiter, taking over for Amador. It made sense. The restaurant needed a replacement. More than two weeks had passed since I'd talked with Amador. I was disappointed not to have heard from him, but I assumed he had taken the job at the Ritz. Ricardo had worked for more than a year under Amador, and he knew what a head waiter at El Torbellino was supposed to do. He would be a logical choice, but hiring staff wasn't up to me.

I shook my head. "Lo siento, no puedo hacer eso."

I was sure he understood what I was saying, that I couldn't hire him or anyone else.

"I be good head waiter. I have idea, Señora." He insisted, handing me a sheet of paper with the words *"Special Dinner Package"* at the top and a list of menu items below.

"You think the restaurant should offer a special dinner package for our guests?"

"Si."

"And you made this?" I couldn't help but be impressed at his initiative and his chutzpah.

"We make dinner package. Romantic. The best," he said haltingly. I looked more closely at the menu he suggested and I was impressed with his ingenuity and the dishes he had in mind.

"The invitation, she will be beautiful," he said, proudly.

"Bueno, Ricardo. It's a good idea." I handed the paper back to him, committing to nothing.

"Por favor, Señora, you try dinner. You see. Very special."

"It looks wonderful, but no, Ricardo. No puedo. No soy la gerenta."

I was not the manager of the hotel, but he and the other waiters thought I had that authority. His shoulders fell. He looked crushed, and I felt sorry for having discouraged him. He could at least have the job temporarily until there was a new general manager and chef for the restaurant who could hire the head waiter he thought would be best.

"Pero, Ricardo, possiblemente por un rato. Maybe for a while you can be head waiter. Until a new manager comes. No promises for later. Esto no es permanente."

"Si, Señora." His face brightened. "Gracias."

Now that he had the answer he'd come for, I thought that would be all, but he wasn't finished.

"The special dinner package, you try?"

"You mean you want me to come to the restaurant to taste the dishes?"

"No. You sit. I serve you like special guest with special dinner package," he puffed up proudly.

It was an excruciatingly tempting offer. I'd been working long, frustrating hours at the hotel with little sleep, grabbing a bite alone at home for meals. A dinner at the hotel restaurant the way I once had experienced sounded impossibly wonderful, and it would make Ricardo so proud. But should I say yes? I could already feel the disapproving looks of the other managers as they saw the special treatment I would be getting. On the other hand, Molly and Luis Felipe would have accepted his offer without question, and didn't they say I was to be their eyes and ears, to represent them?

"What night do you want me to try it?" I asked.

"Miercoles."

"There aren't too many reservations Wednesday?"

"No, Wednesday is good. I will be good jefe de camereros, Señora."

"I know you will and I'll look forward to the special dinner."

"Gracias Señora....y señora, waiters, we say thank you. No mas Señor William."

It was the first time anyone had mentioned William's name to me since he'd quit. Ricardo and the other waiters must have thought I had fired him, and they wanted to thank me for that.

I felt like a triathlete dragging myself to the tape at the finish line, waiting for Wednesday to come. At noon that day, someone knocked at my door. Surprised to have a visitor, I opened it to find a busboy from the morning shift standing with a scroll of parchment-looking paper tied with a red satin ribbon. He handed the scroll to me and scooted away before I'd even unrolled it.

My name was printed in elegant script with an invitation to a special dinner at El Torbellino in the garden next to the restaurant at eight o'clock. I loved the gesture, which was just the touch guests of the hotel would expect. I treated myself to the rest of the afternoon to stay home and rest. I read and wrote in my journal, which I hadn't done since I'd started work. At six I started getting ready. For the first time in months I manicured my nails; curled my hair with the curling iron; put on eye shadow, eyeliner, mascara, and lip gloss; slipped into a sundress and high heels; and gave myself the once-over in the full-length mirror on the back of my bedroom door. Not bad, I thought. Mike would have approved.

Maybe if Mike had come with me to Torbellino, in this romantic setting, we could have started over. I imagined him in his tux, playing guitar in the dining room of the restaurant, smiling at me as I listened adoringly from a front row table. How could he have resisted falling in love with me there in the moonlight with the ocean breeze and my house to share? But Mike had decided to leave me long before Molly called, and even if he'd come with me, I wouldn't have had time to devote to our relationship.

I turned away from the mirror, reminding myself that I wasn't going on a date, I was going to try out a new head waiter and his idea for a special dinner package. I grabbed a shawl and draped it over my arm, knowing it would be chilly later. Ricardo wanted to impress me, and I wanted to look my best and not hurry the evening along because it got too cold outside.

Torches burned along the stone pathways as I put one high-heeled foot in front of the other, making my way to the restaurant as though it were a runway. Under the walkways, blue lights shined through blocks of glass like blue morpho butterflies trapped underfoot. In the daylight, Torbellino's pristine, white bungalows looked mystical, perched serenely between the blue sea and the opulent green jungle, but after the sun went down, the buildings took on a sensual glow, like a starlet draped in black, sparkling with diamonds.

When I made my way into the dining room, I was aware of the waiters' eyes on me, and suddenly felt self-conscious in a dress with a low neckline and bare shoulders. Feeling modest, I pulled my shawl closer across my chest. Candlelight danced against the crystal wine glasses on the white tablecloths. An exotic, voluptuous floral centerpiece erupted from an enormous brass urn on an antique mahogany table in the middle of the room. This was the same room where I worked, checking in with guests, making sure they were comfortable and contented, but the room felt transformed, back to the dining room I once knew and enjoyed as Luis Felipe and Molly's guest.

Ricardo came toward me and grinned approvingly. "Buena noches, Señora," he bowed. In studied English he said, "I will show you to your table, Madame."

He led me back through the front door and outside to a corner of the garden that bordered the restaurant. A table for one had been set for the occasion, its privacy protected by a tall, thick hedge. Light from a candle shone down on the padded white tablecloth and gleaming flatware. One perfect, single, pink rose reached upward from a cut-glass vase. My heels sank into the carpet of grass as I made my way gingerly to the table where Ricardo held out my chair. I breathed in deeply. The scent of fresh orange blossoms, sweet, citrusy and lively filled the air. I felt like royalty. I didn't care that this special night had been arranged for me only because Ricardo thought I had become the manager of Torbellino and he wanted to impress me. I was carried away by the elegance of the setting and his attention.

"Your menu, Madame." He handed me a scroll with selections for each course elegantly printed on parchment-style paper: salad with pumpkin seed pesto, caramelized onions, goat cheese, lettuce and garlic vinaigrette to start;

followed by the chef's special pasta with seafood and herbs; then a main course of surf and turf, including broiled short ribs, plantain, lobster, mint and gremolata; and for the final course, classic churros with dulce de leche, chocolate sauce and dulce de leche ice cream.

"It's beautiful, Ricardo," I said as he waited anxiously by the table for my approval. "Everything. The table. The setting. The menu. It's very, very special. I'm sure our guests will love it."

He smiled, delighted. "You would like something to drink? A cocktail? A bottle of wine?"

"Riesling, por favor. Una copa."

"Yes, madame."

He disappeared inside the restaurant. Lazy, cotton-candy shreds of clouds drifted softly across the moon. The light cast shadows of the Anapole tree against the white adobe wall as the branches swayed in the wind. Couples on the other side of the hedge spoke softly to each other, unaware of my presence behind the hedge, but I didn't feel lonely. I was grateful for all that Torbellino had given me. It was the experience of a lifetime. I will write about this one day, I thought.

Every dish, served with Ricardo's impeccable attention, had been perfection. It was late by the time I finished dessert. I got up from the table and went to find Ricardo in the dining room, to say goodnight, and thank him again for the special dinner. His idea would serve the hotel well. A few guests were still lingering over their drinks when I walked outside to go home. Suddenly, the lights in the dining room behind me went out. I looked around the courtyard at the bungalows and the walkway; the entire hotel was without electricity, and I hadn't thought to bring a flashlight.

I stepped gingerly onto the lawn feeling uneasy about walking home through the patch of jungle and the rest of the way in the coal black night. Clouds had gathered overhead and blacked out the moon. I took a few mincing steps, feeling my way onto the pitch black lawn, when a dot of light flashed across the courtyard, blinked briefly, then went out. I couldn't imagine what it was when it happened a second time, and then a third, a mystery light that blinked off and on and moved slowly across the lawn toward the restaurant. It was bizarre, steady, like a firefly on steroids, off and on. I stood still watching as it came closer and I could make it out for what it was, not a blinking light, but a flame. For one sustained second the flame glowed, and in it its glare I could see Gaspard's face. It was our resident artist, flicking his lighter on so he could see enough to take a step before the wind blew the flame out. He'd flick the lighter on again and take a few more steps. He was stumbling, barefoot and bare-chested, making his way to the restaurant through the dark like an ancient Greek philosopher with a torch held high, searching for the truth. I almost laughed when I saw him. In that moment, all was forgiven, his outrageous nude sunbathing and smoking pot in front of the restaurant, his disregard for hotel rules. In the glow of the special evening, I felt as lovingly toward Gaspard and all the characters at El Torbellino as Christopher Robin did when he said to Pooh, "Silly old bear, I won't ever forget about you." All thoughts of danger seemed silly as my fear of monsters lurking in my closet when I was a child. But some monsters can turn out to be real.

CHAPTER TWELVE

*I*t was later than usual when I left for work the next morning and headed straight to the Bambucco Bar. I couldn't wait to tell the other managers about Ricardo becoming the new head waiter, but I never got the chance. I thought I'd gotten there early, but when I cleared the top step, the entire management team was waiting for me.

"Have you heard what happened last night with Ricardo?" Gerardo asked excitedly.

"No, what happened?"

"Ricardo and a few other guys from the kitchen went to the bar down the road after work. They all got drunk...especially Ricardo. When they got ready to leave, it was three a.m., and Ricardo ordered the new busboy to pay for everyone's drinks. The kid said he didn't have enough money on him. Ricardo got mad and started yelling, and then he shoved the poor guy. You know how big Ricardo is, and the busboy's a lot smaller, well, Ricardo got him on the ground and was choking him," Gerardo said.

"The busboy pulled out a knife and slashed Ricardo from his neck all the way down one arm," Carla chimed in.

"Oh my God!"

"There was blood all over the bar, on the floor and the wall, everywhere," Jimmy said. "I saw the mess when I stopped by the bar later. It's right down the road from my house."

I knew this wasn't chisme, it was the truth. I was furious at Ricardo. How could he have been so stupid and such a bully? It didn't fit with the Ricardo I'd seen the night before. How could he have squandered his chances at success? I was furious, but worried about him all at once.

"How awful," I stammered.

"An ambulance came and took them both to the hospital," Gerardo said. "Maria Elena called me at four this morning, and she was completely hysterical. She gets like that anyway, and Ricardo's her boyfriend, you know. She kept saying, *Ricardo's going to die, he's going to die.*"

"Is he? Is it that serious?" I asked.

"No, that was just Maria Elena. He's out of surgery this morning, I checked. He'll have to stay in the hospital a while, but the doctor says he was lucky. He would have bled to death if they hadn't gotten him to the hospital in time. They still aren't sure how much damage there was to the nerve in his arm."

Knowing the incident had happened unnerved me. Chisme was upsetting and confusing to hear, but violence happening so close to the ranch and involving our employees at the hotel was terrifying. I thought we were rid of the threat when William quit. But now, Ricardo, and I had been the one to promote him. Who would be next? I could think of little else. When I ran into Gerardo I'd ask about Ricardo, but there wasn't any new information, so eventually I stopped asking. The restaurant functioned as it could, getting by without a head waiter, but missing a touch of penache.

Then, one afternoon at the end of the week, before the evening shift, Amador showed up at my office door, dressed in his waiter's uniform, looking as though he'd never been away. He was elegant; he moved like a dancer, not a fighter. He was back to work, fully committed. If William hadn't given him a hard time, he would never have quit, and I had no doubt, now that he'd made up his mind, he'd keep his word and be reliable. I was ecstatic to see him.

"I'm glad you're here. Señor Helu will be happy too, but I'm surprised to see you. I haven't heard from you since our meeting."

"I know. I tried the Ritz, but you were right, it is not like Torbellino. And now William isn't manager anymore...I promise you, Señora, I will come to work every day."

I knew with Amador in charge of the dining room, everything would be fine. The next time there was an electrical outage on the ranch, he directed the waiters to set extra candles on the tables, and move the candelabras where they could shed the best light, without missing a beat. The flames flickered like diamonds in the reflection of the glass walls. The waiters glided between the tables like well-trained ballet dancers, their trays raised high as they turned with demi-pirouettes to exit through the dining room door into the kitchen. The diners were entranced; it was the epitome of a romantic setting and mood.

By the time we talked again, Molly somehow knew that Amador had come back as head waiter. For once, she had good news too; they had hired a new chef, Eric Martin, on the recommendation of their good friend in New York who'd given Eric his seal of approval. He'd be there as soon as he could.

"He just graduated from the Culinary Institute of America. He wants to combine classic French and Mexican cooking with the best of modern American cuisine. He'll really help raise the level of the kitchen. Keep an eye out for him when he gets to El Torbellino."

That was the best news she could have given me, other than to say they were on their way home. A CIA chef from the US could take over the management of the restaurant and kitchen. Just knowing he was coming made me breathe easier.

But the spaces between my moments of despair never lasted long. Carlos showed up unexpectedly at my office the next day. The only other time he'd come to see me before was when William quit and he had magically appeared. He wasn't one to waste time with a social visit, so as soon as I saw him, I knew something was up.

"Good morning, Julie. We have a problem. You know Sebastian, the truck driver?"

"The guy who makes pickups and deliveries for us from Cancun?"

"Yes, this morning he went to make a bank deposit for us, like he does every week. But today he stopped first to pick up some things at the market in Puerto Morelos. He left the envelope with the money in it on the front seat and somebody stole it while he was doing his errands."

I felt like someone had punched me in the gut. "Do you know who did it?"

"No. Everybody in Puerto Morelos knows his truck and his routine and somebody must have followed him."

"Did he break the lock to get in?"

"No. The window doesn't close and it's been that way

for months. It was easy to reach inside and take the envelope."

"How much did he take?"

"Two thousand dollars American. "

"Jesus Christ! Two thousand dollars? How could that have happened? That was so damned careless!" My voice shot up to the ceiling, and I didn't even try to reel it in. Carlos stared at me cooly. Losing control of my emotions was exactly the wrong way to deal with this. I knew it, but I couldn't help myself.

"It was a mistake," Carlos said calmly.

"A *mistake*? Who makes a mistake like that?" I demanded, sounding even more hysterical. How did I know Sebastian didn't keep the money himself? How did I know that Alejandro, the head of accounting who was his boss, didn't put him up to it? Or that Carlos himself wasn't part of the scheme? I didn't trust any of them, not after the missing silver and the lobsters, or Ricardo, and now Sebastian.

Carlos looked blankly at me. "We won't lose that money."

"And why not?" I challenged.

"We will break a window in the office to make it look like the money was stolen here, not in Sebastian's truck. Then insurance will pay if it was at the hotel."

He said it so easily, as though there were nothing wrong with insurance fraud.

"But we can't do that, Carlos."

"This is what Luis Felipe would want."

"That doesn't make it right," I snapped.

"It's his hotel," Carlos shrugged.

I shouldn't have been so surprised. Plenty of business owners are sleazy. Companies everywhere cheat, but I didn't want to be part of one that did. I had been so proud to say I worked at El Torbellino, that I had a house on the property, but I was helpless in the face of a deception that Luis Felipe would approve. I would never mention that I knew anything about it, but I felt like a collaborator and I was ashamed.

Now, I felt my eyes were wide open and I saw so many things that worried me, like the flock of lawyers that came and went from the accounting office constantly like sand flies. Why did Luis Felipe need so many for such a small hotel? And why was there a whole team of accountants? I knew Luis Felipe had other businesses like his furniture factory and his real estate company, but what else?

I tossed and turned all night, trying to sort out the paradise I had loved from my recent suspicions. I wouldn't condemn Luis Felipe without knowing the facts. Money laundering. The phrase was a howling monkey that wouldn't let me sleep.

At nine the next morning, there was a loud, impatient knock at my door. Maria Elena was standing outside, impatiently flipping the ends of her greasy hair over her shoulder as her car idled in my driveway.

"We have to go right away or we'll be late. You have an appointment with an immigration lawyer in Cancun, and it wasn't easy to get." She was in a foul mood. Ricardo wasn't working at the hotel anymore, and he'd been told he couldn't come back. She probably held me responsible for that, and now, she had to drive me into Cancun.

No one had mentioned a green card to me until now, which the hotel needed me to have to work there. I hadn't planned on spending the day in Cancun, but it was too late to object. We drove down the highway in Maria Elena's VW bug with the windows open, which made it too loud to talk, even if we'd wanted to. When we finally got to the large government building in Cancun City, Cynthia, a young, attractive attorney, met us outside. She was very businesslike and brusquely asked for the photo I was to have brought with me. Maria Elena had forgotten about that. Cynthia scowled and told us to go find a photographer and come back when we had the picture. After several tries, Maria Elena found a photographer whose shop was open. He took my snapshot and gave it to Maria Elena in a manilla envelope. She paid him, and we rushed back to the courthouse. I didn't care what the picture looked like, I just wanted to get the whole bureaucratic process over with and get back to the ranch. The city streets were burning up and there was no breeze in the middle of town.

Cynthia looked disgusted when she opened the envelope.

"It needs to be in black-and-white, not in color," she said. Now Maria Elena was really pissed off; she fumed the whole way back to the photographer's studio and then to the immigration office. I knew better than to say a word. By the time we got there, the immigration office was closed for lunch. Maria Elena left me, saying she'd be back for me later. I was glad she was gone, but Cynthia was nowhere around either. A few other people were waiting, scattered around the dull room, holding numbered cards. The sign said the office would be open in an hour and a half. I took a number and sat down, stealing glances at the people waiting with me; women holding babies on their laps, older men, a young woman. I didn't want to be there. I didn't want a Mexican identity card. I had too many questions about Luis Felipe and the other managers to want to be part of their system.

The people around me were used to waiting. I shifted in

my chair trying to get more comfortable and fidgeted with the card with my number on it, listening for someone to start calling people up to the desk. I was afraid I might not understand Spanish well enough and would miss my turn. One woman with a baby sleeping on her shoulder looked over at me and smiled and I let out a deep breath and relaxed. It was good to meet a friendly face. Finally, an official came in and took his seat at the desk at the front of the room. One by one, numbers were called. Cynthia breezed in, handed some papers to the officer, and left, without saying a word to me. When my number was called, I walked up to the desk, my knees shaking.

"Su nombre?" the officer asked, without looking up from the stack of papers in front of him.

"Julie Heifetz."

"Su direction?"

I gave the address of Torbellino.

"Director de Ventos?"

" Si." He glanced through the documents and waved me over to the next desk to another official who held out a rubber pad with purple ink, waiting for my finger to press down. It felt like a defining moment. My fingerprint on that document would make me feel like I was abandoning part of myself, a part that I didn't want to relinquish, my own principles. It was foolish to give it that much importance. I wasn't giving up my citizenship or joining the army, but I was attaching myself legally to Torbellino.

"Por favor." The officer nodded at a document. I inhaled and held my breath, pressing my finger down where he had indicated, leaving my purple stain behind, as though it were blood.

"Siguiente," the official called the next person in line to come forward. I walked to the sink and scrubbed at the purple on my hand. How long would it take for the ink to fade? I started to feel sick to my stomach as I walked away from the desk. Maria Elena was waiting out front in her car. Having an official government document should have made me feel more legitimate, but instead, I felt more vulnerable than ever.

When Maria Elena dropped me off at my house, I couldn't wait to get inside, get undressed, and take a long hot shower. I felt dirty after the time in Cancun walking back and forth to find the photographer and waiting at the government office, dirty from the whole experience. I put my hand on the door knob of my front door and felt something strange under my fingers. I leaned down to see what it was and pulled back, horrified. A string was twisted around the doorknob, tied to a dead bird's head. The bird's sharp bony beak and feathers were matted with dried blood, and its eyes were open. I could hardly look at it. Who would have left such a disgusting thing for me to find? Had it been killed and put there as part of some ritual sacrifice? Many locals believed in voodoo and black magic. Some of the workers thought that Maria Elena was a witch, but it couldn't have been her doing, she'd been with me in Cancun.

I ran to Eliseo's hut to ask him if he'd seen anyone outside my door while I was gone. He could tell me what it meant and get rid of it for me. It took a long time for Sebastiana to answer. It was dark inside the house, when she opened the door and Eliseo stepped out, I could see his face and bare chest were covered with red angry welts and his eyes were so swollen they were nearly shut.

"Oh no, Eliseo, what happened?"

"Mal agua." His face was pinched with pain. "I was swimming in the ocean. The bad fishes, they do like this." It was nearly June, just before rainy season, when the poisonous jellyfish filled the bay. They must have come early this year, before Eliseo realized it, but I felt as though the welts on his body were my fault; a bad luck spell that had been intended for me had fallen on him, because he was my friend.

"I'm so sorry, Eliseo. Can I get you something from the pharmacy?"

"No thank you, Señora." He covered his swollen eyes with his hands, ashamed to have me see him like that. I felt so terrible for him.

"I hope you feel better soon. Let me know if you want to go see a doctor."

Sebastiana closed their door and I went home. As much as I wanted to avoid touching it, I had no choice. The string loosened easily, and I threw the head into the trash. Whatever else it was supposed to mean, one message was clear: Leave. This is not your place.

CHAPTER THIRTEEN

*I*n time, I dismissed the bird as a stupid prank. I wasn't going to let anxiety get the better of me when there was too much else to occupy me. Molly called from time to time, her calls lasting as long as a butterfly's kiss. She doesn't seem to care about me, only about the hotel and Luis Felipe's reaction to what was happening there. I didn't trust him or anyone at the hotel, but I was damned if I was going to quit until I knew for certain what was going on with him and El Torbellino, if I was a pawn in the game, and if Molly was too. I didn't mention the bird to her or money missing from Sebastian's truck. Let Carlos be the one to tell her about the plan to get the money back from the insurance company. I did tell her that Amador was back, even though Maria Elena had probably already told them by the time she called me. And I told her about the fight between the busboy and Ricardo, which she also had heard about.

That day, Luis Felipe took the phone from Molly. It was the first time he'd talked to me directly and not through her. "That Ricardo, he makes trouble, that guy. This is not the first time. Once, Maria Elena gave him my truck to drive and he got in an accident and the car was finished. He didn't even have a license. Maria Elena begged me to give him one more chance, so I did. But now he made trouble for us again."

"He's been told that was his last chance. Neither he nor the busboy can work here anymore."

"That's good, and good that Amador is back. Hold on, here's Molly." He handed the phone to her.

"There's one more thing. Luis Felipe wants you to know you're going to be getting a call from our friend Rick Israel's son, Max. He wants to have his wedding at the hotel the first week in November, and you're to work out the details with him."

"He already called. I've blocked that weekend off in the calendar." I'd been excited when Max called to tell me he wanted to have his wedding at Torbellino. I'd booked a few business meetings, a retreat for a group from the States, plus the ad agency's stay, and a birthday party for a Venezuela family, but Max Israel's wedding was going to be huge. The staff would all benefit, getting extra hours to work when the hotel was full and busy, serving every meal all weekend long, with fishing trips for the men and massages for the women. Max's father, Rick, was a frequent guest at the hotel and tipped generously, but I hadn't seen him since I'd started work in the sales department. It would be nice to see him again. I wondered about the unfinished mansion on the land that François said was being disputed.

"It's important to Luis Felipe that everything goes well. Ask Carla if you need help."

Carla and I gave each other wide berth when our paths crossed, which wasn't as often as I would have expected. I had been poised for a confrontation between us, but her animosity was controlled, kept under the surface, but I certainly wasn't going to rely on her when it came to planning Max's wedding. I'd found a list of providers and knew who to call for flowers, music, photographers, and even had the name and number of a wedding officiant for the ceremony. We wouldn't need to ask for Carla's help.

"There's plenty of time between now and then. This is only May."

Jimmy was waiting for me when I got off the phone.

"We really need to talk to Luis Felipe. It's kind of an emergency." He took off his battered Fedora and mopped the sweat from his face with his handkerchief.

"So what's the emergency?"

"The guys in my department have been waiting for the raise the boss promised, and they're threatening to join a union if they don't see the money in their paychecks tomorrow. Man, if there's one thing Luis Felipe hates, it's the unions. He'd rather close up the hotel than see them unionize." He flipped his hat back on his head. "They say if they don't get their money tomorrow, they'll quit. These guys don't play. I know them. They're out of patience."

"Do you think what they're asking is reasonable?"

"Yeah. They get bupkis. The waiters and the guys in the kitchen make a lot more from the tip pool than they do."

"That doesn't seem fair. Can we adjust the percentages that they all get?"

"That's what I think should happen, but Alejandro pays the salaries, and he won't listen to me. He doesn't want to change things, and he really doesn't give a rat's ass about my guys. They deserve more than they get. They work their asses off for this place."

"When Luis Felipe calls again, I'll tell him what you said, but I don't know when he'll call back, and I don't call them." Molly had a new number in Miami, but she hadn't given it to me. They were renting a condo, and there was no more medical emergency, so I should have been able to call her, but she obviously didn't want that. What kind of one-way relationship did we have? But now wasn't the time to ruminate over my relationship with Molly. Something had to be done about the maintenance men.

"Do you think it would help if I met with them, Jimmy?"

The suggestion caught him off guard.

"I mean I can't guarantee I can get them their raise, but I can listen to them. I want to hear what they have to say. Of course I'd need you there to translate. My Spanish still sucks."

"It's not a bad idea. I'll tell the guys to meet us in the parking lot tomorrow morning right before their shift. This'll be a first for them, meeting with management."

I was trying to buy time until I heard from Molly and Luis Felipe, but I wanted to be respectful. Many of them lived on the ranch, but I didn't know where or what the conditions were like, and I had wondered about that even before Jimmy told me they might go on strike.

The next morning at eight, a dozen workers showed up on the employees' parking lot. They stood facing Jimmy and me, with a car's length distance between us. Manuel, the old gardener, was one of the group. I was sure he recognized me, but he didn't tip his hat when he saw me as he usually did. One of the younger workers stepped forward, said a few words to Jimmy, and then took out of his pocket a wrinkled sheet of paper and started to read. The longer he read, the more confident he sounded. The men behind him were fixated on Jimmy's face. When he stopped reading, Jimmy translated.

"That was a list of their demands; the raise Luis Felipe promised and better conditions in the dorms."

"Ask them what's wrong with the dorms?"

Jimmy asked and the leader answered, with a few others also wanting to be heard.

"They say there are two bathrooms for over two hundred men, and there's no place safe to keep their personal stuff, like radios, money, extra clothes. Everything they have gets stolen."

I was appalled. "Something ought to be done about that."

"Hey, you sound like you should work for the union, not management," Jimmy said sarcastically.

"Just translate for me, please." I stepped forward to talk with the men.

"First, I want you to know that I very much appreciate the fine work you do for us every day. You keep the hotel running smoothly, and the pool looking immaculate. The gardens are the pride of El Torbellino. All the guests comment about them. You were promised a raise, and you need better living conditions. Anything else that isn't there now, you can put on your list. Get the list to me and when Señor Helu calls, I'll tell him those changes are necessary."

Jimmy translated what I'd said into Spanish, but suddenly the group broke into laughter, slapping each other on the head and talking. I was confused and a little embarrassed.

"Why are they laughing, Jimmy?"

"Because...I told them what you told me to say...only, I used a little more colorful language than you did."

When they'd quieted down and got serious again, the leader said something else to Jimmy.

"What was that?"

"He said we have a week to get them their raise, and a guarantee from Luis Felipe that he'll build a new dorm with more bathrooms and closets and cabinets that lock."

That's when I noticed Alejandro at the side of the parking lot. He must have been listening the whole time, but I hadn't noticed him; I'd been too focused on the maintenance men. He walked up to the group and started talking at them. His tone was harsh, chastising, like he was speaking to a bunch of unruly children. They hung their heads as he yammered at them, without taking a breath. When he finally stopped, he turned away and walked back toward his office, without saying a word to Jimmy or me. The group silently disbanded.

"That went real well," Jimmy said as we walked back toward my office. "They appreciated meeting with us."

"Maybe they did. Obviously Alejandro didn't."

"My guys are real glad you're here. Forget Alejandro. He thinks because he's the accountant he's hot shit. He's Carla's brother, and they've got their own thing going on here, their own little Mafia."

"Mafia?" My ears perked up at the word.

"Their father used to be the accountant here, until a million dollars turned up missing. Luis Felipe thought their father was the one who stole it."

"I've heard that story before, but how could Luis Felipe have hired his son if that's true? It makes no sense." I shook my head.

"All I know is, Carla, Alejandro, and Gerardo work together. They get what they want and make trouble for everybody else. Not too long ago, Carla took a year off, and it was really calm at the hotel when she was gone. Everybody got along just fine then. But now she's back, and maybe one of these days Torbellino will be completely in their hands."

"Never! That's never going to happen."

"Oh, don't be so sure. Luis Felipe's in love with Carla."

I was shocked hearing my suspicions confirmed when I hadn't wanted to trust them, but Jimmy knew it was true. "This is his playground, this hotel. He's like those ranchers in Mexico a long time ago. They had houses for their women all over their property."

"What?"

"It's a Mexican thing."

"And Molly?"

"Molly only knows what Luis Felipe wants her to know."

We kept walking. I sensed from the first time I'd seen Luis Felipe and Carla together at the employee party that they'd been having an affair, but I was sure Molly didn't know. She was blind to whatever he did, including his relationship with other women, living like a princess in the life that Luis Felipe had constructed for her. And I had tried to be blind too. But how much should I believe of what Jimmy said? Was there really a Mafia, or was that just what he called it?

We crossed the parking lot. I was following Jimmy aimlessly, but I was thinking about Luis Felipe and Carla and what else Molly might not know about her husband when I stumbled, and Jimmy reached out to steady me.

"I'm okay. I wasn't looking where I was going and I tripped."

"You gotta watch where you're going here. They're putting in a new addition to the dining room and there's shit everywhere...boards, nails. Be careful."

I looked around. Official-looking government notices

were nailed to massive pillars around the periphery of a new construction area. *Construccion Prohibida,* the sign said.

"Hey, Jimmy what's with the signs? We're not supposed to be building here?"

"Those pillars they're putting up are made out of palms that are on the endangered list. The inspector was here today and when he saw them he said to stop building until we get a permit."

"But they haven't stopped."

"Yeah. Boss's orders. Look, this whole hotel was built without a permit. We aren't even supposed to have a restaurant here, but we do." He grinned, amused.

"Yes, we do."

"Probably most of the hotels on this coast operate without permits."

I wasn't thinking about other hotels, I was thinking about Luis Felipe and this hotel, remembering something that had always made me wonder. When Luis Felipe first dreamed about building El Torbellino, he had investors interested in the project. But just as the hole for the foundation had been dug, the Mexican economy tanked, the mortgage rate for construction loans went sky-high, and all those potential partners backed out. I remembered Molly telling me how depressed Luis Felipe was for the next two years, trying to come up with money to finish building his dream. He flew from one country to the next for meetings with potential investors. Who knows if Carla was with him on those trips, but Molly was worried about him. She didn't know whether to tell him to give up his dream or encourage him to keep looking for backers.

But then, suddenly, with no explanation as to where the money came from, the hotel was up and running. At the time, I'd been relieved that the construction could go forward and so impressed with what Luis Felipe created I didn't think more about where the money had come from. Every year after that, I saw new construction added; a temazcal, a spa, a theater, a television room. But now that I was working at the hotel, I wondered how all of that was possible. Where did that money come from? We weren't operating at full capacity, even with only thirty-six rooms. Someone must have been putting money into the hotel that I didn't know about. I thought about François' story about Luis Felipe selling the same land to two different buyers. If that was true, maybe there was more that he and the hotel were involved in; money laundering, banking fraud. I didn't know how those things worked, but I didn't want to think too much about them. I wasn't a lawyer or a detective. I didn't want to judge what I didn't know or understand.

An image came to me of a scene that I had witnessed a few years before. I was walking on the beach when a little girl nearby looked up and noticed Luis Felipe as he rose bare-chested out of the water. Seeing his coal black hair, black beard, and a red sail from his boat draped around his neck like wings, "*El Diablo! El Diablo!*" she screamed. Maybe the child was aware of more than I was willing to see about the nature of the man.

"Jimmy," I said tentatively, "What do you know about money laundering?" Jimmy looked as though he'd been shot.

"We don't ever mention words like that around here," he cautioned in a whisper. I knew I'd overstepped my bounds by asking, but his reaction was enough to make me think I'd been right to be suspicious. We walked in silence the rest of the way to the front lobby where Dulce was bent over the credenza. She was reading a page in the leather-bound guest book filled with glowing accounts of guests' experiences. She stood up quickly, looking guilty, as though she'd been caught stealing.

"Is something wrong?" I asked.

"Yes...Carla told me to look at the guests' comments... it's...you should see this...I'm sorry..."

She moved aside to show me the entry she'd been reading, which was printed in large, child-like letters sprawled across the page.

"Everything at Torbellino is good, but not Señora Julie. She bother the guests."

I felt mortified, sick to my stomach. Everyone would read this and believe it, even though I was sure that wasn't how the guests felt about me. I wanted the ground to open up and swallow me. Jimmy looked over my shoulder and read the entry out loud.

"No guest wrote that, that's for sure. Look at the handwriting...and the grammar. It's like a second grader."

I felt too shitty to say anything.

He shook his head. "I bet whoever it was, Carla was behind this. She's a sneaky one." He laughed and lay a calloused hand on my shoulder. "Don't let her get to you, Julie. That's how they win, little by little."

CHAPTER FOURTEEN

I felt ashamed when I thought about the entry in the guest book, ashamed that someone disliked me enough to humiliate me, that Carla and her little gang didn't want me at the hotel and were doing such a good job of making me miserable. I am an intruder, a gringa. When Luis Felipe and Molly left I thought I would be their savior. I had rushed in to help, coming up with ideas, organizing the beach clean-up, getting William to quit. I was eating humble pie now, withdrawing, feeling uncertain of every move I made.

I would play my hand close to my chests too and trust no one. I avoided eye contact with Carla and had as little to do with the management team as possible. The next time Molly called, I told her that things had gotten more difficult for me since William quit, and once I started talking, I couldn't hold back. I told her about the guest book and the dead bird on my doorknob, and how miserable that made me feel.

"I know how Carla can be. I'll tell Luis Felipe what's

been happening when we're done talking. Maybe he can think of some way to make it better."

"I hope so."

"I'm sure he can. And he says not to worry about the maintenance men. We heard about your meeting and he'll take care of the situation when we get home."

"And when will that be?"

"We'll be there for Thanksgiving. It's my favorite holiday, you know." I groaned. Thanksgiving was over four months away. But I'd made it for this long, and I could hang on until then. Besides, I felt better having confessed to Molly the hell I was going through, knowing that Luis Felipe would try to help.

As I walked toward the restaurant, a burst of raucous laughter exploded and I hurried to find out who it was. Everyone at Torbellino respected the serenely quiet atmosphere of the hotel, which was easy to do since children under the age of sixteen weren't permitted.

Gaspard was in the hot tub with a young blonde red-faced kid I'd never seen before, the two of them slapping the water at each other like teenagers at a high-school pool party. The walkway was now wet and slippery and unsafe to walk on.

"This is for you, Eric!" Gaspard yelped. The spray of water landed in the kid's eyes and Gaspard howled with delight.

The hot tub and swimming pool were off-limits for the employees. Gaspard knew the rules, but he paid no attention to them, which annoyed the hell out of me. He was an artist and Luis Felipe's friend, which he felt gave him special dispensation; he sunbathed in the nude where guests could see, he smoked weed on the patio of the restaurant, and used the hotel cell phone to call his friends and family in France without paying for the calls.

"Gaspard!" I said sharply from the edge of the hot tub.

"Ah, Julie." He stopped and rubbed the water from eyes. "This is Eric Martin. He just came today. He is our new chef!" He squinted to shield his eyes from the sun.

"This is our new chef?" Oh no! He was too young, too frail, he couldn't be the one Luis Felipe had hired to run the restaurant, the heart of El Torbellino? We needed someone strong in charge of the kitchen and the dining room, someone who could command authority. How could this pale faced kid barely past adolescence live up to the sophistication of our restaurant, much less improve it? I had been looking forward to having another American work at the hotel, but not a child. If he had any sense at all, he would have known better than to be playing in the hot tub in the middle of his first afternoon at El Torbellino, even if Gaspard suggested it.

Damn Gaspard. But this was true to form for him. He was a seventy-year-old child himself. "Hello, Eric." I said through clenched teeth. He climbed out of the tub as fast as he could, grabbed a towel and wrapped it around his waist.

"I just got here a couple of hours ago from the airport."

"Molly said you'd be coming, but I didn't know you'd be here today. I'm Julie Heifetz, Sales Manager."

"Hello. It's nice to meet you."

"He was hot and tired from his trip," Gaspard said. "The hot tub would be good for him."

"I'm sure that's what you told him. If you have any questions, Eric, I'd be happy to try to help. My office is on the other side of the courtyard." Gaspard lifted himself out of the tub, toweled off and walked away down the path with the new chef in tow.

A few weeks passed before Eric took me up on my offer. I hadn't seen him around the hotel grounds since the day he'd arrived. I assumed he was working in the kitchen when I was at the restaurant, and I was giving him time to adjust before checking in with him to see how things were going.

When he showed up at the door of my office, his white chef's coat was full of grease stains and dark around the collar; there was no trace left of the youthful glee that I'd seen when I first laid eyes on him. He hesitated before coming in.

"Uh, Julie, um, I was wondering if you've got some time?"

"Sure, Eric. I'm glad to see you. I've been wondering how things are going. Have a seat." I gestured to the couch and walked over to join him.

He sighed and unbuttoned the top of his lab jacket.

"Thanks. I need to talk with someone who can speak English for a change. I don't know a word of Spanish."

"I'm not much ahead of you. It's not easy is it, working with people when you don't know their language?" I felt terrible for him. He was just about my younger son's age, and he looked so lost. I had it easier than Eric did since all of the management team spoke English. But the cooks and dishwashers didn't know how to say more than hello, and he was their boss.

"I was excited about this job, but it's a lot tougher than I thought it would be. The first few days I thought I was doing OK with the guys in the kitchen. I'd show them what I wanted, you know, pointing, grunting, whatever. They smiled and laughed, and I started kidding around with them. They're my age, some of them even younger. I kinda thought we were getting to be friends. But that's not what was happening at all. I show them how to do something and they do the opposite. They laugh at me behind my back and they think I don't know."

I understood perfectly. Carla, the ice queen, and her staff talked about me behind my back too. Once I overheard them calling me "the old lady."

"Look, I know it's really hard being new here." I said, wishing I had a magic answer for him. "We're outsiders here. All I can tell you is to keep on doing what you know is right. Keep showing them what you expect. Didn't Molly and Luis Felipe tell me you were going to work on some new menus?"

"Crap. I haven't even started thinking about that."

"That's OK, I didn't mean to add more pressure, I just thought it might help to focus on something you were trained to do. Just give yourself time. You have a lot to offer." I half believed what I was saying, but who was I to offer advice about how to survive here? My relationship with my own team hadn't gotten any better. If anything, it had deteriorated over the four months I'd been working at the hotel.

Eric shook his head and grimaced. "They were impressed with the way I used the knife, when they saw how fast I was. They put their thumbs up and I thought I'd scored some points. But last night, after we cleaned up and left, somebody came back and stole my good knife, the expensive one I brought from New York."

"Oh, I'm so sorry."

His lip quivered and I thought he might cry. "I need to get away from this bullshit," he said. "I've been on the ranch for three weeks and I haven't had a day off yet. I don't get home until after midnight, and then I'm right back in the kitchen for the breakfast shift, and the guys are so slow, I don't know if it's deliberate or what, but I'm going nuts."

"Can you sleep in a little tomorrow, let somebody in the kitchen prep for you?"

"Yeah, but that's not really the problem. I have no social life, and I'm not used to that. In New York there were always people around and places to go. Here, there's nothing but work. I need to meet some people my own age, not just the kitchen guys. Gaspard says Playa's a great party town, and it's not too far from here."

"How would you get there?"

"When Luis Felipe said I could have the job he told I could share the van with you when you're not using it. That was part of the deal."

"Oh, I didn't know that." I'd been using Molly's old van ever since Jimmy got it back from the previous sales director, and I'd almost forgotten it belonged to the hotel, not to me personally. But Luis Felipe never said anything to me about having to share it.

"I'd like to take it tonight when I get off work. That is, if you don't need it."

Of course I didn't need the van when he got off work. I never went out late at night, but I resented being blindsided about having to share it.

"Sure," I said, trying to sound gracious. "That would be fine. The van's parked in my driveway. I can give you directions to my house."

"It's OK, Gaspard showed me. It's down the path from my casita."

"Right. I'll leave the keys on the floor under the front seat."

"I'll have it back by morning."

I stood to walk him to the door.

Every night after that when I heard the van's engine start up, I ran to the window to look, to make sure it was

Eric behind the wheel. I'd watch as though I were his mother as he backed the vehicle slowly out of the driveway and disappeared down the windy path through the jungle. Even though it meant sharing the van, at first I was happy to think that he was meeting people in Playa, but he was getting home late and not getting much sleep. He was young and used to that, I reminded myself, and would be a happier employee now that he could get away from the ranch after work. Then one morning, I went to the kitchen to talk with him about a menu for a meeting that I'd booked for executives from Argos Communication. But when I got there, the staff said Eric hadn't shown up yet, and it was two hours after his shift had started. Jorge, the Mexican cook, who had worked at El Torbellino for years, was in charge of the kitchen.

"Donde es Eric?"

"No viene."

"Porque?

"No se. No problema, Señora Julie."

It worried me that Eric was sluffing off already when he'd been at Torbellino less than a month. The cook wasn't the kind to complain. He liked being in charge and would have wanted the title of executive chef for himself, which I actually felt he deserved. But I understood that Luis Felipe wanted someone with more sophisticated taste and credentials when he hired Eric. The kitchen was humming along smoothly without him that night, and I wondered if it wasn't easier for the kitchen staff without Eric around. It turned out, our young American chef had missed or was late for work frequently these days, and Jorge covered for him each time.

I intended to talk with Eric about his absenteeism when I saw him the next day, but I never had the chance.

In the middle of the night I woke up from the sound of someone banging on my front door.

"Señora, Señora. Securidad!" someone yelled from outside. I didn't recognize the voice, and I had no idea how long he'd been out there. My watch said it was two o'clock. My first thought was of Eric.

I threw on a sweat suit, raced downstairs, opened the door and saw a security guard, wearing a badge, standing at the doorway, holding a flashlight, and no van in the driveway.

"!Ven!" The guard commanded, motioning me to follow him.

Out of nowhere, Gerardo appeared and took the flashlight from the guard. "Sorry to get you up, Julie, but..."

"What's happened, Gerardo?"

"It's the Chef."

"Was there an accident? Is he OK?"

"He's not hurt."

"Then what...?"

"A cop followed him from Playa... he saw the van weaving back and forth over the median on the highway. He could tell the driver was drunk, so he pulled him over. "

"Shit!"

"It could have been worse. He could have impounded the van or had Eric deported."

"Deported?"

"The police can do that if they want to. But he knew the van was yours, so called us instead."

"Jesus. This is all we need. He could have killed somebody or himself."

"He was lucky the cop stopped him."

"Where is he?"

"He's still in the van. The cop's with him. They're

waiting for us. We have to wait for Alejandro first. He went to the office to get some cash."

He was getting money to bribe the cop. The pitch black night was alive with the sound of frogs shrieking all around us. I shivered from the chill in the air, following Gerardo blindly to his car, which suddenly appeared in the beam of his flashlight. I could feel the adrenalin surging through me, my body tingling with excitement and dread. I didn't trust Alejandro or Gerardo, but I needed them to handle this with the cop.

I climbed into the back seat of Gerardo's VW with my heart racing. How much money would they keep for themselves and say they'd given to the cop when they made out the report the next day? Gerardo and I waited until the car door opened and Alejandro got in, closed the door, and Gerardo put the car into gear and we took off. Neither one of them seemed flustered, but I didn't know anyone could drive so quickly down the dirt road in the dark, careening the car around pot-holes, flying over bumps in the rutted road, speeding through the tunnel of overhanging branches until finally we emerged from the jungle at the highway and turned south. It felt like being in a high speed chase in an action-packed film. The thrill of excitement startled me.

Ten minutes further down the two-lane road, a red light whirled at the side of the road and the high beams of a police car shined hot white in the black night. We pulled up next to the police car. Gerardo left the motor running. Behind the patrol car was my van. The sliding door was open, and Eric was slouched in the back seat, holding his stomach and moaning.

"You'll have to drive the van back to Torbellino, Julie. Mexicans can't drive cars made in the US," Gerardo said.

"I know. I'll drive the van and I'll take Eric with me."

Alejandro got out of Gerardo's VW and walked over to talk to the cop, who never got out of his patrol car, but spoke through the open window. Alejandro reached into his jacket and handed something to him. I didn't how much he gave him, but I knew it was money for the bribe.

I opened the driver's side of the van and got in. It reeked of liquor. Eric was slumped against the back seat, so drunk he could hardly hold up his head. His eyes were bloodshot, and he looked like he was going to vomit. I hoped he felt sicker than he'd ever felt in his life, that he wished he were dead, as long as he didn't puke all over the back seat of my van.

"What the hell, Eric?" I snarled.

"I didn't do anything," he slurred.

"You're drunk. The cop saw how you were driving. That's why he pulled you over."

"Fuckin' cops." His eyes looked like they were trying to focus. "I didn't do a fuckin' thing," he said loud enough that I thought the cop might hear.

"Shut up, Eric. Just shut up! You're in enough trouble. Don't make it worse. You want to go to jail? You want to get deported?"

He closed his eyes. His head rolled from side to side against the back seat.

"Fuckin Mexicans! Fuckin' pigs!" he muttered under his breath.

The policeman turned off the flashing red lights and high beams of his squad car and drove off down the highway. Alejandro walked over to the van.

"I only had half of the money we needed. That's all that was in the cash drawer tonight. Tomorrow I'll have to give him the rest of it," Alejandro said.

"How much did you give him?" I asked.

"Five hundred American dollars."

"Jesus," I muttered under my breath. I was furious. Eric was supposed to take over the kitchen; he was supposed to be a professional. I didn't need to be a babysitter on top of everything else.

"It's lucky the cop recognized your van. Luis Felipe gave orders to them to watch out for you on this stretch of highway," Gerardo said as Alejandro got back into the car.

"How do you know that?" It was creepy that the police followed my comings and goings from the hotel, that I'd been watched without my knowledge, my privacy invaded.

"I know everything about the hotel," Gerardo bragged. "You think I'm just here to manage the house cleaning department? I've been with Luis Felipe a lot of years, even before Torbellino. I take care of everything for him." So that was why the cop called Gerardo after he pulled Eric over. Gerardo not only looked the part, he was Luis Felipe's right hand man, his consigliere.

"Sorry we had to wake you, Julie. You can go back to the hotel now, get some more sleep." Like that would be even a remote possibility. Every fiber of my being was on guard.

"Believe me, Gerardo, Eric's never going to get those keys to the van again."

The VW drove off down the highway ahead of us. "Fuckin' Torbellino," Eric muttered from the back seat.

"Whatever they paid that cop, it'll come out of your check, Eric." I snarled, but I was wasting my breath. He wouldn't remember a thing I said the next morning. I was sick of the chaos, the whirlwind of chisme, and the atmosphere that bred distrust among the staff, while all the guests luxuriated in the illusion of being in paradise. I was somewhere between the two. I didn't know whether to believe my suspicions about Luis Felipe and the hotel or if I had made them up out of loneliness and fear and my own inability. I didn't have enough information to distinguish. I only knew I was sick of not belonging. But I needed to hang on through Max Israel's wedding week-end in late October, then on Thanksgiving, Luis Felipe and Molly would be home.

CHAPTER FIFTEEN

*T*he restaurant was the only place I felt welcome and like myself. One morning, when I arrived to help with the coffee service, Paulo, the head waiter, was standing at the glass folding doors between the dining room and restaurant. He was holding a small yellow bird to his cheek, talking to it softly. It wasn't unusual for birds to die crashing into the glass patio doors of the dining room, which was apparently what had happened that morning. Paulo was unaware of my presence, he was so focused on the bird. I couldn't tell if it was still alive or if its wing was broken. I held my breath as he carefully carried the frail body out of the dining room, placed it on a tree branch and stepped away to watch what would happen. The bird steadied itself, and after a split second, flapped its wings and took off. I felt as if my own balance had been restored by his compassion.

"He is all right." Paulo said reassuringly when he noticed me. Then he disappeared into the kitchen to wash his hands. When he came back to the dining room, he said, "Señora, Walter, one of the morning waiters, you know him?"

"He's tall and thin and sings all the time?"

"Yes, that's Walter. He is moving to Los Cabos next week."

"I'm sorry to hear that."

He nodded. "Do you know anyone I could interview for the job?"

"In fact, I have someone in mind. I'll ask him later today."

I couldn't wait to tell Eliseo about the opening. He'd be perfect for the morning shift. He was bright and quick and charming, and the guests would adore him. He'd been studying English in order to become a waiter. Every evening he listened diligently to his English tapes and filled out the pages of the workbooks I'd bought for him in St. Louis. Even though our lessons weren't as frequent, we caught fragments of time so he could practice pronouncing all the names of the items on the restaurant's breakfast menu and their descriptions. I was sure he was up to the interview with Paulo.

A waiter's job would raise his status significantly, not only on the ranch, but everywhere up and down the coast, and he'd earn more money for his family. Working with Paulo at the morning shift would be better for him than working with Amador, who could be a prick to the waiters under him. Paulo would train him well and treat him kindly. If he got the job, he could still work for me in the afternoons after his shift ended. He was the only one living on the ranch that I trusted implicitly.

"You'll need a pair of black pants; a white shirt; some new, good, black shoes; and a haircut. I'll add the cost of your uniform to your salary this week."

"Thank you, Señora. I will make good job," he said sincerely.

"You will *do* a good job," I corrected. "I know you will. I'll tell Paulo you'll come to see him tomorrow morning. Read the menu for him. Show him what you know."

His interview with Paulo was set for nine-thirty the next morning. I was surprised when he didn't come by to tell me how the interview went, and I didn't see him the rest of the day, but when I got to the restaurant the following morning, there was Eliseo, dressed in a white waiter's coat, black pants, and shiny new shoes. He was setting tables and looked like he belonged.

He grinned when he saw me and gestured proudly at the table with fork, knife, and spoon placed properly. "Mira! I am waiter now! Paulo says I make good job...no, I *do* a good job." Paulo had hired him on the spot at the end of his interview and he and Sebastiana had spent the day shopping for his uniform.

"Excellent," I said.

"Thank you, Miss Julie, for my shoes," calling me by my first name, rather than addressing me as Señora as he usually did.

"I hope they're comfortable shoes. You'll be on your feet a lot of hours."

."Is good. Very, very good." I watched as he held a knife to the light to inspect it, giving it a final polish before putting it on the table. Helping Eliseo get that job felt like my victory too, something to hang on to when so much else that I'd attempted had gone wrong.

That afternoon, I got a call from a man named David Guttierez. He said he was from Cancun and wanted to make an appointment to come to the hotel with his fiancée to tour our facilities. They hoped to have their wedding at Torbellino, and we agreed to meet the next day. I was excited about the call since weddings didn't happen often at the resort. The big hotels in Cancun could easily accommodate them, with separate dining rooms for regular guests and others for the wedding event and enough overnight accommodations for everyone. A couple needed to book the entire resort to have a wedding and reception with us, which was too expensive for most young people and their families, even for one night. It would be a coup for me to put another wedding on our calendar in addition to the one scheduled for Max Israel and his fiancée in late October. A second successful effort in one day was almost too much to imagine.

Twelve o'clock came and went, and then the entire afternoon passed with no sign of David Guttierez and his fiancée. I tried not to feel let-down, reminding myself that Mexicans have a different attitude about time. By the end of the afternoon I had given up hope of ever seeing them, but at eight that evening, Dulce came to the restaurant to tell me a young couple was waiting for me in my office. They said we had an appointment.

"Hello," the young man said from the couch when I walked in. "You must be Julie Heifetz. I'm David Guttierez, and this is my fiancée, Anja. I spoke with you yesterday on the phone."

He was well-dressed and poised, a self-assured man in his mid-thirties who spoke English flawlessly. The gorgeous blonde on the couch next to him must have been a good fifteen years younger than he. I glanced at her left hand, expecting from their appearance to find an engagement ring with a big diamond, but her ring finger was bare.

Anja smiled shyly and nodded hello but said nothing. I wondered if she spoke English.

"It's nice to meet you both. I was beginning to think you weren't coming."

"Well, here we are." He sat back down without apologizing for being eight hours late for our meeting. "I forget, you North Americans do everything by the clock."

I bristled at the critical tone in his voice, but smiled, determined to get along with him well enough to book his wedding at the hotel and work with him. "I think you said on the phone yesterday that you're from Cancun?"

"I was born in Mexico City. Anja's from Germany, but we live together now in Cancun in an apartment. It's temporary. After the wedding we're going to build our own house. How long have you been sales manager at Torbellino?"

"Since February."

"So, you're new here. I understand the owner's away. I'm sorry, I was looking forward to meeting him."

"We miss him, but even if he were here, I'd be working with you if you plan to have your wedding here."

"One night soon we'll have you over to our apartment for dinner. She's a very good cook. You have a way to get to Cancun, I suppose?" She has a name, I thought. He hadn't consulted her about having me to dinner or once looked at Anya; in fact, he hadn't acknowledged her in any way. It was her wedding too that we were there to discuss.

"I don't get many nights off, but thank you for the invitation."

"That's too bad. But I'm sure you could get away just for dinner with a client?"

"Why don't we talk about your wedding first. Do you have a specific date in mind? If you do, I'll check the calendar to make sure that weekend's available. Are you aware that you'd have to book the entire hotel for the night of your wedding?"

"Of course. We'd want all the rooms for both weekend nights."

"Which weekend is that?"

"We haven't decided, actually." He hesitated. "That depends on when Anja's family can get here from Germany." It seemed strange that they hadn't figured that out before our appointment, but I had just met them and didn't know their circumstances.

"I see. Then it's too early to talk about details. But we have a photo album for you to look at and a list of service providers that you might want to consider: florists, photographers, musicians, officiants. Their work's shown in the photos too. Here, take a look, Anja."

I handed the album to her since usually brides are the ones who make the decisions for their weddings.

"You've had some beautiful events here," David declared, taking the album out of the hands of his fiancée. He flipped disinterestedly through the pages and handed the binder back to me. "We'll want the very best of everything for the meal, of course: lobster, steak. I especially love lobster," he said.

He wanted to be sure I understood he was wealthy and that it was his taste that mattered. He was an arrogant chauvinist. I smiled. "Our new chef will be glad to plan whatever you'd like to serve when you're ready to think about that. Then he can give you an estimate of the cost."

"We don't want to spare any expense. That sounds fine, but we'd really like to see the property for ourselves. How about a tour while we're here?"

"Of course. I'll show you the patios and the restaurant. All of them are lovely for a wedding. It just depends on how many guests you have. Let's go take a look."

They wanted to see everything: the dining room, the

patios, the Temazcal, the swimming pool, the guest rooms, and the beach.

"Very nice," David said approvingly.

"And this is our gift shop."

Anja whispered something to David. "Is the shop open? She's looking for a wedding dress, something casual for a beach ceremony."

It was after hours, but Alexa, Charles' wife, who ran the gift shop was still inside, going over the books. I knocked on the door. Alexa opened it, wearing her glasses, looking harried. But once she laid her eyes on gorgeous Anja and heard that the couple was planning to have their wedding at Torbellino, she was all smiles and charm.

"We have a lot of new inventory that would look wonderful on you."

She pulled several outfits off the racks, but Anja was busy rifling through the clothes on her own. She held up an A-lined, calf-length, white linen dress with angel sleeve and I could see in her eyes how much she liked it. She looked at David for permission to try it on, disappeared into a changing room, and came out looking like a vision.

"You look beautiful in that dress," I said sincerely. "It would be perfect for a wedding on the beach, with white sandals and a garland of white orchids in your hair."

She pivoted slowly, modeling the dress for David. He smiled wanly and shook his head.

"It's too soon," he said. Anja looked crest-fallen, but went back obediently into the changing room without saying a word. It struck me as odd and made me wonder if he intended to have their wedding at Torbellino, or if he'd decided against it. I thought Alexa would be disappointed not to make a sale, but apparently she was more interested in having someone to talk to. "I just made a fresh pot of coffee," she said. "Would you like some?"

Without waiting for an answer, she took a few little cups from the shelves and started pouring the coffee, all the while prattling on about her own modeling career, pulling out some ads with her in them from when she was much younger, with David pouring on the charm. By the time I pulled David and Anja out of the shop, it was nearly eleven o'clock.

"We'll call next week," David said as I walked them to the hotel entrance.

"That would be fine. I'll wait to hear from you." I walked them to the lobby, but I didn't feel good about the vibes I was getting. I told them good-bye and went to my office to put away the files away I'd left out on my desk. I'd wasted hours with those people. I was tired and cranky and ready to go home.

The door to my office building opened and closed. I froze in my chair, listening for the sound of footsteps in the outer office. No one worked this late at night; the anfitrionas left hours ago. No one should have been coming in. I could feel the blood drain from my face. My heart pounded as I waited to see who was there.

Ricardo's hulking form appeared in the doorway. His blue-black, long-sleeved shirt revealed his muscular chest and arms. His hair was slick with pomade, his face oily, his eyes wild. I thought he was still in the hospital. What was he doing at the hotel and so late at night? It couldn't be good. Gerardo had already told him he'd lost his job, but I was the one he'd hold to blame for that.

My voice was shaking. "What are you doing here?"

"I waited tonight. You were talking."

"I thought you were still in the hospital." He took a step

closer to my desk. I could see the veins in his neck bulge, rivulets of sweat running down his cheeks. He was breathing hard, his face dark with anger.

"Doctor say go home. But I don't go home without first I talk to you."

"You shouldn't have come without calling."

"I need....I want...I come back to work," he demanded. I was terrified. What if he'd been drinking? There was no way I could defend myself if he intended to hurt me. I was the one who had said he couldn't come back again, and he knew that. I prayed he'd listen to reason.

"I'm sorry but you can't work here anymore." I hoped he couldn't hear my voice tremble.

"Yes. I can." Did he mean I will? Was he threatening me? Or didn't he understand?

"What I mean is...not after what happened at the bar."

"The new busboy had knife...not me," he whined.

"You started it. You tried to make that new kid pay for everybody's drinks."

"I make joke..."

"No one thought you were joking. You got him on the ground and were choking him. Everybody in the bar saw it."

"He cut me...look...here." He rolled up the sleeve of his right arm and bent over my desk to show the thick, angry, red scar and puckered skin from the surgical wound.

I winced. "That looks awful."

"And here there is more." He pointed to the side of his neck, where the scar snaked nearly up to his ear. It was hard to look at the wounds, to realize how close the knife had come to the carotid artery in his neck. Any closer and it might have cut off the blood supply to his brain.

"I'm sorry you were hurt so badly, but you can't come

back to work here. Neither can the busboy. Everybody here is too afraid of you now to work with you."

He must have known that I was talking about myself, that I was afraid of him. Had that been a terrible mistake, showing my fear? Maybe he hadn't sensed that at all. Maybe he was overwhelmed realizing he wasn't going to talk his way back into his job as he had talked his way into it in the first place. He wiped the perspiration from his face with his upper arm and hung his head and stared at the floor. In that moment, he looked like a pathetic child being held in from recess. I felt so sorry for him. Sorry for the Ricardo who had been so proud to serve me the special menu he'd created, sorry for the man with so much potential who'd thrown it all away in a drunken bar fight after work.

"I was very sad and very angry when Gerardo told me what happened, Ricardo. You let everybody down. Especially yourself."

He looked like he'd been whipped.

"I hope you find another waiter's job in another hotel, maybe in Cancun, or Playa."

He shook his head. "I can no be waiter now." He held out his hand and pointed to the searing scar that ran under the short sleeve of his shirt and down the inner arm to his palm. "I can no carry trays. I need head waiter job."

"I understand. It's going to be hard for you now to find a job you can do. But you can't find one here. I hope you find something that's right for you. Good luck, Ricardo."

He stood still in front of my desk, as though not knowing what to do next.

"Goodnight, Ricardo," I said, looking down at the papers on my desk to let him know there was no more reason to stay. I didn't look at him again and pretended to get back to the paperwork on my desk, but I couldn't even focus in front of me. When I finally looked up again, Ricardo had evaporated from the room like a ghost. I kept sitting at my desk, afraid to leave too soon, before he had time to get off the property. I waited another half an hour, just to make sure he was gone before I walked home, feeling I'd dodged another bullet that night.

I had been hungry for change when I came to Torbellino. I'd felt smothered by the suburbs, by a cloyingly close community of family and friends. But it wasn't Clayton that had held me back; I'd let my circumstances define me. I'd been the person I was expected to be. I didn't always color within the lines, but I hadn't been satisfied with who I was. Friends and family hadn't held me back; they were the safety net under my trapeze. At Torbellino, every day I walked a high wire without a net, and I still had months to go before Luis Felipe and Molly would be home and I could figure out how and when to leave.

CHAPTER SIXTEEN

*L*ife in Clayton, Missouri had seemed so boring, but now, every day a new curve ball was thrown at me that I hadn't seen coming. I craved predictability and monotony to my routine, the very elements of my life in St. Louis that made me want to flee. But the more days that passed, the more things changed. I felt like a shape-shifter, raw and sharp-edged. All that I had loved about living on the ranch was being eaten alive, torn apart by what I couldn't help from seeing: the underbelly of paradise. And I felt trapped.

One afternoon, Maria Elena arrived with a fax in hand. It was a new organizational chart with my name in its own box at the top: Director/Coordinator Julie. I'd never seen a previous version of an organizational chart for the management. For half a second, I felt flattered by the title. Director. But I had told Molly how tense things were between me and the other managers and she had told Luis Felipe how unhappy I was. If he thought the chart would help, I knew differently; it would only piss off Carla and make matters worse.

It didn't take long to see that I was right. Carla and Gerardo were huddled together, bent over a piece of paper, when Carla saw me coming and snickered loudly.

"What's so funny, Carla?"

"It means nothing, this chart. We've had charts with Directors' names at the top many times before. You will see what happens now."

I was shaking when I got to the restaurant. The waiters didn't need to see a new organizational chart to think that I was in charge anyway. In a few hours, when I got to my office, Amador called me, not Eric, to tell me he wouldn't be coming to work that day.

"My daughter, she is sick for a long time. She get well, then sick, then well. We take her to the doctor once, but the sickness, always it comes again. Now I drive her tomorrow to the doctor another time." I knew nothing about his family before this. I'd heard that he had a lover, so I didn't think of him as a family man, but his concern was genuine. A week passed before we spoke again. He looked exhausted, and I asked how his daughter was feeling.

"Estoy desperado," he said. "She is sick again today. I don't know what to do. I take her to the doctor. He gives her medicine, but she gets sick again soon." It surprised me to hear the desperation in his voice.

"If the doctor she saw hasn't helped you, then you might try taking her to a different doctor, a private one, not one at the clinic."

"It cost too much, a private doctor. We cannot," he shrugged.

"Well I have the name of a doctor that I've heard is very good. We send the guests to him if they get sick while they're staying with us. I'll call to see if your daughter can get an appointment right away. If he says yes, then you call him yourself and talk with him."

"Yes?"

"Yes, let's just see what he says. It's worth a try."

"But it is expensive."

"Don't worry about the cost. I'll pay for her appointment."

"You do this for me, Señora?" His eyes opened wide in disbelief, but paying for the appointment when he couldn't afford it seemed the only right thing to do. One appointment couldn't cost that much. I hoped it didn't set a precedent with every other waiter whose child or wife or mother got sick, but I'd deal with that later.

"Don't worry. Just get your daughter well." He nodded and gave a half-hearted smile. I could tell he wasn't hopeful that the appointment would make any difference.

The hotel doctor had been trained in family practice in the US and liked the connection he had with the hotel. I told him about Amador's daughter and he said he could fit her into his schedule the next day. I thanked him and told him to send the bill to me.

The next time I saw Amador, I asked after his daughter, and he answered with his signature gold toothed grin.

"The doctor, he looked at my daughter and my wife and other daughter too. Everybody was sick with strep throat. He said my daughter got well from the medicine she took, but then her mother or sister gave the strep throat back to her. Now everybody takes penicillin, not just my one daughter. He is very good doctor."

When I was growing up, and even later when I worked as a consultant, I felt at times as though my very presence had a healing power. "She's better than chicken soup," my grandfather used to say about me when he was sick and I went to visit. When I saw Amador was back to his dashing self, seating the dinner guests with a special flourish, I felt like a healer again. So much happened at El Torbellino that made me feel like I was the disease not the cure, and I saw myself as my enemies on the management team and the people they controlled saw me; fat and old, an intruder and a threat.

A sound came from behind one of the bungalows that I'd never heard before, a blood-curdling shriek that sliced open the night and ricocheted against the buildings and trees. This wasn't the sound of raucous laughter, it was one long unbroken cry of terror. Without thinking, I started to run toward the scream.

Rounding the corner of one of the guest bungalows, I watched, horrified, as two guards dragged a young Mayan boy by his arms, one of which hung from his elbow at an odd angle, like a gate on a broken hinge. His feet trailed along in the dirt behind him as the guards marched him stonily past me. The boy's face was bloody, his eyes swollen; he'd been beaten mercilessly. What had he done to deserve that?

"Alto!" I yelled at the guards, but they paid no attention. Just then, Gerardo headed down the path towards me.

"Julie, let them go. The guards will take care of this."

"But Gerardo, they're hurting him. What did he do?"

"The guest in the Junior Suite had a gold necklace stolen from her room. One of the housekeepers said that kid was the one who stole it."

"Did they find the necklace on him?"

"No. They haven't found it yet, but they will."

"They don't know for sure that he was the one who took it!"

179

"They're taking him to the guard house. They'll get a confession out of him there."

"You mean they'll beat one out of him?" I felt desperate to stop them. I didn't know if the kid was guilty or not, but it was wrong what they had done to him and what they would do as soon as they got him inside. "I'm going to call the police and let them handle this." I started toward my office to use the phone.

"I wouldn't do that if I were you. You think the guards are rough? You should see what they'd do to him in jail. He might never get out."

"Can't they look for fingerprints to prove who did it?"

"You've seen too many detective shows. Police here don't do fingerprints." Gerard chuckled. I stood frozen in place as the guards and the boy disappeared. A few minutes went by and the shrieks faded to a whimper. Then there was only silence, but the boy's screams were seared into my brain.

I was the Director of this hotel in name, but I was powerless to change things. I left the hotel feeling numb and went home, poured myself a glass of wine, and then another. I wanted to drown out the vision of the boy's bloody, desperate face. I would never know what happened to him after the guard house. But what was happening to me? I was changing in small imperceptible ways; my sense of trust and security wearing away like sand castles in the wind. Would I keep shape-shifting over time until there was nothing left of the qualities I admired about myself? I respected honesty, sensitivity, openness, all the qualities that seemed wrong here. Already I was becoming someone I didn't know or like.

I climbed the stairs slowly, undressed, put on my night-gown, and got into bed. In the distance, I heard men's voices. Strange for this time of night. No one came to the residential section of the ranch who didn't own one of the houses or was an invited guest. Whoever they were, they were coming down the path toward my house. Or was I imagining it, thinking they were strangers when they actually belonged here? My nerves had been frazzled since the guards dragged the boy off. But no. What I was hearing were slurred voices of men speaking to each other in Spanish; a gurgle of laughter passed among them. The voices got louder as they came closer.

Oh my God. They stopped in front of my house. Whoever it is, they've come for me. I thought about Ricardo and his hulking presence in my office, about the bird skull left on my door handle as a threat, about the words in the guest book, about Carla and the other managers who wanted me gone. *You'll see what happens next*, she had said. I lay in bed, paralyzed, my heart pounding, my hand shaking, clutching the sheet around me. I could hear the men's rough voices under my window. They were close enough that I could almost hear them breathe. Then, there was a splash of water, and then another, and more laughter. They were in my swimming pool just under my window.

"Julie, Julie," one of the men sang, as though serenading me. I thought I recognized his voice. "Julie," he crooned again. This time I was sure I knew him; it was Amador. He'd had too much to drink and now he was calling up to me. I held my breath, waiting for them to come in, to climb the stairs and into my bedroom. Had I locked the French doors of the living room before I came upstairs? I couldn't remember. If they got in, I wouldn't be able to get away. There were too many of them. Please. Don't let this be like Ricardo. Don't come in. Please, just don't. If they did, would they rob me or rape me? What would I say, or would I say nothing and lie still and mute, waiting for the pain to end? On my God, had Amador misunderstood when I paid for his daughter's appointment?

Suddenly the splashing and laughing stopped. Someone was speaking in a muffled voice that was calm and steady, different from the others and kept talking. When he stopped, there was a pause and the voices started to move down the path away. I listened to the silence, distrusting it at first. I listened harder until I was sure the men had gone. Slowly I got out of bed and crept downstairs to make sure the door was locked and found Eliseo standing in the entryway, looking up at me. I hadn't heard him come in, but he was the reason that Amador and his friends had taken off. He'd been looking out for me. I felt so relieved when I saw him, I didn't care that I was wearing only a silk nightgown.

I put one careful foot in front of the other, making my way down the steps, holding onto the wall to steady myself.

"Thank you, Eliseo," I said gratefully. "Thank God you were here."

Just then Sebastiana walked through the door, looking as though she were expected.

"You are fine, Señora?" Eliseo asked, concerned.

"Yes, I'm OK now."

"No. You are tired. I see. Sit down, Señora, please." He turned and spoke to Sebastiana in Mayan. She pulled out a dining room chair next to the table and pointed. Dutifully, I eased myself into the seat. I had finally stopped shaking. Eliseo bent down and picked up my foot and started to massage it with long, firm strokes. He had a lover's touch.

"No, you don't have to do that for me," I protested weakly.

"I know," he said softly, not letting go of my foot. "Every night I do this for Sebastiana." The gesture wasn't subservient, it was intimate and loving. I was glad Sebastiana was there. Her presence guaranteed that nothing would happen between Eliseo and me that I would regret later, which was why she had come to join her husband. He was young and handsome. I had seen the way he looked at me sometimes, with a flirtatious smile that seemed too interested. The attraction between us was palpable, in spite of our age difference. I was hungry to be touched, to be wanted, to be reassured that I could be loved again. It had been a year and a half since my relationship with Mike had ended and my body ached to make love. But if I gave into an affair with Eliseo, it would ruin everything. I had too much to lose.

I closed my eyes and gave in to the warmth of his hands. I was so relaxed I nodded off in my chair. When I jerked awake, Eliseo and Sebastiana were quietly crossing the marble living room floor, heading to the front door.

"Good night, Julie," Eliseo said softly. The wooden door shut gently behind them. I made way back upstairs to bed as though in a trance. How blessed was I knowing that Eliseo would be right there next door watching over me like a god.

CHAPTER SEVENTEEN

eeks passed with sustained periods of calm. It was June, the rainy season, although the rains hadn't started yet, and it was low season for the hotel. Low season meant more intense heat and fewer guests checking in. It seemed the whole country moved in slow motion normally, and now, activity crawled nearly to a standstill. The staff seemed half-asleep. Only the maintenance department was busy with the gardens and a frenzy of new construction and fresh painting of the empty guest rooms.

Watching the staff sit around with little to do was as annoying to me as having a root canal procedure. I tried to think of constructive ways to fill their time because boredom could only lead to trouble. Fortunately, someone showed up in my office wanting to give English classes, and someone else with a certificate to teach hygiene, and I hired them both. The restaurant had passed its yearly health department inspection, but much of the crew had changed since then, and the many of the new workers from the countryside needed to be educated about good sanitation and safety practices.

I worried about cell phone service on the ranch since outages were more likely to happen with the coming rains. Alejandro was responsible for keeping the cell phones in working order, and from time to time, I'd ask when we'd be getting regular phone service.

"Telmex says they'll be here soon to lay the cables from the road to the hotel," he said.

"But they've been saying that for two years. They won't give us a date when they'll be coming?"

He shook his head and shrugged. "Can't we find another company then?" I pushed.

"They're the only ones who can do it, but I'll call again."

I stormed off, knowing he would do no such thing. He would nod and promise, and that would be the end of it. Mexicans never say no. It was maddening, and though I knew it was a cultural preference for politeness over honesty, I was beginning to feel there was something personal in his refusal to follow through on my requests. Like his sister, he wouldn't give me the satisfaction of doing what I told him to do, no matter how I phrased it.

One evening, I made my rounds, saying hello to our few guests in the dining room before leaving early for the beach to catch the last glimpse of the red sun sliding under the water. Isla Mujeres beckoned from a distance where the little island's shops and restaurants would be nearly empty waiting for the season to end. We were all in the same boat, but I was terrible at waiting.

Raphael, the dive master of the hotel, steered his boat around the bend. He looked up and waved when he noticed me sitting on the beach, jumped out of the boat, and steered it to shore. He gathered his gear and came towards me. His shiny wet suit sparkled with diamonds of water in the sunlight. He was a fine-looking young man, dark haired and slim. I watched him walking up the beach, remembering that he and his girlfriend had lived in my house without my permission while it was being renovated, but I'd gotten over being angry at them long ago. Even though François was his girlfriend's father, the young couple seemed independent of him and very different. He was kind and friendly, the opposite of François.

"Hola, Julie."

"Hi, Raphael. I haven't seen you lately, but I saw the fences and signs you put out on the beach warning people not to disturb the turtle eggs. Do you know when the eggs are going to hatch? I'd like to see that when it happens."

"I keep checking, but not yet. It'll be sometime between now and August. As soon as the babies are born, they head straight for the water. They use the light of the moon to navigate. It's pretty amazing to see, if you're in the right place at the right time."

"I'll keep my eyes open."

He nodded and trudged up the sand toward the shack to store his gear.

"There's a party down at the beach past the hotel," he called over his shoulder. "Crystal and the baby are going to meet me there as soon as I put away all this equipment. You really should come. There'll be wine and a bonfire. Listen, you can hear the music already."

Under the sound of the wind were the faint thumps of drums. I was delighted that he had asked me to the party, but I knew Francois and the whole Lemotte clan would also be there and I'd feel uncomfortable with them, especially François.

"Thanks for the invitation. Maybe later."

"It's going to be a nice night," he said, glancing at the sky. "Think about it." I wished I had more time to talk with him. He knew so much about the cenotes in the area and marine biology in general. I wondered where he'd gained so much knowledge. Maybe he'd be willing to give a lecture for the guests one evening.

I sat at the beach, listening to the rhythmic pulsing of the waves falling on the shore. I wished I could interview Raphael the way I'd interviewed so many others in my past. I thought about Mr. Herman, the Holocaust survivor, a gentle man who picked flowers for me from his garden in the spring and his wife who made schnecken whenever I visited. There seemed to be no anger in them, in spite of all that they'd lost and suffered. I wondered if they were still alive. And I thought about Glenn David, the patient with a brain injury from an attempted suicide who lived with the guilt of his own actions. I believed that the stories I wrote from those interviews helped restore their dignity and allowed them to move on. Raphael was different; he didn't need to talk, but I needed to listen. He would have such a fascinating story to tell.

It was almost dark. As I walked home, a black-winged something flew by me on the path. As I kept walking, another creature buzzed by, and then two more and three, and suddenly I was surrounded by swarms of black flying creatures. They looked like small bats at first, but as they fluttered around me in the half-light, I realized they were black moths. They seemed to come from nowhere and were strange and delightful companions to keep me company.

I had never seen moths like that before, although I'd read about them. They were thought by Mayans to be witches; if one flew overhead it meant someone had put a curse on you and you were going to die soon. But they were too beautiful, too graceful to be frightening.

I never knew what each season might bring; the poisonous jelly-fish that came and then disappeared without warning from the bay; the march of great armies of mud crabs I'd discovered crossing the road in spring; scorpions, usually out of sight, but scurrying for shelter when it rained; and now the black moths appearing in low season. The moths hovered around me as though they had some secret to tell and I hoped they'd stick around for a few more days.

In the morning when I got to the office, Francois was just leaving. He said there was a sixty-percent chance a hurricane would be landing in the Gulf of Mexico in the next few days. From the weather map, it seemed to be headed right for our beach. In 1988, Hurricane Gilbert had hit the property, destroying the glass in Molly and Luis Felipe's front window and flooding the living room with water and debris. They were in Cancun when it landed, but they had to come back a few days later and build a raft to rescue the animals in waist-high water down their flooded road all the way to the highway.

Hurricane warnings since Gilbert had all turned out to be false alarms, but the hotel had to get prepared just in case. Francois and Raphael hoisted the boats out of the ocean and moved them onto the sand far from the water's edge, tied them up, and made sure they were secure. Jimmy's men boarded up the windows in the dining room. All morning, I anxiously watched the sky, wondering if and when guests and staff should be evacuated. Francois scoffed at that suggestion. He wasn't going anywhere, no matter what the prediction said. The masons, too, seemed oblivious of the threat. They kept working at their usual steady pace to finish the new addition to the dining room when there were fewer reservations. Still, a guest with a room close to the construction complained about the noise the crew made early in the morning. I apologized and suggested we move them to a different room farther from the construction site.

By late afternoon, I heard from Amador that the hurricane had changed direction and was now heading further north and inland and I could relax. I was in the dining room and caught a glimpse of myself in the large gilt-framed mirror on the wall. For a split second, I thought I was someone else. My shoulder-length hair had been full and wavy in February. Now, it looked wild and unkempt and ugly. I hardly recognized my own body. My belly bulged under the skirt that had once flattered me. It was true that I'd been less careful than usual about my diet: pan dulce every morning, dinner at the restaurant with guests, and too much bread had added up over the months with too little exercise. I'd also run out of my thyroid pills and hadn't taken the time to find a doctor in Cancun for a new prescription.

I was horrified seeing the way I looked. I had been paying attention ever since I'd started work to everything but my own well-being. I was obsessed thinking about Molly, worrying about what I was discovering about the hotel and Luis Felipe, and trying to meet the challenges that came up day by day. A few days away to rest and read, where I could get a good meal and be completely undisturbed sounded heavenly. I deserved some time off. With so few guests registered at Torbellino, the weekend coming up would be a perfect time to get away.

I'd read about a place called Sian Ka'an, a biosphere reserve designated as a UNESCO World heritage site that had piqued my interest. It was within driving distance of the hotel, but I'd never been there before. The guide book recommended Las Palmas as a place to stay, a small fishing lodge at the tip of Sian Ka'an where I could see many varieties of wildlife. It was rustic, inexpensive, served meals, had rooms overlooking a river, and was only thirty miles past Tulum, which was about an hour from the hotel. I called and made a two-night reservation. No one there would know or care that I was Director of Torbellino.

I told Carla and Amador that I'd be taking two days off and gave Carla the phone number where I could be reached. Then, I packed my backpack with shorts, t-shirts, underwear, a flashlight and batteries, snacks, bottles of water, a copy of *The French Lieutenant's Woman,* and two books of poetry by Naomi Nye. I filled the van with gas at the station down the highway and headed toward Tulum.

Just past Tulum, the road to Sian Ka'an turned out to be one treacherous, continuous sheet of large, loose, limestone rocks, with deep pits where rainwater had accumulated during the recent storm. The drive made our hand-hewn road seem like a super highway in comparison. Scrub trees lined either side of the road. The landscape was desolate. I bumped along in my van at fifteen miles an hour, cursing myself for not having rented a jeep and cursing the guidebook for not advising its readers to get a pick-up truck with high ground clearance, the kind of vehicle that would make a sixteen-year-old boy drool. What would I do if my tires popped and I was stranded out in the middle of nowhere? I gripped the wheel and concentrated on inching the van forward. This was supposed to be a weekend of R and R, two days away from the tensions of work, not fifty kilometers of driving over sharp rocks, with a white-knuckle grip on the steering wheel. I was so relieved when I finally made it to Las Palmas that I didn't care that it had started to drizzle or that the fog was so thick that I couldn't see the water. When I pulled into the parking lot, the scent of the river made me hopeful. I could almost taste the solitude, and my shoulders relaxed immediately.

A fisherman with tackle box and fishing pole was busy loading up his truck as I stepped out of the van. His was the only other vehicle in the parking lot, and since no one else was around, I asked the fisherman where I might register or how to find my room.

"Name?" he asked, pulling a piece of paper from his back pocket.

"Heifetz," I said, spelling it slowly for him, surprised that he spoke English.

"You're up there. Third room on the left. Pay when you leave." He pointed the way to my room, up a steep set of rough-hewn wooden stairs to the second floor. He wasn't just a fisherman, he was management. I smiled to myself, thinking how we greet guests when they first arrive at Torbellino, with a cocktail, a smile, and the words *Welcome home*. Las Palmas was not a place to be pampered and overindulged. The man watched as I climbed unsteadily up the steps, holding onto the railing with one hand, shifting the weight of my backpack with my free hand. I could see him below, wondering what I was doing at Las Palmas without fishing gear or a man, and I was beginning to wonder the same thing.

"There's no electricity," he called. "Except from four to eight at night."

"Thanks," I yelled back to him.

My room was sparsely furnished, with a single bed, a small lopsided cabinet, a wood chair, and one bare light-bulb that hung suspended from the ceiling. I pulled the string cord, and a yellow light clicked on, barely adequate for reading. The rain picked up, with torrents of water falling with foreboding and impenetrable insistence between me and any inclination I might have had to explore.

None of that mattered now, not the rocky road, or the rain, or the bare-bones welcome. I'd arrived someplace I'd never been but that still felt vaguely familiar, like remembering a musty scent from a time long ago. I shivered in the chilly heavy air and wrapped myself in the cocoon of the blanket from my bed. My father would have loved this place, even in the rain.

When I was a little girl, my father took my sister, my mother, and me on a fishing weekend over Memorial Day on the Current River in Missouri. No matter how many times he'd made the trip, Dad would be so excited the night before they left for the river that he couldn't sleep. My father and his cousin, brother-in-law, and uncle went year after year, always on the same weekend, with the same family of guides because the river could be treacherous. Andy Price and his sons navigated our fishing boats adroitly through the rapid currents, dropping anchor where the fish were biting best.

I never did learn the art of casting the way my father could; he made it look so easy, the line making graceful arcs in the air like a dancer's arms. There was a prize given for the person who caught the first fish, another prize for the one whose fish was biggest, and yet another for the one who'd caught the most at the end of the weekend. I didn't care about any of that. The joy was in being on the river on a lazy summer afternoon with my family; sitting by the campfire, listening to the sizzle of the fish frying in Andy's pan. I remember how shocked the rest of us were when my mother stood up, pulled off her jeans, and jumped out of the boat into the river in her underwear to cool off. After dinner, she even tried smoking one of my uncle's cigars. Those were the days.

I opened my book by John Fowles and started reading. By six o'clock I was hungry, so I left the lightbulb turned on in the room, grabbed my flashlight, and went downstairs to look for dinner. There was a tent with its flaps tied back on the other side of the parking lot from the ramshackle lodge. Inside the tent was a sand floor on which were set a few tables covered with red-checked tablecloths and hurricane lanterns for centerpieces.

"Hola," I called. "Alguin aquí?"

The fisherman from the parking lot sauntered in through a screen door, wearing shorts, t-shirt, a stained apron tied around his waist, and a dish towel draped over one shoulder.

"Hello, Julie."

"Oh, hello. Am I too early for dinner?"

"Not at all. What would you like? Fish or chicken? The bonefish is very fresh. They just brought it in an hour ago."

"Then I'll have the fish, of course. Are you the cook too?"

"Cook, waiter, manager. I do everything but clean the rooms, and if the girl doesn't show up to do that, I clean the rooms too. Give me a minute." He disappeared through a screen door, but came back right away bringing a carafe of white wine and a wine glass, although I hadn't ordered it.

I slipped off my sandals and ran my feet through the cool, dry sand under the table and took a sip of wine. I was relaxed and free from worrying about what the wind had done to my hair or if my thighs looked too heavy. I inhaled deeply the sweet, pungent scent of the rain.

The fish dinner took a while, but it was worth the wait. The waiter/chef/manager brought it to the table covered when it was ready, served with a slice of lemon, spicy smoked sweet potatoes, black beans with cilantro and mango, and Mexican rice. The chef waited by my table to watch for my reaction when I took my first bite.

"It's delicious," I said. The fish had been perfectly cooked, seasoned with only salt and pepper and not too much oil to disguise its freshness. Seeing I was satisfied, he nodded, turned, and went back to the kitchen.

The rain was coming down harder now, in heavy pellets, beating against the tent with solid thuds. Two men in fishing caps and rain jackets dripping from the rain ducked into the tent and sat at a table next to mine. They talked until the waiter came back to get their orders.

"Two Dos Equis." They stretched their legs out on the sand floor, and settled back in their chairs. I pegged them for New Englanders from their accents, but they reminded me of my father and my Uncle Dick, born and raised in Missouri. I dawdled over my meal as long as I could, catching the comfortable camaraderie between them as they shared information about fish and lures, eventually sliding into conversation about their families. The sound of their voices was like background music. No meal at a five star restaurant could have satisfied me more.

I climbed the slippery stairs, holding onto the bannister with my free hand, as the rain kept coming. The fog looked thicker in the beam of my flashlight than it had been earlier in the evening, and I was glad to get back to my room and into bed to read more of The French Lieu-tenant's Woman. Suddenly, the generators stopped humming, and the lights snapped off. If I had been at Torbellino, I would have still been schmoozing with guests, listening to exclamations of wonder over the beauty of the hotel, and how lucky I am to live in the property. But I was so glad not to be there. I craved simplicity.

Time at Las Palmas stretched in front of me like a lazy Missouri river. An image of Raphael getting out of his boat with his dive gear flashed in my mind, and I thought again about how much I wished I could interview him. His life had been so different than anyone's I'd known before, and he was verbal and engaging enough that he could describe it well. I missed the intimacy of getting to know someone well, listening to whatever he most wanted to talk about, being surprised, educated, impressed.

But he wasn't the only one at Torbellino who would have unusual stories to tell and language that would make their stories sing. The hotel was crawling with colorful characters. Gaspard and Francois came to mind; working with them was infuriating, but interviewing and writing about them would be a whole different story. The interviews might make me feel better about some of them and seeing the finished performance, the staff might feel better about each other than they did before.

My mind started racing and my heart pounding with excitement the more the plan started to reveal itself. I could come up with a list of people to interview who worked at the hotel in all different capacities, from all different backgrounds. If our conversations turned out to be as interesting as I imagined, I could create a one-woman-show based on them like the shows I'd written and performed before. I'd call it "The Torbellino Family," and I would show each person in his or her best light. Guests would love it and learn more about the people and culture of the Yucatan than they'd ever get from sunbathing, fine dining, and luxurious accommodations.

I was too excited to sleep. I imagined becoming each

person on stage. I would change costumes and accents from French to Spanish to English. With a performance to work on, I wouldn't obsess so much about Luis Felipe and Molly. My success or failure in the sales department wouldn't weigh so heavily on me. I could focus on what I knew how to do well and loved doing. It would give me a life line to my old self. Slow down, breathe, I told myself. There is a lot to consider. First I'd talk with Molly and find out what she thought of the idea, and if she and Luis Felipe gave their blessings, I'd give it more thought.

The rain kept up for the whole weekend, a steady, percussive ping after ping against the tin roof. I never took a boat ride, or went fishing, or walked to town, never had an extended conversation with anyone, but I was completely content. Unscheduled time and solitude were the luxuries I needed, which was what Las Palmas had to give.

El Torbellino felt a lifetime away, and my room had been as protective as a nun's cell. By Sunday morning I was more relaxed than I'd felt in months, but I was good and ready for a hot shower. I would have more energy now and a new idea to keep my batteries recharged. This was summer, and Molly had said they'd be back by Thanksgiving.

CHAPTER EIGHTEEN

$\mathcal{I}$ dawdled before checking out Sunday morning, but the drive back to Tulum seemed shorter than it had been to get to Sian Ka'an. I stopped for lunch in Playa at an Italian restaurant that I knew and browsed in some of the shops along Quinta Avenida, the main street in town. I was in no hurry to get home. The city was too brash, too touristy, especially after a weekend that was a throwback to simpler, more authentic ways. Everywhere in Playa, new construction elbowed its way onto the crowded streets that reeked of sewage from infrastructure that was already strained from over-building.

As I turned down one of the side streets, a woman's voice behind me said, "I didn't know you were going to be in Playa tonight, Julie." I turned around, surprised to hear anyone calling me by name and there was Dulce, one of the anfitrionas, behind me.

"Hi, Dulce. I took the weekend off and I'm on my way back to the hotel soon, just browsing. I'm surprised to see you here," She didn't seem the Playa type; she wasn't a party girl. Carla kept her and the other anfitrionas under tight reign, so I hadn't seen much of her lately, but away from the hotel, she seemed genuinely glad to run into me.

"I'm on my way to a friend's house. Her family's holding a healing ceremony and I'm going to watch. A famous shaman's going to be there. If you've never been to an authentic Mayan ceremony, it's something you might want to see. Would you like to come with me?"

"I'd love to, if you're sure no one will mind." The Mayan culture fascinated me, and witnessing one of their religious ceremonies was an experience I didn't want to miss.

We walked to an unpaved street at the edge of town where locals lived and came to a house made of sticks. The yard was an overgrown jumble of scrappy, reedy palms. Among the stubby trees near the front door of the house a group of Mayan men congregated.

We walked past them and inside. It was dark in the front room where many native people stood shoulder to shoulder waiting silently. The air was thick with anticipation and the fog of incense. The women were dressed in white huipil and skirts heavily embroidered with colorful floral designs, the men in guyabera shirts or t-shirts and jeans. We stood at the back of the crowd in a large room. Since the Mayan people are short-statured, I could see over everyone's heads, for a change, being short myself. No one seemed to notice us, which made me feel more comfortable. I was invisible and therefore free to watch and observe without feeling like an intruder. The smoky, hazy air made it harder to breathe and gave a sense of other-worldliness to the atmosphere. I hoped I could give into a mystical experience like the people around me.

I wanted to remember every detail that happened; it was a privilege to be there as witness among Mayans who followed the old way. At the front of the room, an altar was laden with flowers, statues of saints, and a tall candle holder, like altars in Catholic churches everywhere, except for the shot glass which took the place of a chalice. As we waited, more people piled into the room, our bodies pressed together in the heavy air. I had a flashback to when I was a child, the first time I visited my grandfather's Orthodox shul. Everything about the experience felt so strange; my grandfather and the other men in their prayer shawls swaying back and forth, chanting in a language I couldn't understand. It was unsettling, but it filled me with a new feeling, one I later came to understand as awe and already felt again waiting for the healing ceremony to begin.

"We just made it in time," Dulce whispered. "That man sitting with a bare chest in front of the altar is the patient. He's been so sick he hasn't been able to walk. The shaman's the one standing next to him, the famous spiritual leader and medicine man I told you about. The patient's family paid for him to come, and some people traveled a long distance to be here today."

Without grand dramatic gestures or speeches, the shaman lit the tall candles, poured some liquid into the shot glass and spoke to the patient in a low monotone. He picked up what looked like an animal bone, and dipped it into the shot glass. His motions were so small they were almost imperceptible, especially in the dusky light. I focused with razor-like attention as his hands moved, pressing the bone onto the patient's bare neck and shoulder, maybe a dozen times, while in a steady quiet voice chanting over and over the same Mayan phrase. At first I was frustrated that I couldn't understand his words or his choice of objects to use. What meaning did they have? I realized how foreign my Jewish services and ritual objects must feel to visitors coming to our services for the first time. After a few minutes, I gave into the experience of the healing ceremony itself. The people around me were so intensely still, I could have been alone.

Another phase of the ritual seemed to be happening as the medicine man picked up a bundle of dark leaves, which he sprinkled on the patient while uttering a few more incantations. At the end of each prayer, he circled the leaves above the patient's head. With an upward, spiraling flourish, he waved the leaves as if to draw out an evil spirit from the old man and send it skyward. I could sense that the ceremony was coming to a close and I rode the haunting wave of belief that emanated from the people around me and prayed for the man's recovery.

The ceremony took no more than fifteen minutes. A few men stepped forward from the front of the crowd, lifted the patient from his chair, and carried him out of the front door. I wished the man had gotten up and walked. Maybe the healing ceremony worked and the man did recover later. I hoped he did. Stranger things have happened.

People began moving to the side of the room, clearing the way for women putting out food for a communal meal. I didn't want to stay for that, even though Dulce said it would be fine and that everyone was welcome. I told her goodbye and thanked her having brought me with her, that it was an experience I would never forget. It was nearly dusk, and I didn't want to have to drive back to Torbellino through the jungle in the dark.

Coming outside after the ceremony was like waking

from a dream. It took the entire walk back to my car to shake off the other-worldliness of the ceremony. I wished I had the kind of faith I had just witnessed in the people around me. Life would be so much simpler if I believed certain words and that certain gestures made in the right order could make things whole and all one had to do was learn them.

I was still emerging from the simplicity of two days at Las Palmas and the spiritual world of the Maya, so it was no wonder that I nearly missed the turn-off from the highway onto our unmarked road. The sun had just disappeared behind the trees, and the jungle on either side was blanketed in darkness. But as soon as I made the turn, I could see in my headlights a white barricade stretching all the way across the dirt road; there was no way to drive around it. Beyond the barricade loomed a massive truck, like an animal the length of five or six vans placed end-to-end. The ground shook from the roar of machinery.

I pulled the van over into a ditch at the top of the road, parked, and got out of the car to investigate. What in the world was happening? I was furious. How was I supposed to get to my house now? Floodlights from the truck shined down on muddy, deeply gorged earth, with men standing shoulder-high in the slimy ditch. They had head-lights strapped to their foreheads and looked like three-eyed monsters, with pick axes like giant arms swinging. I couldn't make the leap from the ancient healing ceremony I'd just left into the destruction of modern civilization.

"Que pasa?" I yelled above the din to one of the workers.

"Telmex," he hollered back.

Telmex? I'd been so anxious for them to get here, but seeing how they were tearing up the jungle, I was sorry they had come at all. And why now in the middle of the night? Why hadn't anyone called to let me know this was happening? I'd given the phone number of Las Palmas to Carla, so she could have reached me. She must have warned the hotel guests not to drive off the property knowing they couldn't get back once the trucks got there, because there were no other cars than mine at the top of the road. I would have stayed another night at Las Palmas had I known.

I sure wasn't going to spend the night in my car, and I didn't even think about driving back to Playa. If I could make my way past the machines, I could get to where the road was still whole. I walked back to the car, grabbed my flashlight, and locked my backpack in the trunk.

I had never before walked the length of our road at night, and being away from the familiar parts of the ranch the jungle spooked me. Anything could be hiding in the dense tangle of roots and leaves. Better to keep my eyes straight ahead. Soon my eyes adjusted to the dark, and the full moon was so bright a flashlight wasn't necessary. The road was soft underfoot, and the air was like silk. Soon, the sound of the Telmex truck was behind me, replaced by the screech and whistle of birds, the rustle of leaves, the croak, ribbit, and grunt of frogs. As I walked, a strange thing happened; the farther I went down the two mile road, the calmer I felt. It was too beautiful to be afraid. The sight of the truck and the churned-up road that had made me so angry dissipated as I slowed down and breathed in the fresh earthy scent of the jungle. I would never have chosen this experience of walking the road alone at midnight if it hadn't been forced on me by circumstances. I felt so grateful for the moonlight and the solitude and the chance to experience it all.

There is an ancient Mayan legend that says a King from

the heavens had arrived on Earth in a spaceship and would one day return. The workers at El Torbellino believed that spaceship had returned to earth a few years ago. They had seen it hovering over our very jungle, and they were sure it would come to visit us again. I thought that was a bunch of hooey. But as I walked, I had the sense that I was being accompanied, as though all my relatives were gathered around me. Maybe it was a remnant from the Mayan healing ceremony I had just witnessed, but I felt my grandfather around me. I felt him in my bones. He would always tell me *Take a chance, Dooliebug. Columbus took a chance.* He had emigrated alone from Austria when he was sixteen and moved to Broken Bow, Oklahoma, which was still Indian territory. He knew what it meant to seize life as one long adventure. It struck me as I walked down our hand-carved road what an extraordinary adventure I myself was having, this whole maddening, wild ride of a year; the good, the bad, and the ugly of it. I had made a leap into a world I didn't know, and I was making my way through the dark. I had been that foolish, and that brave, and I would survive. I was my grandfather's legacy.

El Torbellino was not my place. Molly was the planet revolving around Luis Felipe's sun, constant and accepting. I had admired her loyalty, their romance. But I was not Molly. I needed more room to be myself. I knew that now, and for the first time, I didn't feel ashamed of that. I had come for an adventure, the beach, the jungle, my house, but I hadn't put it to use for anything creative, and it seemed such a waste. I hadn't worked on a single writing project since I'd arrived in February; I'd been too consumed by the hotel, too controlled by what I thought Luis Felipe and Molly wanted of me.

The weekend away had been like standing on a high

cliff, seeing my future spread out below me, the details too far away to be clear. At the next bend in the road, the white stucco wall of my house rose proudly above the hedge of bougainvillea.

Reluctantly I went inside, still not ready to let go of the magic of the night.

CHAPTER NINETEEN

*T*hat night, I had a disturbing dream about Molly. When I woke up in the morning, I couldn't remember any details, but it upset me. My feelings about her were so complicated. I had always admired her courage and her talent, decorating all the rooms at the hotel with an artistic flair, choosing natural fabrics with neutral colors and subtle woodland designs. She created the art for the front of the menus, selected the china and tableware, hunted down fine Mexican antiques and unique pieces of art crafted by local artisans. I was impressed by the way Spanish tripped off her tongue as though she'd been born to it. She was a gourmet cook and hostess, roles she carried out with ease and lack of fanfare.

But when I thought back to all of our conversations since her move to Mexico, I had mostly been the one listening. She talked to me about Luis Felipe, her life on the ranch, the Mayan culture, the hotel, the people who worked for them. I was delighted that she had metamorphosed from the shy, withdrawn young woman of her earlier years into someone who wanted to tell me the details of her life. I was proud to be the only friend she'd kept from her years in the States, honored to be the one she confided in, when she was still so reserved and private with others.

Any imbalance in our relationship was as much my doing as hers. I realized that now. I had been contented just to be with her, sipping wine under a full moon and starry sky with the cool breeze blowing softly from the ocean. When Mike left me, I told her how devastated I was, but I wanted to submerge my grief in the healing warmth of the Yucatan and Molly's quiet companionship. She didn't need anyone other than Luis Felipe and her animals, who were her children.

But ever since she and Luis Felipe had gone to Miami and left me to work at the hotel, she had become so distant over the phone it was as though we had never been close. She was as much of a mystery as he was. I was hurt that I heard from her so infrequently, and when she did call, it was to relay something I was supposed to do. She didn't ask how I was or seem to care. I began to wonder if the relationship had ever been as mutual as I had thought.

I was determined to talk with her about a "Torbellino Family Performance". I so badly wanted to work on it, but I was nervous when I brought it up. I wasn't sure how she'd react to the idea, and the project might have ended then. When she called the next time, I sold the idea to her as best I could, explaining that it would be a chance for guests to learn more about Mexico. The audience would be able to see themselves in the stories, one human being to another, and appreciate the dignity of the workers. I reminded her that I'd done similar projects in the US and it had always worked out well.

"I think it's a great idea," she said enthusiastically when

I took a breath. "I'll tell Luis Felipe and see what he says. I hope we can see a performance when we get there."

I was thrilled that she was enthusiastic. Knowing I had her support, I got to work making a list of people I wanted to interview, starting with Gaspard, our resident artist. He was so flamboyant and outrageous, I was a bit surprised when he seemed reluctant, but he changed his mind quickly and told me to meet him at the house he shared with Alejandro so we could talk. His housemate was rarely there so we wouldn't have any interruptions, he said.

The house he lived in had a privileged position down from the front of the hotel in front of the ocean. When I knocked, no one answered. I tried the handle, opened the door, and let myself in.

"Gaspard?" I called, finding my way to the kitchen where he was standing over a stove, stirring something simmering. The kitchen smelled like chicken soup: comforting and delicious.

"'Alo, Julie," Gaspard said in his French accent, glancing up at me. The ashes from his lit cigarette dangled over the pot as he continued to stir. Before I'd even settled into the chair, he put the lid on the pot and began without waiting for me to ask a single question. He'd been thinking about the interview once he'd agreed to it.

"So. You are here to talk to me about my life? Sit down and we will talk." He gestured to the kitchen table and chairs. "It would be arrogant of me to refuse."

From my chair, I could see the whole length of him. He was shirtless, a nipple ring pierced his tanned, wrinkled chest, and his shorts were so skimpy his penis hung out. He wasn't trying to come on to me, or shock me, he was unconcerned, completely oblivious, and so like Gaspard. But I was embarrassed anyway, and from that moment, for the rest of the interview, my eyes never left his face.

I realized I had forgotten to bring a note pad or tape recorder because it had been so long since I'd interviewed anyone, but I had had enough experience to remember the important things he would say and the way he would say them. He was too colorful a character to forget, and I was hooked from the beginning.

"I am not at all sorry about my parents," he said, starting with his childhood. "My father, he was always angry at me. My mother was beautiful, but she had her boyfriends and no time for a little boy. When I was one year old, one day, my father kicked me across the room. That was the best moment of my life!"

"The *best* moment? What could have been so good about that?"

"My father was free to do that, and so he taught me by his example that I am free. Man is half animal, really. Any man who doesn't know that is only half a man."

"You must have had quite a life."

"When I was a young man, I lived with Picasso and his wife. I had affairs with both of them. Everything I know about painting I learned from watching Picasso paint, and that's all I need to know."

Having seen both his paintings and Picasso's, I disagreed, but my opinion as an art critic wasn't being asked, or what mattered. I was here to listen to the story of his life as he wanted to tell it, and he continued to regale me with such incredible stories they seemed too outrageous to be true. But then this was Gaspard, and I'd never thought of him as less than honest. In fact, his openness was so guileless that it was hard to reign his behavior in.

"At the time I knew Picasso, my life was in the theater as a choreographer. At twenty-two I had a big success. I got an eighteen-minute ovation after my ballet. It was the longest applause in history...Maria Callas only got fifteen minutes. After my ballet, I started producing and directing for the theater. That's when I met Gene Kelly. I coached him in the film where he kisses a black woman. It was a big moment for film...a white man kissing a black woman. It was terrific. When they finished filming, Kelly took me to America to work at MGM. He was a bastard really, that guy."

"That's quite a career," I said, wondering why I'd never heard how famous he was from anyone at the hotel. I only knew Luis Felipe was amused by him and liked having him around. In a way they were kindred spirits, two free artistic souls.

"When I came to Mexico I directed 'Hair.' That was the best. It was the first all-nude production in the country. The police came and arrested everybody," he chuckled. "It was wonderful for sales."

He paused and took a final drag of his Delicado cigarette, which had burned down to a nub and dropped it on the tile countertop, letting it die.

"But I take it you don't direct plays anymore."

"No, it's finished. I was tired of it all: the crowds, the parties, the press. I had no appetite for ambition anymore. I live here at Torbellino now because of Luis Felipe. I love that man. I am waiting for him to come back when he is well. It is wonderful for me here. I can be alone and paint every day, then go out and lie in the sun. I don't have to talk with anyone. But I love the Mayan workers, they smile and are so kind, and I talk with them, even if we can't speak the same language. My daughter likes it here too. She's thirty-six. You will meet her when she comes from France to visit soon."

"I didn't know you had a daughter."

"She was here last year for a month, but you weren't here yet."

"That must have been nice for you to see her."

"Yes, we are friends now, and she likes my girlfriend. You will meet her, too, but I haven't seen her in a while. She lives in Merida, and she's a very fine artist and she's been very busy getting ready for a show. She's a little younger than my daughter. I had my nipple pierced because she thinks nipple rings are sexy. Have you seen it?" He stuck his bare chest out so I wouldn't miss it.

"I see. Very brave of you. So now you live at Torbellino and paint," I said, changing the attention to the unframed canvasses lying against the wall near me.

"Yes, I made this one of my mother," he pointed to one of the portraits. It was a garish, sexualized caricature of a show girl, a painting I found particularly distasteful.

"She was beautiful," he said flatly. "And this painting is of my wife. She died years ago. We were divorced by the time she died, but she always loved me even after the divorce. You have to know how to handle those difficult moments in life. Like Clinton. Oh, I love that man. Okay, maybe it was not so good for his wife, but maybe she understood him like my wife understood me." He nodded at the painting he'd done of her and said proudly, "Every time I hurt her, she was there for me."

"She must have really loved you. You've had such a full life: a fascinating career, lovers, a child. Is there anything you've done that you regret?"

"No, not at all."

He took the lid off the pot, bent down and breathed

deeply, then dipped the ladle and tasted the broth. "Good," he pronounced, his eyebrows raised in satisfaction as it dribbled down his chin until he wiped it away with the back of his hand.

"I want to put all the past behind me now. My relationships, I want them to be very superficial." He waved the ladle in the air like a conductor signaling the upbeat. "I don't want to talk with the guests. I want to paint and stay all day in the sun and be alone. Happiness hides in the imagination."

"I can see that's true for you."

"And I am learning Spanish from Pepe in the palapa bar. I want to know all the important words: '*fuck you, asshole,*' and '*I have to go to sleep now. I have to work in the morning.*'"

I had to laugh. He was a total trip.

"I think I'm done talking now," he said. "I have to get back to my painting."

"Of course. Thanks so much. I think you've given me all I need. It'll make a great monologue."

"If I can help you with the production I will. I would do anything for Luis Felipe. If he doesn't come back, Torbellino will be just another hotel."

"I miss them too."

"When you talk to him, tell him I'm making a painting for him...one with a little girl in it."

I thought that was really creepy. What did it mean about Luis Felipe and his relationship with young girls? Men can get away with most anything if they're arrogant and clever enough, but I didn't want to think about that. I wanted to go home and work on writing a monologue from the information Gaspard had given me about his life.

It wasn't until much later that I was in the little theater

watching a film from our collection. When it ended, the credits scrolled by, and there was Gaspard's name in black and white letters. What he had told me about himself had been true. As long as I lived at Torbellino, it was difficult to sort out fact from fiction.

$\mathscr{I}$ went home and put the material from the interview with Gaspard into monologue form. It was easy to come up with a list of several others to include in the performance: Manuel, the gardener; Roberto, a waiter; Raphael, the dive master; Pedro, the salty old sea captain who ran the fishing trips; Nancy, the woman who led the Mayan rituals in the Temazcal; and Dulce, from guest services. The greater the differences in personality and in-services they performed at the hotel, the more interesting a performance I could make. I thought long and hard before including François on the list. He was the only one of them I didn't like, but he was such a colorful character, such a big personality, omitting him would have been a mistake. I didn't have to date him, I only had to interview him and represent him fairly in the performance.

I wanted to start with Manuel, since that seemed most challenging. I wasn't sure he'd agree to talk with me about himself or to have Dulce with me us as a translator since he spoke no English. But she told him what I had in mind and he agreed to sit down with us to talk about his life. On

Wednesday afternoon when he finished work, he met Dulce and me at the employee outdoor lunchroom.

"I am fifty-eight years old," he said. "When I came to El Torbellino looking for a job they told me, 'No, you are too old. You won't be able to do the work. It's manual labor and long hours in the heat. But now they see I work more than anybody here, from four a.m. to three p.m."

"Yes, and we're so lucky to have you here. But you work such long hours."

"I like my work. I am happy here for the most part, but I haven't had a vacation or seen my family in ten months," he said wistfully. "My wife is very understanding. We've been married forty years. She works hard taking care of the children and the pigs and goats and turkeys and chickens. She supports me going away to work, leaving them at home. It is what my grandfather taught me when I was young: to be respectful, to be a hard worker, and to make the ground give something to us even when it thinks it can't."

"He taught you well."

"I am from Veracruz and grew up on a ranchera, a place smaller than a village. My grandparents were the only parents I ever knew. But then, when I was twenty-two, my grandmother died and a new family moved to our ranch. They had a fifteen-year-old-daughter. Four months later, I won her for my wife."

"You sound proud of her."

He nodded. "Si. Mi esposa es la mejor."

He seemed surprisingly at ease, looking first at Dulce as he spoke, and then at me.

"It was very hard, especially in the beginning. When he had only been married a little while my grandfather sold our ranch. Then, there were big problems for me and my wife. Her cousins thought my grandfather had given me the money from the sale, and they threatened to kill me if I didn't give it to them. We moved away, but my wife was already pregnant, and with this worry she lost the baby. She needed surgery, but it cost thirty-five hundred pesos and I only had fifteen hundred. A man loaned me the money and gave me a job, but I worked five years to pay him back." He spoke without self-pity or anger about his past, having accepted that this was the way life was and should expect nothing more.

"That must have been so difficult for you both."

"Yes," he nodded vigorously. "When we came back to Veracruz, I bought my own little piece of land so my family could eat. All my life before and after I got married, I have made the plants grow, the maize, the corn, the beans. This is what my hands know. In Veracruz, where I am from, it isn't easy during the dry season. The plants stay tired, even though I try to give them all the water they need."

"And at Torbellino?"

He smiled. "At El Torbellino, the plants are always green. It's paradise for sure."

"I know you start work here very early, before anyone else. Why so early?"

"Every morning I come to water, to wake up the plants. I like that time when I'm alone with them. I don't think about my family then, only how the plants will look when I am done, how beautiful is the garden. I love them all, but my favorites here are the ones with the red leaves and that little spot behind the Boutique. I made that myself.

"You're happiest when you're working?"

"When I'm not working, I think too much about my family. Most of my children are grown. I am very proud of them. They are good boys. They never did anything to get into trouble to this day. But we have two adopted ones still at home with my wife. They are young and they miss me. I worry about leaving enough when I am gone so they can make it. I did this for the others and now it's their turn. I send home every penny I can. This is why I work."

"And how do you have the strength still at your age to work so hard?" I asked tentatively, respectful of his age.

"I trust in God. When I die, I will be at peace. Heaven and hell are right here on this earth and I have already suffered enough. I will go back to the earth and my body will help to fertilize the soil and help the plants grow. This will be my job, even then. I only worry about my family. Who will help them when I'm gone? While I'm here, I only want to be able to choose what to plant and when."

Listening to him talk was the way I'd felt as a child listening to my grandfather tell stories about his life in Broken Bow, Indian territory. There is a Jewish tradition that says there are thirty six *Tzadiks,* 'righteous ones,' living among us at any one time disguised as beggars, so we never know who they are, but it's on their merit that the world continues to exist. I felt I had just met another tzadik, my grandfather having been the first.

That night, when I finished writing a first draft of Manuel's monologue, I began to think about my next interview and Francois' name leaped out at me from my list. Francois was so different from Manuel, which was exactly the variety the performance needed.

I didn't like François, but he was a charismatic figure. The guests were smitten by him and his philosophizing about freedom, which he did for every passenger he took out on his boat. The audience would want to know more about him. I hadn't talked with him since the incident with his dog, but I thought maybe I'd find more to like if I could get him just to concentrate on telling his story. The next time he came to the office to use the fax machine, I stopped him to explain about the performance. He jumped at the chance to be part of it. I told him to pick a day to meet me. He said the next afternoon after lunch he'd be at his waterfront hut where the boats and snorkeling equipment were kept.

I'd never been inside the hut, and I was surprised to see how roomy it was. There was a high ceiling and a lot of light coming in through the windows, with a little table and a couple of chairs at one side, and a thick piece of fabric spread out on the floor with pillows — the kind I imagined I'd find in an Arabian tent. I was reminded again that François and his wife and two children were French Algerian. There were bottles of sea glass with wildflowers along the storage shelves that his wife must have put out. They made me think I might interview his wife Claire, too, at some later time, if she were willing, but she was awfully reticent about speaking English. I could relate to this, considering my hesitation about speaking Spanish.

He was tying up a sail on a hook from the wall when I ducked into the hut. He was wearing shorts and no shoes, his blonde hair stiff as straw from too much sun and wind. From the doorway, he gave a youthful appearance, without an ounce of fat on his lithe body, but as I looked more closely for the first time, his face didn't lie; he was in his middle to late fifties.

"Hi François. Is this still a good time to talk?"

"Of course. It is our choice what we do. We are free, so let's go." He said in his charming French accent. He sat down on the blanket and I sat next to him, cross-legged, ready to hear his philosophy on freedom and how he came to live it out.

"We talk now about the life. It is huge. Look where we

are living. We are in complete harmony with nature. We are free. We do here what we want to do."

I was thinking of Manuel and the difference, even physically, between the two men, though they were of similar age. Manuel, humble and reliable, works the land until it turns to lush gardens bursting with yellow, rose, and magenta; François, a mop-headed rogue who makes his living wind-surfing and snorkeling, takes time off whenever the mood strikes him. I was curious as to how he turned out this way and I wondered how much he would tell.

"You have chosen this beautiful place and every day that the wind is good I see you out on the ocean on your boat sailing. You're the picture of freedom."

"I have always been like this. When I was young, living in Algeria, my grandfather had many businesses. He make a lot of money. We had houses, cars, Mercedes. Our family, we love the cars. My grandfather give all his grandsons a building each one. He tell me to go to school in business, then he say he will give me a building too like my cousins. But I hate this. All my years in school I hate. They want children in a little box. I won't stay like this. I do what I want, always. I go like this and like that." He made a winding motion with his hands back and forth through the air, like a boat on a sea. "You must find your course. Is right word in English, course? I speak more Spanish."

"You are saying it perfectly."

"I tell my grandfather, teach me to sail, and he did. I love this! I follow him like, how you say, a *perro*, a puppy dog. We were French, but Algeria was our country. We love it. One day in 1962 we wake up and they say 'This is not your country anymore. Get out.' So now we don't belong there anymore. We lost everything. EVERYTHING. It all goes to the new government."

"That must have been so awful to have everything taken from you."

"When I say goodbye to my country, in one night, I learn all I need to know about the world."

"You learned not to trust a government?"

"There is no country for me anymore. We move to France, but then, a man came to Paris to find my father. He asked him to come back to Algeria to work for him, to run a factory, because my father, he was the best. So one more time we go back to Algeria, but it is not our country anymore. We are colonialists. For me it was OK. I discover then the desert. I love to be alone with the sand all around me. It is strong like the ocean. I learn to eat all the things the Arabs eat and drink tea the way they do. You must have three cups. It takes many hours. The first cup you drink quick. It is like a young woman, fresh. The second cup, it taste more mature. The third, because it sits so long, the leaves they make the taste bitter, like an old woman, angry with the life. But we must drink this too."

I was charmed by his accent and what he was telling me about Algeria. I knew nothing about the Algerian revolution and the loss it meant for French citizens who had lived in the country for generations. I could understand how that experience had formed or at least added to his innate disregard for authority. As long as I was learning from him I loved being there.

"And do you still drink tea like that?"

"Yes. Claire and I drink tea every day. It is like being home."

"Did you meet Claire in Algeria?"

"She is like me, French Algerian. But I didn't know her in Algeria. When I move back to France, one day, I went to a cabaret. I play guitar like Bob Dylan. I play at this cabaret and I see this young woman sitting with friends from the University. I love this face. We talk, we sing, we drink, we laugh a lot. I know she is the one. So we marry. We have a child, a house, a car. But I am so unhappy in France. We have money, but no time to live. No time for the sea.

"You were in a little box again, like in school."

"Just like that. But I am a sailorman. So one day, we sell everything. We say goodbye to everyone. See you one day, have a good life, like that. We go to Canada six years, we just live and spend all the money and we are so happy. But then, the money, it is gone. I say to Claire, come, we go to Mexico. When we arrive at Punta Allen, we have nothing, only our two kids and Claire and me and our car. We live like Gypsies, ten months in our car. For me it is perfect. The most happy time of all. But Claire, she is tired of this at the end."

"I can understand that."

"Yes. So we look where we want to go next. I hear about El Torbellino. They tell me is the most beautiful place with the most beautiful beach in all Mexico. Paradise. So we come here. They have the boats, the equipment, the tourists. I can make money here. I can teach them to sail and to snorkel, so we stay."

"It seems to have worked out well for you here."

"Ah, but still, we don't have many things. We are without a country. But what is a country of our own? Forget it. One day it's yours, the next, who knows? One day we have to leave Mexico, too."

"But for now..."

"Everything is perfect. You can be unhappy any place if you choose to be, but this is not for me. I am free."

"And now I understand why that's as important to you as the air you breathe."

"Luis Felipe, when he comes back, he will not be so free."

I decided this was a good place to end the interview, before he started in on Luis Felipe and his theories about why he and Molly hadn't come back yet. I thanked him for talking with me and told him I'll try to represent him well when I used our conversation for "The Torbellino Family".

"That will be good. We will want to see that."

I didn't envy him his past, but I was jealous from what he had made of it; learning to live in the moment, letting go of everything else. Both he and Gaspard were happy at El Torbellino, free to live and play as they wished when I felt so miserable and lonely much of the time. We were such different animals.

I'd only interviewed men from my list so far because they seemed to have the most compelling stories and personalities, but I needed to hear a woman's voice, to hear about life from her perspective. Surely they'd be more like me, even if they were younger and raised in a different culture than mine. I asked Dulce if she'd let me interview her.

"Of course I will, but it will be boring. You should talk with Araceli if you want to hear an interesting story, and she's the sweetest person. Everybody loves Araceli." I didn't know Araceli, other than to say hello, but she worked with Dulce in the guest services department and was her room-mate. I said that would be fine if she would set up a meeting for me with Araceli in the executive dining room.

We met the next afternoon after lunch. She was wearing the same white uniform as all the other anfitrionas, but on her it looked like a little girl's party dress. The elastic neckline sat primly high up on her shoulders rather than pulled down on her arms in a sexy show of skin. Her wavy hair was pulled back from her face into a short pony-tail and she wore no make-up and thick clunky black sandals rather than little heels like the other women in her department wore. She could have been a young novitiate nun, she looked so pure and innocent. Right away something in me softened.

"Hello, Araceli. Thank you for coming to talk with me. Dulce says you have quite a story to tell."

"Dulce and I talk a lot. She is almost like a sister to me."

"Do you have other sisters?"

"Oh yes. My three sisters and I have always been close. My mother always took care of us and pampered us, but she was strict when she had to be. We listened to her advice when there was a decision to be made. But when my parents separated nine years ago my sisters and I became even closer. Never before did we have to worry about money, but then my mother and my older sisters had to go to work. We moved from our little town of Celaya to Cordova."

"That was so much change for you with your mother and sisters working and living in a new big city."

"Yes. It was hard coming home from school not finding my mother at home waiting for me."

"You went to school in Cordova?"

"Yes. My mother's family lived in Cordova and paid for my education. I went to San Batiste de la Salle for high school, which was the best school. There were only twenty women out of a hundred students. Every two weeks one of the teachers took us to the Sierra, deep into the jungle. The people there live in so much poverty with no water or electricity. I learned to give my time and part of myself at that school."

"It sounds like it was an education for your soul."

"I had many friends at school, but never a boyfriend. I think I am maybe afraid of this kind of relationship, especially with someone I don't know well. I didn't come from the same town as they did or know their families. My sisters were not so unsure of themselves with men. One is married with a baby, the other has a boyfriend for many years."

"You are the youngest?"

"My younger sister is the baby. We thought we knew what suffering was about when my parents separated, but five years ago we learned the true meaning of the word, and also the opportunity that suffering can bring. My younger sister was nineteen years old when she began to have trouble with her kidneys. At first they thought it was just an infection, but after many tests they found she had an unusual syndrome. Both of her kidneys stopped working. She was so bad the doctors thought she wouldn't live without a kidney transplant."

"How frightening that must have been for all of you."

"It was. We sat down together, my mother and my other sisters and I to decide which one of us would be the one to donate her kidney to Ilyana. My mother said she wanted to do it, but my sisters and I said no, that is not possible. She isn't really old, my mother, but she is older than the rest of us. My oldest sister, Charo, had many kidney infections when she was young, so the doctor told her no because of her medical history. My other sister had just gotten married and started a new life, so it wasn't a good time for her to go through something like this. I had finished my education, I was healthy and not committed to anyone. I had no problems in my way, and I really wanted to do this for my sister."

"That is such a big decision to have a surgery like that. Weren't you afraid?"

"Not about the surgery or the future, but I was scared

about the injections I would have, and Ilyana knew I was afraid of needles. Every day we went to the hospital for different tests. I talked with a psychologist so they were sure my family wasn't pressuring me into doing this."

"How old were you then?"

"I was almost twenty-one. The doctors told me it is a paradox. You are accepted for the surgery because you are healthy, but after the surgery, you won't be so healthy anymore."

"And you weren't worried even then?"

"Only that they would say my kidney wouldn't be compatible for her. If it wasn't, who else was there to do this? We had to wait many months to find out. When we heard the news that we could go ahead with the transplant, Ilyana cried. She was so happy, but she was worried about me. She was so strong, even when she was so sick. She always told me don't give up, I can do this, and now she had new hope."

"She was lucky to have you do this for her."

"After the operation, when I came out of the anesthetic, at first I didn't know where I was, but I asked the doctor how it went. He said it was a success. Look, there she is. And I could see Ilyana lying on a bed near me with tubes coming out of her everywhere, and then they took her to a different room. She was in isolation for five days."

"And what about you? How were you after the operation?"

"For me the pain was so deep, but I was so happy. I love all of my sisters, of course, but Ilyana is like an angel for our family. It was a great opportunity to do something for her, and to make my mother smile again. After four months I was fine. It is always true that when you give something, even a smile, you get something bigger back. And now I have my sister."

She was so unassuming, such a calm quiet presence in the hotel, and she looked so young. It was hard to think she'd been through so much. Her story was less unique, in a way, than the ones I'd heard from Mañuel, but no less important. So many people suffered from illness, but her experience with her sister and her own surgery only added to her gentle manner. To look at her in her white lacy uniform, no one would have guessed that she had serious surgical scars underneath and probably still lived on a daily regimen of medication.

"I hope you feel well now. You certainly look wonderful."

"It has been good for me to work here by the sea in such a beautiful place. Looking at the flowers and the birds help me heal. I like helping the guests, whatever I can do for them. And I like the three women I share a room with. The waiters are all so kind to me. I am used to being away from my family now, but I miss them terribly. I think one day soon I will go home."

She looked down, as though to hide what she was feeling. She would never complain if she was unhappy. She had learned to mask her sorrow and tell her story matter-of-factly, a part of her removed from it emotionally. In one brief interview, she was not about to go there with me. I thought of how many hours it took for me to earn the trust of the women who were Holocaust survivors when I was interviewing them for *Too Young to Remember,* a book about young Jewish children who had survived the war in camps and hidden as Christians in the countries where they lived. The scars, the fear, the anger at their parents for not protecting them still lingered, along with the guilt they harbored for real or imagined reasons. After what they'd endured, something as ordinary as getting up every day and brushing their teeth seemed a victory to me. But those children had had no choice about the horrors they endured. Araceli's was a chosen suffering in order to achieve a positive result, which made all the difference. My purpose in interviewing the Holocaust survivors was very different from my reasons for interviewing the employees, and keeping it lighter was fitting. Still, I was sorry when the time she had set aside from her work schedule for our interview was over. I was grateful to know a young woman like Araceli worked at Torbellino and gained something more from it than the measly salary she was paid.

CHAPTER TWENTY-ONE

*T*rarely saw Claire, François' wife, without her husband with her, but one morning early, a week after I'd interviewed him, I saw her sitting on the beach by herself and asked if she would talk with me. She knew the reason for the interview from François, but she was reluctant to speak with me because she said her English was too poor. I had the sense that the problem wasn't so much about the language, but about confidence. If I was patient and spoke slowly, I was sure we could manage together. I asked if she'd give it a try and see how it went, and she agreed to meet me for coffee in the restaurant one afternoon after the guests had finished lunch.

"I'm glad to have a chance to talk with you," I said as she sat down at the table where I was waiting.

"But why you talk with me? François, he tell you all the story," she said, confused.

"He told me his story, but François is not you. He doesn't know all you think or do or feel. Only you can tell me your story. Do you understand? Please tell me if I'm speaking too quickly."

"Yes. You are...I like how you say words...I understand. You say I have my story."

"That's right. That's what I want to hear. And Claire, I think you know more English than you think you do."

She smiled. "I am, how you say this word, *she*?"

"You mean shy?"

"Yes, shy. François, he is strong. Not like me. All the night he talk about him. He don't let me talk."

"That must be hard."

She nodded. "Yes. But I am used to this. I am from Algeria. When I have ten years, I went to France to school. It was very hard. People treat me like stranger, a bad French person. I am French, but I am born in Algeria. In France I am alone. It is cold there. France is not very beautiful." She sighed.

"And Algeria?"

"I think is most beautiful country in the world. The sea. The mountains. The desert. The smell of the Mediterranean. When I am in France, Algeria says I cannot go back. I am not Algerian. This was very sad, the most important moment of all. But now, I know I can leave a place, go someplace new. But I love too many people. I am too emotional when I say goodbye. Sometimes I am afraid. I think this is normal, yes?"

"Of course."

"I have four children. One has baby. We leave three but the young one comes with us. We go to Quebec. In Quebec there are no smells. Just McDonald's, Burger King, Gasoline."

"So, you didn't love Quebec."

"No, not at all. François says we come to Mexico. Now I am old here. My body, she hurt when I walk. Swim is better. Every day, very early, I sit in front of the ocean. I close my eyes. I feel the sun on my face. I think." She crossed her legs, closed her eyes and lifted her face as though meditating. "I need this time in the morning alone. It is hard. Always, François, he want me. And I have young child. She goes to school in Puerto Morelos, but she is very sad. She has no friends here. I understand. I want too a friend, someone like me."

"You don't have friends here?" It hadn't occurred to me that she might be lonely with her husband and children around.

"One, but she will leave soon and go to her family. This is what she choose."

"That will be another sad day for you when she leaves." My heart went out to her. I identified with her need for friends.

"Sometimes, I have big anger with my husband. Sometimes, I wake up and feel angry. I can choose to be bad girl all day, to fight. We can fight if we need, but I want peace. My friend, he say, 'You come stay with me.' But I love him more than I am angry."

"And love isn't easy to find."

"It is hard, so many years together. When I see François, I must see myself. This is what makes it so hard to live here. So many people from so many places. We see them every day. They are our mirrors too. This is the challenge, to be happy for the other person. It makes us strong."

I'm surprised to hear her sound so wise. "And how do you find peace within yourself?" I asked, really wanting to know.

She had a ready answer. "It is something only for me," she said, showing me the shell necklace that she was wearing. "When I make my necklaces, this makes me happy. When I make my perfume too."

I remembered seeing the bottles of sea glass that lined the shelves of the storage hut when I interviewed François, and now I understood what they were for.

"I love the perfumes, but when we come here, we have no money and I can't buy, so I make. I find little bottles on the beach, or I buy. Very little money I pay for bottles in Isla Mujeres. I buy oils there too. I mix, I shake like this and like this." She demonstrates the motion. "Some perfumes smell like flowers. Some like the trees, like the fruit. Some is blue like the sea. Some is orange and sweet like mango. One is fresh, it smell like the morning." Her face was alive and her pleasure obvious as she described the process.

"And can you make the same perfume the next time if it pleases you?"

She shook her head. "I never know to make the same. It is for the moment. No moment is for long. No moment will come back, even if you want. Someone say I can sell this in the gift shop. You think is true?" She studied my face as I had studied hers, looking for answers.

"I think people would love it." I imagined her starting her own little cottage industry, perfume made at El Torbellino.

"Money for me, not for François." Her expression fell as her husband came through the door of the restaurant, spotted us, waved, and headed over to our table.

"I have loved this time, Julie," she said quickly. "My interview. Now, I know I can speak with my heart in English. Is easy with you."

As I left the two of them, I thought about their relationship. It seemed unlikely that she'd follow through with her dream of selling her perfume at El Torbellino. Her need to please her husband and be available to him would likely defeat any effort she made to claim herself as an independent woman. I would have to be careful in the way I told her story. I didn't want François to be angry at her for revealing too much or to give any reason for her to regret her honesty with me.

Each night, I worked on crafting the monologues from the interviews. Once all eight were finished, only one more remained. No performance about "The Torbellino Family" would be complete without including Luis Felipe. He was the foundation, the very heart and soul of the hotel. At least they'd meet a version of him if they came to the performance.

It was easy to remember so much of what he'd told me because it had seemed so remarkable at the time; the way he spoke was permanently etched in my head.

Molly tells you she met me in my bar in Cancun. It's not exactly true, this coincidence. I'll tell you the way it happened. Molly, she don't know.

One night, it was a Sunday, and El Tomate, my little bar, was closed. I was riding on my motorcycle in my black leather jacket — very sexy, vroom, vroom — and I passed this restaurant and saw these two Americans, these two young women sitting in the window, and in that moment, and I tell you this is true, I thought, that one I'm going to marry. I don't know why. I'd been divorced ten years and met many beautiful girls, Americans, but I knew this one in the window, she was different.

My friend was maître d' of this restaurant, so I went in and told him, see those Americans sitting over there? Give them my card and tell them to come to El Tomate for the best music in Cancun. Jazz. I like this very much.

The next night, Molly, she came to El Tomate with her friend. I heard her tell one of the musicians she lived in New York, so I stopped near where she was sitting, and I said,

"How's New York?" "Cold," she said. I sat down to talk with her and that night I told her I was going to marry her. She laughed. She didn't believe me. I told her, "You wait, you'll see."

We had very nice week. I took her on my motorcycle all around downtown Cancun to see the lights, and I told her on Sunday, "I'm gonna take you to the most beautiful beach you've ever seen." There was nothing but 500 acres of bananas and coconuts and a little hut for the foreman on this property. And this very private beach. We stayed all day on the beach, drinking and swimming, and I taught Molly how to snorkel. She loved the fish and this very, very private place. I told her the big story, how I was working in Cancun and flew over and saw the property, and I knew, even from the plane, it had a power. You can feel it too, can't you? It isn't just beautiful, it's spiritual.

I think the whole history of Mexico started right here on our beach with Gonzalo Guerrera, a Spanish explorer who was shipwrecked here in the 1700s. He stayed and married a Mayan woman and had a child with her, a mixed child of their two cultures, and so started the Mexican people. Right here. Some people say that shipwreck happened on Cozumel, but I know it was here, because the tides make a whirlwind and many shipwrecks happen. And that special magic makes everybody want to stay and be Mexican, just like Guerrero.

Molly and I watched the moon come up that week and we slept there on the beach, and I told her, "Molly, I have a dream. Someday I'm gonna build a house here, after we get married, and then make a hotel. It won't be like other places, I told her, and it will be magic too."

When she went back to New York, I hired some mariachi singers to serenade her over the telephone from El Tomate, and I went to see her in New York. I could see her place was *very nice, and she cooked very well. I said, "Why don't you come to Cancun to marry me?"*

I don't think her mother liked the idea so much, but Molly, she said she'd try living with me for three months first. Every Sunday, Molly and I had a picnic at the ranch with different friends. After we built our house, we flew to St. Louis to get married in her mother's house.

So you see, it was true what I said to Molly. I can see all the things, and I can wait for something good to happen. Many things we're still gonna do here. It is important to have a place where people can create. Musicians, writers, artists, we must give these people much room. The sea makes people creative. Lights, furniture, art, all must come together to create a certain mood, to stimulate, to be provocative.

Everybody must do his part. Even the guests. We invite them to our home and they make it interesting. People come from everywhere around the world to talk, to dream, to make love. Have you seen our guest book? There are many compliments, but there is one that I want you to see. I think it's page 119. This lady, she wrote, "After ten years of marriage, I have had my first orgasm at Torbellino. Thank you, thank you, thank you!" And then she signed her name! I think this is the best compliment of all for our hotel. I want to create romance. Magic. That is how Torbellino began.

But now I have to go talk to the masons. They are building a wall between the bedroom and the kitchen in the old chef's house, and I want them to finish while we're in Miami. Sometimes, they get confused and forget things, but they are the best, these masons. I really like talking to them. Maybe I like talking with them more than with anyone else. Well, maybe not more than with the birds.

. . .

It felt good remembering what I'd loved about him. Luis Felipe, the romantic, the charming, talented artist, entrepreneur, creator of the world-class El Torbellino, with a wicked sense of humor. He had raised the hotel above all the others on the coast with its combination of isolated location; white, Moorish architecture; and handmade simplicity and style. It was audacious of me to think of wearing his clothes and imitating his walk and his manner of speaking, of becoming him on stage. I would try to present him at his best as I would for every other person I'd interviewed. I hoped the real people behind the stories would come and revel in the audience's appreciation of them. I wanted them to feel proud and hoped that the show would bring them together in appreciation of their shared humanity.

I put the monologues together, considering their different accents, genders, and moods. Luis Felipe would come at the end and have the final say. The total performance would last about fifty minutes, plus an introduction. That seemed just right, but to keep the audience's focus, it needed something more to break the monotony of listening to a single voice for that long. When I'd given one-woman performances in the past, Mike had worked with me, adding a cover song after each monologue, accompanying himself on his guitar as he sang. The songs we chose added to the themes of the stories and gave me time to change costumes between each character. When Mike left me, performances weren't the same without him. I thought about finding someone else to work with, but I'd tried other musicians in the past and none had seemed right. I stopped wanting to write shows altogether, until the idea for The Torbellino Family came along.

But I needed a musician to work with. Music had been part of every theater piece I'd created, and when I performed, the music fed me. Diego was a guitarist and singer who played in the restaurant at El Torbellino on the weekends. He did jazz standards, show tunes, pop songs, plus a few standard Mexican favorites. I hadn't spent time talking with Diego, but he had a pleasant voice and was an accomplished guitarist. I always enjoyed listening to him play. As he was putting his guitar back into its case after he'd finished a set one night, I told him about the performance and asked if he would be part of it. He didn't hesitate before saying yes. He seemed flattered to be asked and immediately showed me his song list.

"Thanks, Diego. Some of those will be perfect. We can choose which ones when we get together to rehearse, but that won't be for a while, when we have a performance date."

Screw you, Mike, I thought as I left Diego. I don't need you anymore. The loss of Mike as a creative partner had been as important as the loss of him as a lover. The two had been inextricably wound together, and it was such a relief to know that I could go on without him.

I made a list of costumes: a straw hat and cotton drawstring pants for Manuel, an anfitriona's uniform for Araceli, and a waiter's coat for Pedro from the housekeeping department. I had an old t-shirt and baggy shorts in my closet that would work for François and a sarong and bikini top I could wear for Claire. I'd ask Nancy if I could borrow the red print mini-dress she wore for ceremonies in the Temazcal. With a floral guyabara shirt and carved walking stick from Luis Felipe's house and a bathrobe from Gaspard, I'd be all set, although I should have played Gaspard in the nude to keep it real.

Molly talked with Carla about the performance before I did. She told her to get one of the waiters to come to the little theater to serve wine and cheese for everyone who came to the performance. I scheduled it for the last night in September. The week before, the anfitrionas put fliers in the guests' rooms advertising the time and place for the show. I was thrilled that they were participating in their own way. Everything was coming together so nicely, it seemed *beshert*, meant to be.

CHAPTER TWENTY-TWO

*T*he night of the performance, the maintenance crew set up rows of chairs in the little theater. I got there way too early and paced uselessly back and forth outside, watching guests pass on their way to their rooms or to the restaurant. It was such a beautiful evening, I wondered who among them would want to come inside for the performance on a night like that.

At seven, Pedro, the waiter I'd interviewed, set out wine glasses and cheese on silver trays, smiled and raised a thumb, wishing me luck, reassuring me that all is well.

The program was to start at eight. At seven-thirty, I disappeared into the storage room of the theater that we used for audio-visual equipment. This was my make-shift dressing room with just enough room in it for me to turn around. I put on my first costume and laid out the others in order of the characters I'd present. My palms were starting to sweat as I practiced the lines of the monologues in my head for the umpteenth time. Please, God, I don't want to have to pee now.

I peeked through the slots of the bamboo doors of the

storage closet as the room filled with tanned women in high heels and sunglasses and men with slicked black hair and Rolex watches. They were sipping wine, nibbling cheese hors d'oeuvres, and talking with each other. The room was full, I had to hand it to Carla. She'd done an outstanding job getting people to come.

"This is such a great idea," I overheard one guest say as she sat down close to where I was waiting.

I spotted Araceli and Nancy. François, Claire, and Raphael were in the crowd too. François greeted guests like a rock star as if this was his show. Finally, their group took their seats in the back row behind people they seemed to know. Gaspard tripped into the theater just as Carla lowered the overhead lights and took the last open seat as one white spotlight shined on center stage.

Diego stepped up to the stage with his guitar and sat while I entered from the dressing area, wearing a gardener's uniform. The crowd hushed instantly.

"Good evening, everyone. I'm Julie Heifetz, and this is Diego Alverez. We and the other employees of El Torbellino are so pleased you're here to share with us tonight the real stories of the people who work and live here. We are fortunate to have them with us. They are the ones who make our intimate resort so extraordinary. They come from many places, many backgrounds. No matter who they are, no matter where they come from or what they do, they feel fortunate to be here at El Torbellino, to share the beauty of our beach and this Mayan jungle. They are the Torbellino Family, and they invite you to become part of them."

The room was silent as I paused, giving myself time to think about Manuel, my first monologue. I wanted my admiration for him woven into the fabric of the performance. But then, something transformative happened to me, as I suppose happens to all actors. I wasn't pretending to be Manuel, I *was* him. I was the humble, simple servant, wanting only to give the best of myself to make life grow and flourish.

The audience hardly moved until Manuel's monologue was over, and I left them in Diego's capable hands while I went off-stage, changed costumes, and shifted gears, opening myself to François.

"It's huge, the life!" I threw my arms open wide as I re-entered the stage barefoot, wearing baggy shorts and t-shirt. "When a big wave comes and slaps over the sides of my boat, even if it gets me soaking wet and it's cold in the wind, I say thank you. I love you. And I know you love me too." I embraced François, knowing that part of me was like him too, the hippie, the undisciplined braggart, without a country, charting my own course, feeling free.

As the performance moved from one character to the next, I found each one of the people in me. I was Araceli at times: quiet, loyal, and kind, loving and missing my family who were far away. I was Gaspard: outrageous, artistic, feeling forever young. I understood Nancy, the leader of the Temezcal ceremonies, spiritual and focused, because I had experienced those feelings myself. I had been like Pedro, suave and charming; like Claire, sensual and earthy; like Raphael, an observant student. So, too, was I Luis Felipe, a romantic dreamer inspired by Molly to create an exciting, complicated new world. As the characters moved through me, time expanded endlessly. Suddenly the hour had passed and the stage went dark.

The audience applauded loudly, with François shouting above all the other voices, *"Bravo, Bravo!"* I walked off the stage in a daze and into my make-shift dressing room still lost in the kaleidoscope of characters, but the audience kept applauding, waiting for me to come back. Moving on autopilot, I went back to them and called Diego over to take a bow with me. Then I raised a hand and thanked everyone for coming. "Help yourself to another glass of wine and stay as long as you like."

I barely made it into the dressing room before I started to sob. I felt like an empty vessel. The applause had not really been for me, but for all the people whose stories I had told. The negative thoughts I'd had about Luis Felipe and Carla and the management fell away. None of the frightening disturbing moments I'd had since Luis Felipe and Molly left mattered. My heart was full of love for the people I'd become on stage and for El Torbellino itself. Maybe this would be a new beginning or me and the staff. Together we could begin to repair our little world.

People were waiting at the front of the theater to talk with me after I changed clothes. "When will there be another performance? I want to tell everyone who wasn't here about it. Everybody should see this," one of the women gushed.

"I don't know when we'll do it again, but I'm so glad you enjoyed it. This was kind of an experiment."

A young man standing nearby with his attractive companion leaned in. "How about having a drink with me and my girlfriend in the restaurant? We're both actors from New York and we really loved your performance."

I was flattered, but thanked them and begged off his invitation. I wasn't up to making conversation with strangers, even ones I'd like to meet at some other time. I wanted to get home, get something to eat, and review the performance in my mind. I wished Eliseo had been there to see it, but he hadn't come, and neither had Manuel or

Jimmy, which was no surprise. Carla had disappeared from the theater once she was done working the lights for the performance. I wondered what she thought of it.

Once I got home, it took a while to unwind. I was thinking about what I could have done better, what I'd change when Molly and Luis Felipe saw it at Thanksgiving, but I went to bed feeling satisfied that it had gone well enough for a first performance and more like myself than I'd felt since I'd come to Torbellino.

The next morning, Dulce apologized for not having been at the performance.

"Carla wanted me to take her office hours because she was going to be at the little theater."

"Maybe next time," I said.

She frowned. "Carla told us at our meeting today that if there's another performance, we shouldn't put fliers in the guest rooms again if you ask us to or put the show on the schedule. I wasn't supposed to tell you."

I felt the energy drain out of me, and I turned into a pillar of stone. "Thank you for letting me know."

I should have expected Carla's reaction, but her help in gathering an audience, in setting up the wine and cheese party before the show, and in working the lights had lured me into thinking she appreciated what I'd done for the guests and for the hotel. It had been my own need for a creative outlet that had driven me to write and perform, but now I imagined that Carla saw it as a selfish and inappropriate thing to have done. I didn't feel like tangling with her over a gift I wanted to give to others. Maybe the performance had gone too well, had been too successful with the guests.

No one mentioned the show at the managers' meeting. Carla avoided walking out with me when it was over.

"She's just so jealous," Jimmy said.

"She doesn't need to be. My position as manager is only temporary until Luis Felipe gets back. And I'm not going to do any more performances for a while."

"It's not about the performance. She won't let anybody get in the way of her running things here. I hear she told Luis Felipe you want to fire everybody."

"That's not true! I want to do no such thing!"

"She's always had the power behind the scenes with Luis Felipe, if you know what I mean," he winked.

Carla had free rein with Luis Felipe because they were lovers, he implied. She called the shots with her brother Antonio in accounting and with Gerardo in housekeeping, too. But Luis Felipe was the voice that mattered, no matter how far away he'd gone, or how seldom he called.

CHAPTER TWENTY-THREE

$\mathcal{T}$he performance hadn't made a difference to anyone but me. It had brought me back to what I loved in my old life: listening to people and turning their stories into performances, which would often initiate change in an organization. I missed that part of me and having friends to share my work with who valued it.

Patti had once been my fairly constant sidekick and supporter when I lived in St. Louis. We'd been best friends since our children started kindergarten together. Many days we spent together at my house, under the guise of working; she would quilt while I would write, but we ended up spending more time talking than we did on our work. It bothered me that now I couldn't remember what we actually talked about in all that time. Had our friendship been that trivial that not a word of it had stayed with me? I must not have been paying enough attention.

I winced remembering that I had felt trapped by our closeness. I resented her cloying jealousy over any other friendships I had. When Mike came along, I made little time for her for years while he and I were working together creating shows and traveling to give performances and workshops around the country. By the time the relationship with Mike ended, Patti was barely speaking to me, and I could hardly blame her for that. She too had moved on. Even if I went back to St. Louis after Mexico, there would be no repairing my relationship with her, and she was the one I missed the most.

I had left my suburb of Clayton, shunning friendships that were ordinary and familiar. I had run from a love affair that had ended against my will and had shattered my confidence. But now in the midst of a community where I didn't fit in, I grieved for what I'd lost.

Within a few days of the performance, my relationships with the people who had given their stories went back to what they had been before the interviews: cool, aloof, and polite to my face. I had been foolish to hope for more.

I was surprised when I learned one day that Dulce had quit her job in the guest services department. She left in the middle of the night without telling me goodbye. "That's how people do at El Torbellino," one of the other anfitrionas said.

But now, thanks to Telmex, we finally had land lines and internet access. I couldn't wait to start sending emails to old friends and family.

The computer Alejandro gave me for my work in the sales department was a fat dinosaur of a machine, but that didn't worry me so long as it worked. The computer had only Spanish symbols, and I couldn't figure out how to turn it on. I called Alejandro and asked him to please send over someone to fix whatever was wrong and give me a tutorial on how to use it.

"I'm sorry, but everyone in my office is very busy. I'll send someone soon, though."

I could understand that, especially since a large flock of lawyers had descended again on the hotel to work with Alejandro in the accounting office. But once they left, still no one showed up to help me, and I called him again.

"I haven't forgotten. Javier's our computer guru. He'll be there soon. If not today, then mañana."

Soon could mean anything. A few days. A week. A year. I remembered the story Molly told me about buying a refrigerator the first year she and Luis Felipe lived on the ranch. She had ordered one from the only store that carried large appliances in Cancun. The clerk told her they didn't have the model that she wanted in stock, but it would be there *mañana*. A week passed, and Molly called to check on the order. The clerk said the fridge wasn't in yet, but they'd let her know as soon as it came. Another few months went by with no word from the store, and she gave up on it and went back to using an icebox for food. One day, a year later, a delivery truck pulled up to their house, two men got out and dumped the new refrigerator she'd ordered on her front lawn. I realized when I heard that story that when a Mexican says *mañana,* he may not really mean tomorrow, he may just mean *not today.* Who knew how long it would actually take for Javier to show up and get my computer working? I was beginning to think Alejandro was playing me, deliberately making me wait.

I called again, this time sounding more impatient. A week after that, a heavy-set, twenty-something-year-old, wearing glasses, a sloppy shirt, and baggy pants dragged himself and a box of tools into my office, moving at sloth speed. I told him how glad I was to see him and left him alone in the office to do his magic. When I came back an hour later to see if the computer was fixed, Javier said it still wasn't working and packed up his tools.

"Do you know what's wrong with it?"

He shrugged his shoulders. "Maybe something with the wires. I'll be back."

It was days before Javier showed up again. This time didn't go any better. Frustrated, I called Alejandro and asked if he could give me one of the computers from his office.

"We need all three of ours right now, and Carla has to have one for guest services. Javier will fix yours soon, don't worry."

Javier did come back the next day. He crawled under the desk, fiddled with the wires for a few minutes, shrugged nonchalantly, and ambled off, leaving the computer a clunky, useless ornament on my desk. I wasn't sure if the problem was the computer, Javier's incompetence, or Alejandro's way of frustrating and undermining me.

"If Javier can't fix it, hire a computer technician from Cancun to come."

"They won't make service calls this far away." I had a laptop at my house I'd used for writing the monologues, and now that we had internet, I could use it for sending personal emails, but I wasn't about to mix anything I did for work with my private account when it could be too easily broken into. I would have to wait. I didn't care as much about being more efficient with my work in the office as I did about being deliberately stone-walled by Alejandro.

He was the one who scheduled the transports to bring workers from Cancun and Puerto Morelos to El Torbellino and back again when their shifts ended. One morning, I overheard a group of workers complaining that the truck was always late picking them up. Sometimes, they waited at the bus stop for more than an hour.

"And it's dangerous. The law says we're not supposed to

have more than eight passengers, but there are more than ten or eleven of us. Alejandro doesn't care about safety."

If we added one more truck to the schedule that would take care of both problems, and I told that to Alejandro. He said he'd take care of it, but after two weeks, I saw the same workers piling out of the van. They were late for work again. Nothing had changed. I was livid and sick of getting the same run around from Alejandro, which I took as a personal challenge to my authority, adding to the frustration of having a damned computer that hadn't been fixed.

I marched into the accounting office and demanded angrily that he take care of the problem once and for all. I knew I shouldn't have lost my temper, I should have talked to him more calmly in front of other employees, but he did add another truck to the schedule soon after that and the workers arrived more or less on time.

Alejandro's accounting office was steps away from mine, and for weeks, I had noticed a fairly steady flow of men carrying books in and out of the office. Miguel, one of the young men who worked for Alejandro and came with the transport from Cancun, was outside one afternoon taking a cigarette break.

"Hola, Miguel," I said as I walked by. When he saw me he threw the cigarette butt in the dirt, crushed it under his shoe, and waved. We had never said more than a few words to each other before that morning, but I had gathered that he understood English.

"How are you?"

"I'm fine. But I want you to know my last day at Torbellino will be Friday."

"Really? I'm sorry to hear that, Miguel. Why are you leaving us?"

I was surprised he was quitting when the transport problem had been resolved.

"Torbellino is such a beautiful place. I was proud when I got the job here, but I didn't know..." He looked back over his shoulder to make sure we were still alone.

"What didn't you know?"

"About Alejandro. He makes us stay late because...we have much to do now. We have new accounting records to keep. One set of books is for Luis Felipe. And a different set of books for the government shows different numbers. I never saw these books before. It is confusing. Maybe it's okay what he is asking us to do, but I don't think so. Please don't tell Alejandro I told you this. You want to do good things here. You make Antonio put an extra transport on the schedule. So I tell you the truth about why I leave. Anyway, my new job in Cancun is very close to my house. I think it will be better for me to work there. I don't want trouble."

I believed Miguel's story. The accounting department was doctoring the books so Luis Felipe could avoid paying higher taxes, and who knows what other shady business they were involved in running. I had no more illusions about Luis Felipe, the hotel, or the Torbellino Family, and no more misconceptions about my relationship with Molly. Her loyalty was with Luis Felipe and not with me.

She had been his muse, the inspiration behind the hotel. Her style and taste was everywhere, but she didn't understand his business. She was like a mafia wife, closing her eyes to anything she didn't want to see. Realizing that, I felt as if someone I loved had died. My dreams about living on the ranch and working at the hotel, and all of my illusions about my sophisticated friends, had shriveled to nothing. I would plod on until they were home. I'd get through their friend's son's wedding and Thanksgiving and Christmas week. I couldn't leave until I'd talked with Luis Felipe and made arrangements to sell my house. Now that I had an internet connection, I could start looking for a job and figure out where to go next. It wouldn't be St. Louis. I missed having friends, but I wouldn't go backwards. El Torbellino was not my place, but I'd find somewhere else in the States where I would be happy. By February, I'd be gone.

It was October 31, the Day of the Dead. The holiday recognizes death as a normal part of life, but mocks death at the same time. *Death is skinny, weak, and she can't carry me,* the sayings taunt. It was the national day of mourning and an extension of my own grief. I went into my office and sat staring at the blank walls, feeling numb.

A new anfitriona took Dulce's place. She came to my office to introduce herself and said she wanted to show me the decorations her department had put up for the Day of the Dead. We walked into the dining room where petals of marigolds trailed along the floor.

"The petals are so the souls of the dead can find their way to the altar." She pointed to a profusion of purple, pink, orange and red flowers, and a magnificent display of marigolds set on a narrow side table at the back of the room.

"And the colors of the flowers all mean something different. Purple is for the pain and suffering when we remember a loved one who has died. Pink stands for celebration, because on the Day of the Dead we also celebrate the lives of the dead. The orange color represents the sun, and the red flowers are for the blood of life. The marigolds are most important of all, because they mean death itself."

She was saying something else about the holiday, but I was distracted by the rest of the display: ghoulish skulls with photographs next to them, and cards with names. I stood still in horror in front of the display.

"Who are those?" I demanded.

"Oh, yes, those are the ones who have died recently."

"But that's my picture and my name on that card."

The young woman covered her mouth with her hand. "Oh, I don't know why..."

"I'm sure you don't." I felt the sting of humiliation and shock at seeing my own photo on the altar like my own tombstone made ready for my death. It was terrifying, but I wasn't going to let the new anfitriona see how upset I was. I wouldn't give her boss Carla the satisfaction of hearing about it later.

"Thank you for showing me the decorations," I snapped, dismissing the young woman abruptly. As soon as she had gone, I took my photo down and wandered around the grounds of the hotel, aimlessly wondering what to do. An image of Luis Felipe from one of my past visits came to me. He was still young then, his black hair and beard glistening with water. A red sail was draped across his neck as he rose from the sea like el Diablo. He was behind it all, everything that happened at the hotel. Carla carried out Luis Felipe's wishes. So did Alejandro. In spite of having giving me a job and a title, there was too much he didn't want me to know. He had a vested interest in keeping me confused and frightened, disguising the truth.

There are too many problems at the hotel, Eliseo had warned me when I first told him I was going to work at Torbellino. My suspicions had names. Banking fraud. Money laundering. The words kept playing over and over in my head, tormenting me.

I didn't have actual proof of money laundering, but I felt in my bones that that was what was happening, but I needed to see evidence to be absolutely sure. If I knew beyond any doubt that Luis Felipe was a criminal and that the hotel was being used as a front for hiding money that came from drug deals or other illegal sources, I could leave without a whit of guilt. But I was afraid of what Luis Felipe might do if he knew what I suspected. He paid other people to do his dirty work. He was a dangerous man who might do anything to protect his hotel and his own reputation. He owned the land my house was on and I needed him to buy me out or let me sell it to someone else.

I was sure Molly had no idea about Luis Felipe's affair and didn't suspect anything about the operations of the hotel. Although she had questioned the reason that the flock of lawyers descended on the place constantly, she closed her eyes to everything. On the one hand, I admired her loyalty to her husband. On the other hand, I was appalled that she preferred blindness to facing the truth. How could she have trusted Alejandro, whose father supposedly stole a million dollars from the hotel? How could she have not wondered about the argument with the son-in-law that triggered Luis Felipe's heart attack and kept them away from home for months afterward?

She and I had known each other for more than thirty years, but for most of those years we'd lived in different cities and for the last sixteen in different countries. Our relationship, when it came down to it, consisted of telephone calls every few months and once-a-year-visits. The truth was, I didn't really know her at all.

I had been wrong to want to be like her. Over the last few months, I had found more to admire in myself than I had when I'd arrived. I was loyal, sometimes beyond the point of when loyalty was deserved. Even though I'd moved away, I had friends and children I was proud and pleased to have raised. I was a fighter, trying to figure out a way to hang on. My son had told me once, Mommy, you're like a big soft rabbit with great big teeth, and he was right. I snapped when I was hurt, but I liked my scrappiness, my creativity. I was too direct, too American, too much in need of love to live where I was not wanted. The longer I'd been away, the more I appreciated my own needs: close relationships, work that I believed in, and honesty. I would not find that at Torbellino. But I wanted to stay to the end of the year and finish what I'd started.

Alex Israel's wedding was coming up soon. I had met Alex's father, Rick, at a dinner party once at Molly and Luis Felipe's before I started work at Torbellino. He was a long-time friend of Luis Felipe's, an investment banker with a big brash New York personality, but I liked him in spite of it. I had worked with his son to plan the wedding and I wanted to be there to see it went well. According to François, it was his land that was being contested, and if the rumor was true, Luis Felipe would be especially worried.

"Ask Carla if you need help with any details," Molly reminded me again on one of her brief calls the week before the wedding.

"Don't worry. I've spoken with Alex several times recently. We've gone over what they want. They've been easy to work with because they were so organized and clear. Everything's been taken care of."

CHAPTER TWENTY-FOUR

One afternoon, a few days before the wedding weekend and coming from an interview with a new potential masseuse, I saw a bear of a man with a walking stick in hand coming down the path toward the restaurant. I froze in the path where I stood, unable to say a word, realizing who he was. He was wearing the same blue flowered shirt and khaki pajama style pants he always wore. It took a minute to find my voice again.

"Luis Felipe! You're here!" I stepped up my pace to close the gap between us. Molly had told me they'd be home for Thanksgiving, but she hadn't said anything about coming home now. Why hadn't she let me know?

"Hello, Julie," he said distractedly as though he'd seen me a few hours before, when, in fact, it had been more than nine months. He leaned forward to kiss me perfunctorily on both cheeks.

"What are you doing here?" I asked, still reeling from the shock.

"We wanted to be here for the wedding. Everything is going okay?"

"Everything's fine with the wedding plans. I'm just so surprised to see you. You look great, by the way, so healthy." It was true. He didn't look like a man who'd been seriously ill. He hadn't lost a bit of weight, and his skin color was as ruddy as it had always been.

"When did you get here?"

"This morning. We took a ship from Miami to Puerto Morelos Carnival. It was very bad. I guess for the lower class it is OK," he wrinkled his nose as though he'd tasted a spoiled fish. "They don't sell one-way tickets, so we had to buy round-trip ones and let them think we would be back in time for the ship leave. They'll figure it out soon. We aren't going back," he said with a chuckle. No matter how long he'd been away, he was true to form, playing by his own rules.

"You should have let me know you were coming. I could have picked you up at the ship."

"It was not necessary." He shifted his weight from one foot to the other, impatiently, wanting to move on.

"Excuse me, please, Julie. I'm supposed to meet someone at my office."

"Of course. Is Molly home?"

"She's unpacking."

I could only imagine how happy she must be; home with Lulu and her cats and parrot and geese. I was hurt that she hadn't called or come by to let me know she was there. She'd seemed so different from the friend I used to feel I knew.

I was too insecure to go to her house uninvited. The next day, I caught a glimpse of Molly leaving the kitchen of the restaurant. She was wearing a pair of black shorts, a blouse, and sandals. Her fine hair was pulled into a loose bun. She looked as natural in her surroundings as ever, as though she'd never been away.

"Hi Julie," she said as soon as she saw me. "I'm sorry I haven't had a chance to talk with you," she said, giving me what felt like an obligatory hug. "The masons started work on a new outdoor living room, and the house is a mess, and I'm trying to unpack in the middle of it."

"I know you're busy, but it's so good that you're here in time for the wedding. Rick will be so pleased. Oh, and I ran into Luis Felipe a couple of days ago. He looks really good."

She nodded. "He's glad to be home. Me, too. I was worried that Lulu wouldn't remember us, we've been gone so long."

"She must have been excited to see you."

"I think so."

"I see you're coming from the restaurant. Have you had a chance to talk with Eric?"

"Yes, and with Amador."

"Eric's been really unreliable."

"Why?"

"Too much partying in Playa. Maybe you can do something to motivate him."

"I hope so. The wedding this weekend is very important to us."

By Friday, October 8th, everything was in place. We only needed the guests to get there. Rick had chartered a bus to bring his family and son's friends from the airport to the hotel, including his eighty-five-year-old parents, his ex-wife, his Argentinian girlfriend, the bridal party, six musicians (some of whom had been part of the original Spiro Gyro band), plus several other friends and relatives. I'd hired extra waiters for every meal from Friday dinner through to Sunday breakfast and rented professional sound equipment for the New York musicians for the wedding.

Alex said to expect them before five-thirty on Friday, but it was already six and no one had even called to say the flight from New York had landed yet. I hoped the bus hadn't gotten stuck trying to navigate our narrow, winding road. Concerned, I tried to call, but neither Rick nor Alex answered his cell phone. I imagined they were running so late that everyone on the bus would be in a shitty mood by the time they finally got to Torbellino.

The patio had been transformed from its usual rustic elegance into a youthful party atmosphere, with Tiki lamps and colored lights strung around the perimeter. The formal china had been replaced with pottery plates set on runners of blue and red serapes, just as Alex wanted. Steam trays lined the buffet table, and mariachi musicians waited to burst into a rendition of Lindo y Querido as soon as the guests arrived.

Six thirty-came, then seven, with no word from the Israels. I paced from patio to restaurant, checking unnecessarily on last minute details. By this time, the waiters had loosened their starched white collars and untied their black bow ties in the relentless heat. Eventually, the wait staff disappeared into the kitchen and the Mariachi musicians sat down at the tables, taking surreptitious swigs from flasks they tucked inside their jacket pockets.

At seven-thirty, finally, Rick called. Their plane had been on the runway in Cancun since six, and he was pissed. The charter company in New York had promised they could by-pass customs when they arrived, which had not happened, and they were only just leaving the airport.

At eight-thirty, the bus finally pulled up to the front steps of the hotel. With a groan, its doors heaved open and spat out its disheveled passengers. Surprisingly, no one complained about the delay. The adventure of driving two miles through the dense jungle from the highway had disarmed them. They oohed and aahed at the sight of the peacocks and the geese in the reflecting pond when they stepped off the bus.

Welcome home, the anfitriona and I said as we greeted each guest. A waiter handed out special Torbellino cocktails, which guests sipped as they wandered dazed around the small lobby as though the gates of heaven had opened for them. Attendants dressed in fresh white uniforms with colorful cummerbunds took the suitcases and showed the guests to their assigned rooms.

Rick was at the back of the group.

"Julie!" He called as he walked over and folded me in his arms in a tight bear hug. "Alex, Mom and Dad, Cindy, this is Julie."

"Oh hi," Alex said. "I've been looking forward to meeting you."

"I know. We've been working on this for months now and finally it's here!" I said.

"Honestly, this place is way more beautiful than even Alex said it would be." Cindy, the future-bride, said in awe. "I can't wait to see the rest of the hotel."

"Don't I get an introduction?" an elderly man standing next to Rick teased. "I'm Alex's grandfather. My wife and I are eighty-four years old and we're so glad we could be here to see our grandson married. What a place this is!"

"Well, I'm so glad you're here," I smiled.

"She helped us plan everything, Grandpa," Alex said.

"It was a pleasure getting to know him," I assured his grandfather.

"Isn't he a sweetheart?" his grandmother cooed.

I felt proud and excited now that the weekend was underway. The dinner went off without a hitch and the young people stayed drinking and talking long after I left, but Luis Felipe and Molly didn't show up at all that night.

Early the next morning, Rick and Alex went fishing with the captain in his boat, promising to be back by noon. Cindy and her friends got up late and lounged at the beach and by the pool while the groomsmen played golf at a course not far away. It looked as though it was going to be a perfect day for an outdoor wedding, but by eleven o'clock the clouds rolled in and the skies turned a bilious gray.

"It really feels like it's going to rain," Cindy said, frowning up at the sky.

"Don't worry. If it ends up raining you can get married on the balcony of the dining room and your guests can watch from below the staircase. It would be very romantic, very Romeo and Juliet," I said.

She nodded, but she wasn't buying it. She had counted on having an outdoor ceremony overlooking the ocean and she sounded like she would be really upset if it didn't turn out the way she had planned.

Alex and his father were back at the hotel around noon as promised.

"I think it's going to rain," Cindy said to Alex.

"I'm sure it'll be fine by the time of the ceremony," he said reassuringly. I hoped he was right. The plantings on the patio looked especially vibrant and voluptuous that day, the hibiscus and shaving bush trees burst with new blossoms, as though they'd been told it would be a special night and they'd better make a good show of it.

By four, as if on cue, the breeze cleared away the clouds and the sky turned silky blue. I breathed a sigh of relief and double-checked my list to make sure I'd forgotten nothing before going home to rest for a bit, although I was too nervous to sleep. I showered and changed into a navy blue cocktail dress, with showy pink and yellow flowers cascading from the bodice to the floor-length hem. Even though I wasn't going to be a guest, I was dressed like one.

At five-thirty, I went back to the hotel. The bridal party was already gathered in the entryway to the dining room, getting ready for the processional at six. The bridesmaids looked magnificent in their coral dresses, transformed into goddesses from the lotion-lathered, bikini-clad sun-worshippers I'd seen at noon. There seemed to be some confusion as they huddled together trying to figure out the order for the processional since they'd skipped the rehearsal the night before. Finally, the maid of honor took over and organized everyone.

"Where's the officiant?" one of the bridesmaids asked me quietly.

"Isn't he here?" It was five forty-five. I panicked for a minute, thinking I'd forgotten to call him, until I remembered that Alex said he'd spoken to him earlier that afternoon. He had said he didn't need directions to get to the hotel since he'd performed other weddings at Torbellino. He promised to be at the hotel at least half-an hour before the ceremony, but it was past that already.

"What are we going to do?" the bridesmaid asked me nervously.

"Let's give him a few more minutes to get here. It's only five forty-five." The guests were already gathered, standing around the patio waiting. Alex's grandparents and only a handful of others had chairs, but the ceremony would be brief and the others would stand to watch. I didn't want them to have to wait too long. By now, the whole wedding party, except for the bride herself, who hadn't come down from her room where she was waiting with her father, had realized the officiant hadn't shown up, and they were getting more nervous by the minute.

By ten minutes after six, I had decided what to do. A wedding performed in a civil ceremony in Mexico is considered legal no matter who officiates. Alex and Cindy were going to a Justice of the Peace when they got back to New York anyway to make their marriage legal in the US.

I went out to the patio and grabbed one of the anfitrionas who was busy greeting the guests and pulled her aside.

"You and I are going to have to do the service ourselves. The official who was supposed to marry them hasn't shown up," I explained quickly.

"I can't. I've never..."

"You will," I said. I'd brought a copy of the legal version of the vows in my purse, just in case the officiant forgot his. "You'll be fine. Here, you read this part in Spanish. When you finish, you can go sit down. I'll read the English translation."

I took her hand and moved us to the head of the line of attendants and told Alex and his father to go stand at the altar before the procession started. I was thinking about what personal words to say to Alex and Cindy at the altar, when Cindy floated down the stairs in her wedding dress looking as radiant and as magnificent as any bride could hope to look, clueless that anything was wrong.

"Everybody ready?" I asked from the front of the line. "There's been a bit of a change in how this is going to go. Erika, who works for us in guest services, is going to read the vows in Spanish and I'm going to read them in English. Cindy and Alex, this is your moment. Enjoy the heck out of it."

The guitarist was playing the prelude, Julia Florida, the cue for the procession to begin.

"OK, here we go." I walked slowly out onto the patio toward the arch of white blossoms that formed the wedding chupah. Luis Felipe stood off to the side of the crowd scowling. He turned his head away when I looked in his direction. Molly must have been next to him but I couldn't see her.

We all took our places on the patio at the chupah in front of the ocean. When Cindy's father kissed her and moved aside for Alex to take his place next to his bride, I stepped closer to the microphone. Trying to keep my voice steady, I welcomed everyone and explained the two- part reading of the vows.

After saying "I do," Alex and Cindy exchanged rings and the best man placed a glass wrapped in a white napkin under Alex's foot. With one enthusiastic stomp, the glass shattered and the crowd burst into shouts of "Mazel Tov!" Alex swooped Cindy into a passionate, dramatic kiss that lasted so long everyone laughed, and I breathed a sigh of relief that the ceremony was over and we'd averted a disaster.

The sun had set by this time, and the patio glowed with little lights. A man in a loin cloth stood poised on a boat stationed on the water in front of the patio and after the kiss fired a series of lit torches into the air in dramatic celebration of the occasion. After the flames fell into the water and fizzled out, the crowd began to break up and the musicians took over with trumpet, bass, guitar, and drummer sending up their hot jazz fusion. The patio came alive as people started dancing.

In the middle of the party, a short, stocky man hurried out from the restaurant onto the patio walking unsteadily, his face dripping with sweat. He stood for a minute looking around, and when he realized that the wedding ceremony was over, he turned and helped himself to a glass of champagne from the tray of a waiter passing by, disappearing back inside the restaurant. The officiant had finally arrived.

A few minutes later, one of the musicians interrupted the music to announce, "Ladies and Gentlemen, please welcome the new Mr. and Mrs. Israel."

The newlyweds moved to the center of the patio for their first dance. Rick Israel looked over to catch my eye, smiled, and gave me a thumbs up.

When the party moved inside for dinner, my responsibilities were over, but I decided to hang around and see how dinner went.

The first course took forever to come out of the kitchen; the next course, even longer. So long, in fact, that guests started looking around for their waiters, frowning, and whispering to each other, wondering what was wrong. The soup course was only just being served to some when others were finishing their entrees and the rest were just getting their salads. The problem wasn't with the waiters, it was the kitchen that was holding things up. It would do no good to stand over Eric trying to prod things along, but I felt as nervous as if it had been my job to get the food on the table. I wondered if this was the first large formal dinner party he'd ever managed. Whatever the problem was in the kitchen, Luis Felipe was going to be furious.

When all of the guests had finally been served and finished eating, Alex signaled to Amador that they were ready for dessert to be served. A red-faced Eric emerged from the kitchen with Amador, the two of them carrying a magnificent many-tiered tropical rum cake, layered with roasted-coconut, slathered with jam between the layers, frosted with vanilla bean and passion-fruit buttercream, with mango slices on top. The room burst into applause for Eric when they saw the cake, unaware that our pastry chef, not Eric, had been the one to create the masterpiece. The dinner ended on a high note, but it had been a disaster until then.

When the guests had lingered long enough over dessert and went back out to the patio to dance and drink some more, I went home and fell into bed. The tension had been exhausting and I had a headache. I was glad my part had gone well, although, I'd gotten a funny vibe from Luis Felipe during the service. In the morning, after everyone had had breakfast, I went to the lobby to see everyone off.

"You did a wonderful job, Julie," Rick Israel said. "I was going to give you a nice tip, but Luis Felipe didn't want me to do that. So I'll just say thank you so much for everything. The weekend couldn't have been better." He leaned down, took me in his ample arms, and kissed me on my cheek. His pleasure washed over me. I was hungry for praise, for kindness. I hadn't seen Luis Felipe and Molly all weekend, except to catch a glimpse of them in the audience at the wedding service and at the head table at the wedding banquet.

I was just saying goodbye to Rick and the newlyweds when Luis Felipe saw me. Quickly, he turned away and left, without a word to me. I hadn't imagined it the night before, he was angry. But why? What had I done that displeased him? Was it because I'd stepped up to officiate at the ceremony? Did he blame me for the delays at the wedding dinner? Bastard. I didn't deserve that.

Molly was still in the lobby after everyone had left. She was not smiling.

"I'm glad this weekend's over," I said. "Alex and Cindy

and Rick seemed really happy with everything. But what about Luis Felipe? I get the feeling that he wasn't pleased."

"Actually, he's very upset. He thought the patio looked awful Friday night when everyone came. It was not the Torbellino style, using serapes for tablecloths. And he was so disappointed with the way the patio looked for the wedding. There should have been more flowers, more elaborate decorations. It looked so ordinary."

I was shocked. The decorations were what Alex and Cindy wanted. Friday night, they said, should be a Mexican fiesta: informal and fun. The patio for the wedding should look simple, but elegant. More flowers would have given less room for people to dance, especially with the band and all the equipment. I felt defensive about the plans I'd made.

"Alex wanted to keep it simple, and they wanted Friday night to be casual. They're young. The weekend was all about honoring their choices."

She shrugged. "Luis Felipe says it could have been much better."

"I'm sorry he's unhappy." I was crushed that she seemed to agree with him and to be disappointed in the job I'd done.

"He's not only mad at you. I don't know what's with Eric. I tried to work with him, but it obviously didn't do any good. The whole dinner was terrible, not just the service. Jose Luis is going to talk with him later, but we're both tired. I'm going home now to make sure he's OK. It's not good for him to be so upset."

I stood in the empty lobby and watched her walk away, feeling hollow. Had I really failed them? I had stayed at Torbellino in spite of all the difficulties and the unpleasantness I'd experienced for the eight months they were away. I had been a fool to care.

A taxi cab pulled up to the front steps of the hotel and a

tall man in a muscle shirt, with a ponytail and a sleeve of tattoos on his arms, jumped out of the cab, looking as distraught as I felt. He was one of the musicians from the band who played at the wedding.

He hurried up the steps to where I stood. At six-foot-three, he towered over me.

"Say, could you help me? I'm Don Harris, the horn player with the band last night, and I've got a big problem."

"I recognize you. You guys were great. You're the trumpet player, right? What can I do for you?"

"I guess we were all blitzed last night. Luis Felipe kept pouring us more shots of tequila out on the patio. We left, and once we got back to our hotel, which was about forty minutes away, I looked around in the cab for my horn and realized, shit, I must have left it on the patio. I made the cab driver bring me all the way back to look for it, but I couldn't find it, so I left. I'd like to look for it one more time. Maybe somebody found it this morning."

I was happy to focus on someone else's problem rather than my own. "Let's check with the waiters and the maintenance men who cleaned up last night."

"Please. I've had that horn for years. It was made special for me. And it's real gold." He bit his lip to keep it from quivering. "The maintenance guys looked for me last night when I came back but we didn't find anything then. Christ, I never leave my horn lying around when I finish playing...I always keep it right with me."

A solid gold horn? God. What are the chances of getting something like that back if somebody did find it? We asked the maintenance guys and the waiters and cooks but nobody had seen it.

"Guess I'm out of luck."

"If we find it after you've gone, how do I reach you?"

"I'll give you my address. The horn's in an instrument case that looks like this." He took an old receipt and a pen out of his pocket, made a quick sketch of the case, scribbled his name and address on the paper, and handed it to me. "Thanks for trying, but I gotta go now. Everybody else already left for the airport. I can't afford to buy another ticket home if I miss our flight."

"We'll keep looking."

"Yeah, please. This has been a shitty few months," he muttered, pulling a rubber band off his pony-tail, rubbing his hand across his hair to smooth it before tying it up again. "First I lost my girl, and now my horn." He hurried out of the lobby, down the steps, and into the idling cab.

I didn't have the energy to walk home. I sat down on the front steps, when a car pulled up to the entrance. The driver got out and walked around to his trunk, opened it, and lifted out an instrument case exactly like the one in the drawing in my hand. It was like seeing a burning bush in the middle of the desert.

"Who are you?" I demanded, standing up as the man walked over to me. "And where did you get that case? I was afraid we'd never see this again!"

"I'm the owner of the sound company you used last night," the man holding the horn said.

"When the guys were packing up, I saw this horn and case lying on the patio with the rest of our stuff. I knew it wasn't ours, but it was late and nobody was around, so I thought I'd better keep it overnight and bring it back today. Somebody's really going to be missing this. It's a special horn."

"Bless you," I said, taking the case from the driver, cradling it like a baby who'd been kidnapped and recovered unharmed. "Thank you so much for bringing it back. The trumpet player was just here looking for it and I've gotta get it back to him before he leaves for New York."

One of the hotel vans was parked by the side of the driveway; the driver was behind the wheel, napping. I ran to the passenger's side, threw the door open, and climbed into the front seat.

"Al aeropuerto." I ordered, clutching the horn case as though it were an archeological find. It took forever to get to the airport parking lot. The van barely stopped before I jumped out and ran inside. In front of me, an escalator ascended, crowded with people. I could see Don Harris's pony tail, but before I could call out his name, he turned around to talk to someone on the step below and spotted me holding the horn case over my head.

He blinked like he'd been blinded by a meteor.

"I can't believe it! Sweet Jesus, you found it!" he yelled. Seconds later, he was standing next to me lifting me and the horn so tightly his grip nearly took the wind out of me. "Thank you, thank you, thank you," he sang. To him, I was the hero I'd hoped to be in Luis Felipe's and Molly's eyes.

CHAPTER TWENTY-FIVE

*O*nce the wedding weekend was over, Molly and Luis Felipe disappeared as mysteriously as they'd come. I was glad they were gone. I needed time to recover before diving into plans for Christmas week, which was the most important time of year for the hotel. Guests who wanted to be there over the holidays were required to stay from Christmas through New Year's, and I was responsible for scheduling special events each day.

I had a tentative list of programs in mind, but wanted to check them out in person, which gave me a perfect excuse for spending time away from the hotel. I spent afternoons in town, talking to visual artists and fine jewelry makers and evenings attending concerts and performances as a way of holding auditions. The time away and the performances themselves were like breathing life into a hot house plant. I began to have enough energy to give serious thought to where I would go when I left Mexico.

A tall, immaculately dressed stranger in a grey suit and starched, white shirt stood outside my office, waiting for me one afternoon when I got back from Cancun. He looked to be in his forties, with a buzz haircut, a narrow, pale face, and chiseled features. Even before he spoke, I had the sense that he might have been Russian.

"How do you do, Madame?" he said, in a Russian accent, bowing his head slightly. "I am Sergei Popov."

"It's nice to meet you, Sergei. I'm Julie Heifetz," I said, extending my hand. He held the tips of my fingers in a courtly gesture and bowed from the neck again.

"You are Director of Torbellino," he said.

"Some call me Director. Some say Manager. But I prefer to be called Julie. What can I do for you?"

"Maria Elena, the secretary of the owner, told me to introduce myself to you. I was just in her office."

If Maria Elena told him to come see me, that meant Luis Felipe was sending him.

"And why is that?"

"I came to help you, if you would like," he said crisply. "I have been a hotel manager many years for big, international hotels in Russia and then in Europe."

My heart froze. It wasn't a coincidence that this man showed up. Someone had gone looking for someone with his qualifications. Luis Felipe wanted to get rid of me.

"Oh?" I hoped he couldn't tell how threatened I felt. "What is it you would like to do for me?"

"I would be your assistant," he proclaimed imperially. It sounded like a command, not a request for a job.

"Thank you," I said, "but there isn't any job right now available for an assistant manager."

His thin lips pursed into what he intended as a smile. "I see," he said. "My wife and I are staying in a hotel in Playa now. If you change your mind, Maria Elena knows how to get in touch with me."

I should have felt relieved knowing there was someone

waiting in the wings for my job since I was planning on leaving anyway, but I felt too criticized and resentful of the sneaky way Luis Felipe was treating me. He should have had the decency to talk to me himself. And I wanted to leave when I was ready, not when I was being forced out.

"Thank you," I said. "It's good to know she can find you. If you'll excuse me now, I have a lot to do today."

He didn't click his heels or salute, but he might as well have. When he left, I knew I was only delaying the inevitable and hadn't heard the last of him.

Luis Felipe and Molly came home again for Thanksgiving, as they had said they would. I knew Molly would be looking forward to having a traditional meal at the restaurant, turkey with all the trimmings. I was looking forward to it more than usual; a taste of America, a taste of home.

The day before Thanksgiving, I ran into Eric. He was walking with someone who looked like an older version of himself, with the same blonde hair and fair complexion, but a few years older. I hadn't seen Eric since the wedding dinner. Any comments to him about it would come from Molly and Luis Felipe, not from me. I'd given up on him long ago, but I figured I would be pleasant, particularly since he had company, so I stopped to stay hello.

"Hey, Eric, good morning. You have someone with you who must be a relative, you two look so much alike."

Eric nodded woodenly. "This is my brother." He didn't tell me his name.

"I'm Julie. Welcome to Torbellino. It's nice that you came to visit. You'll be here for Thanksgiving dinner tomorrow?"

He nodded.

"I'm sure your brother's glad to have you here for the holiday," I smiled.

Eric shifted his feet and looked toward the hotel, eager to get going. I figured he still thought of me as the heavy in the story about his arrest, and he wasn't about to forgive me for that. So be it. He's young. Maybe one day he'll learn to take responsibility for his behavior.

"Well, enjoy your visit."

They scurried down the path away from me.

When I got back to my office, a message from Maria Elena was waiting. Luis Felipe wanted me to meet him out on the patio of the restaurant. It's about time, I thought, but I was nervous about what he was going to say to me. I wasn't ready to tell him I was leaving until I knew I had a job lined up in the States. I had just sent off an email to the vice-president of Einstein Healthcare Network in Philadelphia, a woman who had hired me to give a workshop for her staff. I told her I was thinking of relocating to Philadelphia and was looking for work, but I hadn't heard from her yet.

Paulo showed me to the table where Luis Felipe was waiting. The waiters were on the patio setting up for lunch, and I knew they were watching. Luis Felipe didn't stand to greet me, or give me a perfunctory kiss. This was not about friendship.

"Good morning, Julie," he mumbled. "Would you like something, some coffee or juice?"

"Just a glass of water." I sat in the chair across the table from him.

"Paulo, some water please, for Señora Julie," he said, putting down his coffee cup. "So...now we are home for Thanksgiving."

"I'm glad you're well enough to be here."

"We're here for a few days, and then we'll be back for Christmas week. We have some...business to do in Miami."

"There are so many things I need to talk about with you, Luis Felipe...problems with the staff, and I need your help."

"I will. But today, I want to talk with you about what I see when I come back to Torbellino. Things look very bad here. The beach chairs, the umbrellas, the employees, they have never looked so sloppy. It is very important that everyone looks good and smells fresh and clean." He was not mentioning me by name, but I felt his criticism was aimed at me.

I had gained weight and hadn't bought new clothes to make up for the extra pounds. I'd stopped wearing perfume, and my hair was wild from the wind whatever I tried to do with it. I had no idea, though, what he was talking about when he said Torbellino had never looked so bad. He was looking for things to blame me for, the way he had been critical of the wedding weekend.

The hotel was doing well: sales were better than in the past, new employees were efficient and responsible, the feedback from the guests was outstanding as always (except for the one bogus entry in the guest book aimed at me). I had initiated a hygiene training program for the kitchen help, started English classes for any of the staff who might be interested, and had averted a crisis with the workers in the maintenance department. I worked endless hours with no training, no one to direct me. None of that mattered to Luis Felipe now that he was home. I felt like disappearing under the table.

"Maria Elena tells me someone came to see you looking for a job, a Russian. You talked with him?"

"Yes. We talked for a minute." My back stiffened. I knew what was coming next.

"He worked for many big hotels in Europe. He wants to help us. You said no, you didn't want help."

"You hadn't mentioned him to me before he showed up, and I didn't get a good vibe from him anyway."

"No?" he sneered.

"No, I can't tell you why, it was just a feeling."

"But you can work with him anyway, can't you, even if you have this feeling?"

He wasn't asking, he was giving me an order. He sat back in his chair, one hand on his thigh, the fingers of the other hand playing with the new necklace he was wearing, a wooden pendant that hung from a leather lace around his neck. It must have been a good luck charm, a talisman that someone had given to him recently to ward off evil spirits.

"I think it is maybe a good idea," he pronounced. "Make Sergei your assistant. This is good for the hotel."

"If that's what you want," I said, reluctantly.

He pushed his chair back and reached under the table for his walking stick, then stood, ending the conversation. "I have to go see the masons now. They are waiting for me to talk with them about the new restaurant."

I couldn't bear to walk past the waiters. They would have seen that I wasn't happy and would know the meeting had been too brief to have gone well. I stepped over the low wall of the patio to avoid walking past them and took the path down to the beach. I was oblivious of the sound or smell of the sea or swelling of the waves. Molly was outside when I passed her house but she didn't see me and I didn't go over to say hello.

When I went into the front room of my office, I was relieved to see Abril, the young woman I had hired to work the late shift, sitting behind the desk. She was a good addition for me: sweet, friendly, bright, efficient, and not attractive enough to be a threat to Carla, who had left Abril alone and hadn't tried to make her life miserable yet. Abril's parents were internationally renowned painters, and their daughter hung around with local artists, writers, and musicians. I liked talking with her when we had time.

She looked up from the book she'd been reading and put a ticket stub between the pages to mark her place.

"Have the guests in the one-bedroom suite checked out already?" I asked, remembering that I'd intended to tell them goodbye before they left.

"About an hour ago."

"Did you get a chance to meet them? They're really interesting people."

"No, they just paid their bill and said to tell you good-bye. But I did meet Señor Luis Felipe."

"Really? Was he here?" My guard was up. What did he want?

"He came to the office about eleven o'clock last night to introduce himself. He stayed and we talked for a long time."

Luis Felipe didn't make it a habit of dropping by to meet new employees. He was checking up on me.

"How long did he stay?" I asked, trying to sound casual.

"Maybe an hour. He was very nice. He asked how I like Torbellino, and how I like working for you."

"Oh? And what did you tell him?"

"I said I like you very much. You're a good person, and you care about the guests and the workers too. And then he told me he's an artist or he was when he had more time before they built the hotel. Did you know that?"

"I did. You must have enjoyed talking with him."

"Yes, until Carla got to her office. Then he went to talk with her."

"Were they alone?"

"Yes. I could see them huddled together on the couch.

By then, the transport had come to pick me up and I left and went home."

I stewed all afternoon about Luis Felipe, wondering why he'd been asking Abril about me, why he'd been so critical of me ever since he'd been home. Maybe I wasn't doing a good enough job or maybe he didn't want me to be too successful and uncover the truth about him and the hotel.

"Madame," Sergei said, when I looked up to find him standing in front of me.

"Sergei, I didn't know you were here."

"Luis Felipe said I should start work today and you would show me around."

"Of course."

We walked the grounds of the property as I pointed out the lounge area for the guests, the suites and private rooms, the spa and waterfront hut, the kitchen and restaurant, and the guest services' office. I introduced him to Eric and the waiters and anfitrionas.

"Luis Felipe says my wife and I will live in the new casita and I am to share the van with you."

"Oh, did he?" My eyes narrowed. He was taking over already.

"If you will be so kind as to give me the keys I can go pick up our things from our hotel in Cancun. I took a cab to get here."

"Of course, but I don't have them with me, they're at my house. I can meet you there after I finish taking care of a few things."

"Seven-thirty this evening?"

"That's fine, I should be home then. My house is the one..."

"Yes, I know where you live."

"You do?"

"I'll be glad to have our own casita on the property. Before we move in, my wife and I will perform some black magic to get rid of any evil spirits that may still be there."

Black magic. The feel of the beak of the dead bird and its bony skull on my doorknob came back to me. I shuddered, remembering the dried blood, the glassy eyes that still seemed to see, even though I didn't rationally believe in any of that crap. A lot of the workers did, though. Black magic. Voodoo. My skin prickled like something was crawling on me, but I showed nothing of my fear.

"I'll meet you at seven-thirty at my house."

It was already dark as I walked home and passed the chef's casita. A car's engine idled with its headlights turned low. It was parked on the footpath next to the casita with the passenger side back door open, but no one was in the car.

It was so strange to find it there on a path too narrow for cars. A shadowy form came out of the casita carrying something heavy, leaned inside the open rear door, turned, and disappeared back inside the house. Whoever it was didn't want to be seen, and I felt uncomfortable watching, unsuspected. It was well past seven-thirty, and I didn't have time to figure out what was going on. Sergei was coming to meet me any minute, so I walked on to my house, gave Sergei the keys, and forgot about the car idling on the path next to Eric's house.

The next morning was Thanksgiving Day. I was already imagining the smell of turkey and pumpkin, seeing the kitchen of the restaurant humming with preparations. But when I got to the hotel, Gerardo was waiting for me. "Have you seen this yet?" He thrust a piece of paper into my hand with a note written on it in pencil.

To Carla, Gerardo, Julie, Alejandro, and all the other so-called executives.

You think you're in charge? Hah! You don't know what the hell you're doing. Luis Felipe is an ass, and Torbellino is a joke.

I quit. Fuck you all.
Happy Thanksgiving!
Eric

CHAPTER TWENTY-SIX

I felt like a bomb had exploded inside my head. It was cruel what Eric had done, walking out the day of an important holiday. I had seen him and his brother the night before without understanding what was happening; the two brothers loading the car so they could sneak off in the dark. I shoved the paper inside my pocket, ran into the kitchen, and opened the refrigerator to see how much he'd done before he left. There was nothing in the fridge or the freezer or cabinets. He'd bought no turkeys, cranberries, pumpkin, or stuffing for the Thanksgiving feast for the hotel. I didn't gave a damn what Eric thought about any of us, but now what were we going to do?

"No hay nada, Señora. No Señor Eric," Jorge, the Mexican cook said apologetically when he saw me frantically looking for ingredients for the meal.

When I went outside again, Luis Felipe happened to be walking by. I stopped him and showed him the note. A look flashed over his face as though he'd been stabbed, but when he spoke, his voice was too calm, like the quiet before a tornado.

"So..." he said, handing the note back to me.

"So, Jorge can cook tonight," I filled in quickly. "He's very good. He's worked in the kitchen for years and I'm sure he knows how to cook a turkey. He can go to Cancun and buy whatever he needs."

"Tell him not to forget the pumpkin pies with whipped cream. Those are Molly's favorites."

Jorge assured me he knew what to do, but he called later to say he had bought everything but the pumpkin. He'd tried every grocery store in Cancun and there wasn't any, so he was going to make chocolate pies instead. I knew Molly would be crushed not to have her traditional dessert, but in the middle of the afternoon, Maria Elena pulled up to the front entrance of the hotel in her VW Beetle and unloaded a carload of ready-made pumpkin pies from Walmart. No wonder everyone had been so excited when the new Walmart in Cancun opened. They sold everything.

I felt confident with Jorge in charge of the kitchen. Later, Molly sent a messenger to deliver a note asking me to join her and Luis Felipe for dinner at the restaurant, which surprised me. Maybe they weren't so mad at me after all. I was looking forward to sitting down to a meal with them, just the three of us, but when I got to the dining room, they were standing outside with a woman I'd never seen before. They introduced her as Henrietta, and she would be joining us. She was British and owned a travel agency in London. Apparently, she'd been a friend and supporter of Torbellino's since its inception.

Amador took us to our table. None of the guests in the dining room were aware of the near disaster that Eric had caused and were enjoying their Thanksgiving dinner with turkey and all the trimmings. As soon as we were seated, Luis Felipe turned to Henrietta and began asking her about past clients she had sent to the hotel. He wanted to know how her travel agency was doing. She sounded stuffy and pretentious, partly due to her crisp British accent and partly because she seemed in awe of her clients who had royal titles. I listened for a bit, but after a while my mind began to wander. The name-dropping of Lord or Lady so and so didn't impress me. No one noticed that I'd stopped paying attention. I may as well not have been at the table. I felt like a place holder, someone's relative who had been invited to join the party but who was too old to contribute to the conversation. I didn't have the energy to try to insert myself into the chatter.

I ate my meal without tasting the dishes that Jorge had prepared that rescued us from humiliation. All I could taste was loneliness; it was like a bone that had stuck in my throat and wouldn't dislodge.

I was relieved when Luis Felipe stood up, indicating our dinner had ended and that I could go home to bed early. Starting in the morning, I needed to finish getting ready for Christmas and New Year's, my last big responsibility at the hotel. I would email other contacts in the States if I didn't hear soon from Einstein Hospital.

The next morning, Henrietta, Luis Felipe and Molly's British dinner guest from the night before, swept through the door of my office in a get-up that made me smile: a striped caftan, flip-flops, a straw sun hat with pink and purple flowers on the front brim, and a pair of cat-eyed sunglasses.

"May we speak privately?" she asked in her upper-middle-class British accent.

"Of course." She was there early, before anyone else was in the office.

"Last night was not the time to talk about this." She took

off her hat and sun glasses, sat on the couch, folded her glasses carefully, and set them on her lap. Her eyes were bright blue, accentuated by dark, curled lashes.

"You are new here, Julie. I don't know you, but I would like to talk to you about my account because you are the manager now, I understand."

"Yes, but you should speak with our accountant about that. Alejandro handles the accounts, and his office is just across the way." I couldn't tell her anything about her account. I should have been more aware of the finances of the day-to-day operations, but I never looked at the books. Alejandro gave reports about how the hotel was doing, but I didn't trust them. And the truth was that numbers and I had never been on very good terms anyway. I could not have understood enough to analyze whether or not the figures were accurate. I had no background or talent in accounting.

"Yes, I know about Alejandro," Henrietta said with a tone of contempt. "I've tried speaking with him many times, both in person and by mail. Yesterday, when I arrived, I called his office to speak with him, but he never got back to me."

"Can you explain to me the problem you're having with your account?"

"Over the years, my agency has sent many prestigious clients to Torbellino. In fact, Baroness Cumberledge of Newick is planning a trip here in February."

"I'm sure Luis Felipe appreciates the business you've sent us."

"I had a very good relationship with Luis Felipe from the beginning. I believed in his vision for the hotel: a low density, intimate, casually elegant inn that would protect the jungle habitat. I wanted to support him in this. But in the last year, I have not received much of the money I am owed for commissions. When I have been paid, the amount is incorrect. I have an exact statement, pointing out the errors, which I have sent to Alejandro many times. When he didn't respond, I sent the letter by certified mail. He answered, but not to my satisfaction."

Why was I not surprised? The only surprise was that I was hearing the facts from a client rather than guessing about Alejandro and the accounting department. I leaned forward, eager to hear more.

"I apologize for any mistakes we've made in the past. We certainly need to straighten those out."

"No, it's more than mistakes," she shook her head emphatically. "In the beginning that's what I thought, a mistake, but now I think there's something more going on than that."

"Oh?"

"I don't trust Alejandro or his sister."

This was music to my ears. "And why is that?"

"Two years ago when I visited El Torbellino, Carla came to talk with me. She said she wanted to learn the travel business and asked if she could do an internship in my agency. She's a very, shall we say, aggressive young woman."

"I knew she took a year away from the hotel, but I didn't know she worked for you."

"Luis Felipe suggested it. He said she's very smart and capable and that she'd learn quickly. And she is smart, I will give her that. But after a few months, she started telling people she was an agent, my assistant. No one in my office liked her. They felt she was trying to take over."

"That must have been difficult."

"After she'd been there six months, she said she wanted to take a week's holiday. Her brother was coming to visit on his way to Europe for a week. That was fine with me. I was ready not to have her around for a while. But the day Alejandro was supposed to arrive, I got a call from the customs office saying that he'd been detained at the airport. They found fifty-thousand American dollars on him that he hadn't declared when he came into the country."

"Fifty-thousand dollars in cash? How bizarre!"

"Yes, fifty-thousand. Now you tell me, what was he doing with all that money when he was only planning on spending a week in Europe?"

Hallelujah. She was giving me more evidence of some-thing shady going on. Alejandro must have been involved in off-shore banking or money laundering or drug dealing. The cash must have come from the hotel with Luis Felipe's instructions as to what to do with it once he got to England or Europe. Now I was sure of it. I hadn't been paranoid to be so suspicious.

"That's certainly bizarre for him to travel with so much cash. What happened after they stopped him?"

"Alejandro told them he was visiting his sister and that she worked for me. They called to verify, and I said yes, she was an intern in my office, and she was expecting her brother to come for a visit. Then Carla called Luis Felipe from our office, and I don't know what happened after that, because I really didn't want to get involved. Carla left on holiday, and when she came back, we agreed it was time for her to go."

"That's really weird about Alejandro."

"Frankly, I was surprised when I arrived yesterday to see Carla still works here. And I'm surprised Luis Felipe hasn't fired Alejandro. But if I don't get things worked out with my accounting when I am here, I will have to stop sending clients to Torbellino. I do this for a living, you know."

"Of course you do."

"I've told Luis Felipe about this, but he said he's been away and I should talk with Alejandro."

"I will speak with Alejandro about your account. Please let me know if he takes care of it to your satisfaction." I knew speaking with Alejandro would be useless, but I would start with him, and then go to Luis Felipe.

"Thank you for that." She looked me over and nodded approvingly. "It's good that you are Director here now, " she said putting on her sunglasses and hat as she stood. "Now, I think I will go to the beach for a bit, before the sun gets too hot. My skin is very fair, and I don't want to go home looking like a radish." Brushing the bangs back from her high forehead, she strode out the door.

Bless Henrietta and her proper British heart. In the months since Luis Felipe had been away, and I'd been working at the hotel, there had been too many stories not to believe there was some truth to them: the report from Miguel about the accounting office keeping double books; the admission by Jimmy that all the construction projects proceeded without obtaining permits; and the rumor from Francois that Luis Felipe had sold the same piece of land to two separate buyers. Luis Felipe's nephew told me himself that he would handle the cash stolen from the hotel's delivery truck by lying to the insurance company about where the theft had happened. And now I'd heard Henrietta's story about the fifty-thousand dollars in cash that Alejandro took to England.

When Molly had called me in St. Louis from the hospital, she had told me she was worried because she didn't know anything about Luis Felipe's business and she wouldn't know what to do if he didn't recover. She didn't understand why so many lawyers worked for him. She was clueless about his business because Luis Felipe didn't want her to know. They had an unspoken agreement; whatever he said, she chose to believe. In exchange for her blind faith in him, she lived like royalty.

I had followed her to the jungle of the Yucatan just as she had followed Luis Felipe. I had admired her courage and her ability to reinvent herself in Mexico. I thought she was sophisticated and a gracious host. I had hoped, after living in the jungle long enough, I would be the same. I'd be like her, living in a dream house, content to work in the sunshine in one of the most beautiful, secluded places on the planet.

But I wasn't Molly, and I didn't want to become her. She had lived a sequestered life in the Yucatan for nearly a quarter of a century. Over that time, she had turned into a mafia wife. I was still a nice Jewish mid-westerner from the suburbs at heart. And there was no shame in that. I needed to love and be loved, to trust and be trusted. Everything else was wind pudding and air sauce.

I wouldn't stay a day longer than it would take to sell my house and find a job. I called my contact at Einstein Hospital from Cancun. We talked about creating a position as Writer-in-Residence at MossRehab, a rehabilitation in-patient facility that specialized in brain spinal cord injuries. I would work with patients, offering a therapeutic interven-tion. I would help them write about who they had been before their traumas, who they were at present, and who they hoped to be in the future. She said she would write a grant to cover my salary for the first year. We'd discuss the details once I got to Philadelphia. Knowing I had a job waiting for me was like a shot of adrenaline. I was sure it was all going to work out: the job and the sale of my house. I'd find someone to buy it somehow and tell Luis Felipe and Molly once I did. I had only to get through Christmas week.

The day before the employees' holiday party, Luis Felipe sent a message that I was to give the annual end-of-the-year speech. I worried for days about what to say that would be upbeat and yet honest. When I thought about the individuals I'd come to know, some of the waiters, cooks, housekeepers, and gardeners, I felt immensely grateful. My life here would have been so much worse without their friendliness. Seeing them around the hotel lifted my spirits. I would thank them and wish them a positive year ahead, although I had no intention of being around after the holidays myself.

My Spanish had improved too little over the months to write what I wanted to tell them in Spanish. I decided to write it in English and to ask Erica, the shy anfitriona, to translate for me. I gave her a copy of what I wanted to say. The morning of the speech, she turned over the translation to me. Confident that I now could give the speech, I waited a while to look at it, as I had other things to do. Later, I took the paper Erica had given me into my office to practice, but I stumbled clumsily over pronunciations of unfamiliar words, and I started to panic. There wasn't enough time to get it down, to deliver it smoothly. The party was going to begin soon.

It started at dusk. There was no music, no high mood of holiday excitement, although lots of traditional food was served. The anfitrionas had been too busy getting ready for Christmas week to pay attention to the employees' celebration. It was an obligatory gathering for everyone, and I felt no more comfortable that day at the party than I had on Valentine's Day ten months before, when I was introduced as a new member of the Torbellino Family. Molly and Luis Felipe watched from the side of the patio as people filled their plates and stood around talking. Because they avoided looking at me, I didn't have to pretend everything was all right between us.

I wandered through the crowd, greeting people I now knew by name. Before long, Luis Felipe walked to the microphone on the patio and welcomed everyone, but then called me to the mic to take over. My hand shook as I unfolded the piece of paper and looked out at the expectant faces. I could smell Luis Felipe's musky cologne as I took the microphone. The Spanish was too much for me. I looked desperately around for someone to deliver my message for me. Sergei was in the front row and sprang forward to stand next to me as I handed the mic to him. He spoke Spanish fluently.

"Feliz Navidad y prospero ano nuevo, todo el mundo!" His voice wafted over the crowd as he delivered my gratitude and love in slow, fluent Spanish. Luis Felipe smiled, and the crowd seemed to believe the words and sentiments were Sergei's own, the way an adoring public falls in love with an actor for the role he assumes in a film. I felt in that moment that Sergei was the new Director, and I was the one who had handed him the job.

CHAPTER TWENTY-SEVEN

$\mathcal{I}$ steeled myself for the ten day holiday celebration, the most expensive and elaborate time to be a guest at Torbellino and the most challenging for the staff. Everyone was on high alert, ready to cater to any guest's request, no matter how extravagant or demanding. Every room was filled, and many of the guests had celebrated Christmas week at the hotel over the holidays before.

Luis Felipe had silver medallions made for the guests as souvenirs, and Alexa had designed lovely caftans for every woman, hand-sewn by some of the local seamstresses. I had planned a variety of nightly entertainments. Carla and Luis Felipe had planned a surprise for New Year's Eve, but weren't giving away any details.

Decorators from a design studio in Cancun had spent two days creating Christmas splendor in the restaurant. A towering tree that reached the twenty-foot ceiling shimmered in gold and white. Not a millimeter of bare branch showed through the hundreds of bows and ornaments on its limbs. Garlands of white and gold ribbons adorned the walls and doors of the dining room.

I still had to confirm details for a jewelry show with a jeweler from Mexico City and to talk with the pastry chef from Cancun who was going to demonstrate tortilla making on one of the nights. I needed my computer for the contracts, but it was still not working. I had told Molly about Javier on the phone when she was in Miami, and she had assured me that Luis Felipe would handle Javier when he got home. He was going to move him off the ranch and give him a job in Cancun, but that hadn't happened yet, and as long as he was still there, he was the computer guy to go to. I mentioned the problem I was still having with him to Luis Felipe and he brushed me off. I brought it up a second time, in passing, because Luis Felipe was never available to sit down with me to talk. The third time, Luis Felipe exploded in a torrent of rage.

"Can't you think of anything else? It's almost Christmas week!" And then he stormed off, and I had my answer.

On December 24th, Carla and I waited at the entrance for the first of the Christmas week guests to arrive.

"Welcome home!" she said warmly to one of the couples she recognized. A waiter handed them each a Torbellino cocktail, a first sip of the magic that waited to enchant them.

By dusk, all of the guests had checked in. On the walkway of the inner courtyard, a group of workers gathered, wearing new, brightly colored uniforms. They lined up by department and silently stood waiting to begin the opening processional until it was nearly dark. Carla and I passed out battery-operated candles, and on cue, the workers started singing a villancico de Navidad, a traditional Mexican Christmas tune. Guests spilled out of their rooms onto their balconies to watch the procession as it glided slowly around the courtyard, the parading employees' faces illuminated in the white glow of their candles. I forgot about Luis Felipe and whether or not he and the people who worked for him were crooks, forgot about my own inadequacies. I was overwhelmed by the beauty of the procession and the pride I felt in the employees.

When they processed back to where they had begun, they shouted, "Felix Navidad!" Torbellino's holiday season had officially begun. I was busy every day that week checking on details and attending the events I'd planned for the guests. At the Mayan dance performance, held under the roof of one of the outdoor patios, I saw Luis Felipe's scowling face, but I was finally beyond caring what he thought. I knew nothing I could do would ever please him, and I wondered if he'd hired me counting on the fact that I wouldn't succeed and could be replaced, preferably with a male director, once they were home. He had warned me in one of our brief conversations the night before they took off for Miami that being a woman would be my biggest challenge. The sexist attitude toward women was his. Certainly Molly never challenged this. She kept to her place.

After the dance performance, Amador came to find me.

"Would you come with me, Señora?" I followed him to the kitchen, worried that some problem had come up with the staff, but that wasn't it at all.

He flashed his gold tooth smile and handed me a large white box of Cocoa Creme chocolates tied with an extravagant red velvet ribbon.

"Felix Navidad to you, Señora,"

"This was lovely of you, Amador." It was an unusual gesture and it confused me, until he said, "It is from my family. Thank you for what you have done for us, for my daughter."

Little things matter, a hand reached out in kindness

when someone is suffering. There was so much I couldn't achieve in my year at Torbellino. I hadn't rescued the staff. I hadn't been the manager I thought they deserved. I hadn't stopped illegal activity from happening or reduced discrimination against Mayans or the underclass workers. The hotel would go on just as it had before I came. But I had done some things right while I was there, one human being to another, and that kindness had been returned by individuals. The year had changed me. I would leave knowing more of who I was at fifty four years of age and who I would never be. Friendship was not a contractual arrangement, a relationship easily won. Trusting, loving, enjoying the gifts of this world together was the closest to heaven that I would get.

One of the guests with us for Christmas week owned a hotel in Merida and told me she raised black labs on the side. She showed me a picture of one of her dams who'd just given birth to a litter of eight pups. When I said how adorable they were, and that I missed having a dog, she asked if I'd like to have one from that litter. The puppies were just about seven weeks old, and by the end of the week, they'd be ready to leave their mother. The woman said she'd be happy to have someone bring the puppy to Torbellino if I couldn't go to Merida to pick it up myself. I told her I'd think about it and let her know.

The photo of the puppies was irresistible. I hadn't had a dog since my beloved golden retriever, Ginger, died a few years before my move to Mexico. With all the traveling I did for work at the time, it wasn't practical for me to get a new puppy, especially since Mike didn't like dogs and we were living together. But I didn't have to think about what Mike wanted anymore. A puppy would make a great companion for the rest of the time I'd be at Torbellino. With all the tile floors in my house, training would be easy. I did some research and found out I wouldn't have to quarantine the pup when I returned to the US if I had a record from a vet of all its shots.

"I'd love to have one of your puppies, if the offer's still good," I told the breeder at the end of her stay. "I don't care if it's male or female, just as long as it's healthy."

"Our dogs are purebred English labs from good lines. Normally we charge $700.00 for a puppy, but we'll sell one to you for $450.00"

"I'd appreciate that," I said. I didn't care if it was pure-bred, I just wanted a dog that would be a good companion.

"I'll bring one to you with registration papers and records from the vet."

I could hardly wait.

The morning of New Year's eve and after the last guest had finished breakfast, everyone was told the restaurant would be off limits for the rest of the day and lunch would be served on the beach, adding to the anticipation of the evening's festivities.

I had heard nothing from Molly about joining them for the New Year's Eve party, but I wasn't surprised. I wasn't looking forward to it, but I was expected. I changed into a cocktail dress before heading back to the hotel. The dining room had been transformed into a forest of pink and purple. Mylar streamers were intertwined with pink and purple balloons hung from every square inch of the soaring arched white stucco ceiling. The streamers dangled low over the heads of the dinner guests.

Amador showed me to the place that had been reserved for me to the right of Charles. Alexa sat next to him, wearing a long fishnet dress she'd made out of a shower curtain. Gaspard and his girlfriend were seated next to Charles. Two of the hotel guests, the Richardsons, were to my right. I spotted Molly and Luis Felipe at a table in the center of the room sitting with a silver-haired man I'd been introduced to several times, a friend of theirs from New York. I couldn't help but feel a pang of envy, wishing I'd been invited to join them.

Charles and Alexa were already slurring their words when I sat down at the table. It was still early and the party had just gotten started. Charles leaned over to whisper to me that Alan Richardson, the stranger next to me, was a muckety-muck from *The Washington Post*.

"I'm Julie Heifetz. It's nice to meet you."

"Ah, yes, Julie. Do I understand correctly that you own one of the houses on the property here?"

"Yes, I do."

"We asked Charles if there were anything for sale because we love Torbellino. We've been here many times. My husband always feels much better when we're here in this climate. We were disappointed to hear nothing's for sale."

"I told him that," Charles said, tipping his glass to get the last swallow of champagne.

"Are you just curious about the houses or are you looking to buy?"

"Oh no. We're wanting to buy. We want to get out of D.C. as soon as we can, now that Alan's retired."

"Why don't you stop by my place? I'd love to show you it to you," I suggested quietly to Anne Richardson. My back was to Charles. He was talking with Alexa as she poured him another glass of Dom Pérignon Brut and didn't hear me.

"That would be wonderful. Would two o'clock tomorrow be okay?"

"It's a date," I said. The waiters brought dinner and everyone's attention turned to eating. I couldn't believe my luck to have been seated where I was. The Richardsons might make the perfect buyers for my house. I'd have to come up with a price before they got there to see it. Just before dessert, Anne Richardson stood up.

"I'm sorry we have to leave so early. Alan doesn't do well in crowds." She walked over to Alan and leaned down to help steady him as he got up from the table.

"I'm glad we had a chance to meet," I said and watched as the two walked slowly arm in arm out of the restaurant.

"The guy's got bad emphysema," Charles explained. "He can't get from the restaurant to his room without stopping a couple of times to catch his breath. His wife thinks the air here would be good for him."

My mind was running laps around me. If the Richardsons wanted to buy my house, I'd have to talk with Luis Felipe and get him to agree since he owned the land the house was on. If he refused and tried to stop me from selling, I'd tell the Richardsons all that I suspected about Luis Felipe. That would be a story Alan just might pass on to his contacts at *The Washington Post*. Luis Felipe wouldn't want that, which would give me leverage to make him agree to the sale. When I finished one glass of champagne, I told our waiter no more. I was feeling high without alcohol from having found a potential buyer.

As soon as dessert was over, there was an explosion of music, as a Mariachi band appeared in the restaurant wearing red and black charro suits, serenading the diners with a rendition of Mujeres Divinas, a song about and dedicated to all the beautiful, divine women of the world. The room vibrated with sound as diners stood to watch and clap along with the musicians. At the end of the second song, a curtain of mylar streamers parted behind them, revealing the new addition to the dining room. The anfitrionas herded everyone into the new space to continue the celebration. Five enormous screens had been fastened high onto the rounded walls of the new room, each screen with a televised New Year's Eve celebration coming from five different cities around the world; New York, Beijing, Mexico City, Cairo, and Tokyo. A large digital clock suspended from the middle of the ceiling clicked off the minutes and seconds left until midnight on the ranch ushered in a new century.

The world beyond Torbellino fretted over a potential catastrophe of computers going haywire when the century changed, but not at the resort. People worried only about spilling their drinks as they stomped and swayed to the music, undulating shoulder to shoulder. After a few more selections, the Mariachi band disappeared and were replaced by pop music through the loud speakers. In the middle of the room, Amador, who had been serving cocktails, took off his black waiter's jacket and started dancing in his shirt sleeves with one of the female guests. The perspiration glistened on his face as he stunned the audience who had stepped aside to give him room for his athletic graceful moves. More people joined in. It was hot and crowded. I stood staring at the television screens for a while but ducked out just before midnight, hoping no one would notice.

It was a relief to get outside into the night air, away from the televisions, the crowd, and the thumping music. The sky sparkled clear and bright. We had made it to the first moments of a whole new century. Luis Felipe had survived. So had Torbellino. And so had I.

I walked slowly back to my house, undressed, put on my

nightgown, and crawled into bed. I thought about what to name the puppy the woman had promised me, hoping that the Richardson's would show up the next day and fall in love with my house. The last time I checked before I fell asleep, it was two a.m.

I woke with voices over me, calling, "Julie, Julie! Get up!" and someone grabbing me by the arm, trying to drag me out of bed. My eyes flew open as I tried to focus in the dim light of nearly day. It was Charles and Alexa. I'd forgotten to lock my door.

"Get up! Get up! They're here! Come see!" They were staggering drunk.

"They're on the beach! Come with us!"

It would be safer to go with them than to resist and have them keep tugging on my arm. I couldn't imagine why they'd come for me in the middle of the night and why they sounded so excited and insistent, as if the whole world were on fire. Barefoot in my nightgown, with Charles gripping my hand like a zombie, the three of us hurtled to the beach and down toward the water's edge.

"There it is!" Alexa yelled stopping in her tracks, pointing out over the water.

"What? There what is?" I asked, dumbfounded. I could see nothing but water and the grey horizon in the mist.

"Don't you see that light?" Charles shouted over the sound of the wind and the waves, his face glowing with excitement.

I looked again out over the water, trying to see what they were seeing that was so remarkable.

"It's the people from outer space. They've come back to Torbellino. Don't you see how that light over the water doesn't move, it just stays bobbing up and down? It's the light from their space ship. They're here! I knew they'd come back!"

As my eyes adjusted to the night sky, I could see a small light moving slightly up and down, hovering low over the water. But it was no light from spaceship, it was a light at the top of the mast of a sailboat that was bobbing on the waves.

"It's a sailboat, Charles," I explained, but he was too far gone to listen.

"No! They've come back! You'll see." They shouted as they ran frantically down the beach, their eyes fastened on the light over the water. Each of us was certain of what we had seen and believed, clear reflections of who we were as individuals. Charles and Alexa would stay at Torbellino long after I had gone. They belonged, and I most decidedly did not.

CHAPTER TWENTY-EIGHT

The last day of the Christmas week, I was walking in the courtyard of the hotel when a woman came towards me carrying a tiny black bundle under her arm. As she got closer, I could see four black paws hanging down against her side and a soft furry black body snuggled comfortably against her chest. I could hardly make out the puppy's eyes from the rest of her face she was so black all over.

"Hi, Julie. I have something for you," the woman said. "I asked someone who works for us to bring your dog this morning."

"I didn't know she was coming today! What a wonderful surprise! Thank you for bringing her to me. Hello, puppy," I said as I folded her into my arms. A pink tongue licked my hand. She looked up at me with soft brown eyes that locked with mine. I swear, she already knew, somehow, she belonged with me.

"What will you call her?"

"Roo," I said without pause. I'd been thinking of a name ever since I'd been known she'd be coming.

"Roo?"

"This is the state of Quintana Roo, right? And Roo is also a name of a character in Winnie the Pooh, which is a book I loved as a child. So Roo's the perfect name."

"Well, Roo, you will be happy here. But I've got to get back to Merida now. We've been at Torbellino all week and we're never away this long. We have a guest coming for dinner tonight," the woman said, as she watched the puppy settle into my arms. "I brought some food for her. It'll be enough for a few days until you get your own supply. She's a very good girl. She's already nearly housebroken."

"Thank you so much. She's adorable. I have your money at home if you'll come with me."

"She deserves a good home," she smiled.

We walked to my house and I handed my new puppy to the breeder to hold as I went to get the envelope I had waiting for her. After I got Roo inside, I sat on the floor holding her, savoring her warmth until she started wriggling, wanting to get down. I took out a little dish from my cabinet and filled it with water, then put some food in another dish and set the dishes on the kitchen floor. Roo scurried right over to the bowl of puppy food and stuck her nose all the way into it. She didn't just eat the food, she vacuumed it up so quickly the little pellets were flying out of her bowl, landing all over the kitchen floor. I wondered how much actually made it into her belly.

"Take it easy, Roo, there's more where that came from."

I scooped her up and took her out into the front yard. "Go potty," I said, and just like that, she squatted and peed.

"Good girl." I patted her, picked her up, and took her inside. She sniffed around the kitchen, exploring until she found a spot she liked next to the center island, circled once, lay down, closed her eyes, and was out. There was nothing I wanted to do but watch her as she slept.

I didn't know how long I'd been sitting there with her before there was a knock at the door. *Crap*, I thought. Who is it now?

"Hello, Julie? Anne Richardson here."

Ann Richardson? I glanced at my watch. It was two o'clock and I'd been so absorbed watching Roo's soft, sweet sleep I'd forgotten my appointment to show the house.

"Please, come in. Isn't your husband with you?"

"Alan really isn't able to walk this far so it's just me. But I can tell him about it later."

She looked around the arched entryway, her eyes landing on Roo curled up on the living room floor asleep.

"Oh, look at that darling puppy!"

"I'm afraid she doesn't come with the house," I said. "We'll leave her here while I show you around."

Taking her on a tour of the first floor and then upstairs to see the bedrooms, I felt so proud of the sparkling marble tile, the soaring ceilings, the round bedroom in the trees, the view from the third floor that looked out over blossoming hibiscus and bodacious bougainvillea. A wave of grief came over me at the thought of actually leaving it all.

"It's perfect," she said when she'd seen the whole house. "I can't imagine why you'd want to sell. Is it really on the market?"

"Not yet but I've been thinking about it. It's been my dream house."

"How much will you sell it for?"

"I'm not sure yet. Can I get back to you? When are you leaving?"

"We'll be here for a few more days. The airport in D.C.

is going to be a zoo with everybody getting back from Christmas vacation."

"I'll get in touch before you leave."

I needed to get the money back that I'd invested in the house and the renovations, plus what I would have made if the money had been invested. I had to talk with Luis Felipe to tell him I intended to sell before I got back to the Richardson's, and I prayed he'd be reasonable. I thought about the joy that the house had given me before I went to work for the hotel, the dinner company I'd never had since that time, the bedrooms where my children had never stayed because I'd been too overwhelmed, too busy running myself ragged to have them there. All for what? I picked up Roo and held her warmth against me, burying my face in her soft fur to stifle a sob.

By the end of the day, after most of the hotel guests had checked out, Luis Felipe called a meeting of the managers. We were all exhausted. I thought the meeting would be to congratulate and thank everyone for a job well done, but as soon as we had taken our seats in the little theater, he turned to me and demanded to know how much money Torbellino brought in each day on an average and what our expenses came to. I was shocked and stared at him in dumb silence. I didn't know the answers and he knew I didn't.

"You said I should leave the money matters to Alejandro," I objected feebly.

"A Director of a hotel ought to know," he said accusingly.

"I'm sure you're right."

"Sergei, can you tell me how much Torbellino brings in every day?"

Sergei answered crisply, providing the numbers he had asked for. It was a set up. The entire meeting had been designed to humiliate me. The meeting moved on to other matters, but I didn't hear a word of it. I was the first one out of the Little Theater.

Jimmy caught up to me as I hurried away. "Do you know why Luis Felipe did that?"

"Because he's an ass?"

"No, it's because since the day he came home, Carla and Gerardo have been telling him all kinds of shit about you that isn't true. I warned you that Carla's out to get you."

Whatever she said or did, Carla couldn't hurt me anymore. I had a buyer who was interested in my house and a job waiting for me in Philadelphia. I'd keep to myself and take care of Roo until I sold my house and could get away from the ranch for good.

$\mathcal{T}$he next day, after most of the Christmas week guests had checked out, there was a knock at my front door.

"Quién es?"

"Un mensajero."

I didn't answer. A messenger? I trusted no one to be who he said he was.

"Señora." There was another insistent knock. "Señora, por favor. Tengo una invitación para usted."

"Una invitación?" I asked through the closed door, afraid to open it.

"Si. De Carla et las anfitrionas." An invitation from the guest services department?

A slightly built man from the maintenance department stood with an envelope in his hand with my name beautifully scripted in calligraphy. I opened the door and took the invitation. "Momentito," I said as I read the invitation to an employees' party at the Little Theater that night at six o'clock. Who were they kidding? Did they really expect me to come after the insulting way I'd been treated the day before? Maybe Luis Felipe and Molly wanted to show there were no hard feelings, that they weren't angry anymore, but I was done with all of them.

I got a pen and wrote on the envelope, "Thanks for the invitation, but I just got a new puppy and I need to stay home with her. Enjoy the party."

I was up most of that night with Roo, waiting for morning when I could go talk to Luis Felipe about selling my house. I hadn't told him or Molly I'd be coming. I was afraid he'd be away from the house if he knew when I'd be there.

I walked down the beach and up the stone path to the courtyard, my stomach churning. The parrots' cage sat perched on the ledge of the wall as usual, the birds quiet under their cover from the night before. Morning sun streamed through the skylight into the dining room. Lulu came scampering through the open kitchen door and ran over to greet me with her tail wagging, stopping to sniff Roo's unfamiliar puppy scent on my leg. The house was as it had been the last time I'd visited, yet everything for me had changed.

Molly followed Lulu onto the patio looking startled when she saw me.

"Hi, Julie, is everything OK?"

"Everything's fine. I hope it's not too early, but I wanted to make sure to catch you and Luis Felipe before you went anywhere this morning."

"We missed you at the party yesterday."

"I just got a new puppy so I stayed home to help her get adjusted."

"That's what your note said. I thought maybe you'd show up later."

I nodded. "It must be nice being home again, getting back to normal."

"It is. I was just making coffee. Can I get you a cup?"

"That's OK, I've been up for hours. I already had breakfast, but I'll sit down with you while you have yours."

She carried her coffee cup outside and we sat down at the dining table.

"Luis Felipe will be downstairs in a minute. We slept later than usual. We're still recovering from the party yesterday and New Year's Eve."

"That was an incredible way to celebrate the new year."

"We were so pleased with the way the new addition to the dining room worked out. They just finished it in time to get it ready for the party. Did you see our friend Jeffrey on New Year's Eve? He was sitting at our table with us."

"I did. From a distance. Why?"

"I guess he had too good a time at the party. He stayed really late, but around two he said he was supposed to meet some woman in Cancun and he borrowed our car. Before he got off the property, he hit a tree and totaled it. The maintenance guys had to go lift the car off the road."

"He wasn't hurt?"

"No, only the car."

"He was lucky."

"You sure I can't get you some coffee?"

"I'm sure, thanks. I won't stay too long. I know you have things to do."

She ducked back into the kitchen. I smelled his cologne before I saw him.

"Good morning, Luis Felipe." I hadn't seen him since the managers' meeting and I dreaded talking with him now. I wished I could tell him what I thought of him, but I had too much at stake. I didn't want this to turn into a confrontation. Our friendship was dead to me, the body barely warm.

"You've come to take breakfast with us?" he asked, coming to sit at his place at the table.

"No, I have some news I wanted to talk with you about."

"Oh?"

"Yes. I've been offered a job in Philadelphia at a hospital as writer-in-residence, and I'm excited about it. You're home now and I've been here almost a year. It's time for me to go back to the States."

"You're leaving us? But, why are you leaving? You don't like us anymore?" There was a suspicious edge to his voice. "If you don't want to be Director, we will find another job for you." One reason came to mind as to why he would try to convince me to stay: he was worried that I might know too much and tell that to the authorities if I left.

"Thank you, but I need to get back to doing the kind of work I'm meant to do, using stories to help patients heal. I did that before I moved here and I miss it."

"But, you have a house here. You moved here to stay."

"Yes, that's what I want to talk with you about. Alan Richardson, the editor from *The Washington Post*, and his wife want to buy it. We haven't talked price yet. I needed to talk to you first about selling, but they're waiting to hear from me. He and his wife would like to make a deal as soon as possible."

"But you are part of the Torbellino Family." His eyes narrowed and a chill ran through me. *Part of The Family.* Did that mean I couldn't leave the way the Mafia meant it? My hands were clammy and I was starting to feel claustrophobic even though the dining room only had three walls.

"Luis Felipe, she wants to go home," Molly said quietly. It was the first time I had heard her weigh in with her own opinion about anything that countered her husband's. Eliseo had been right when he said that Molly was my friend. Luis Felipe reached down and patted Samantha absent-mindedly.

"People move on, and we have to let her," she said earnestly. I held my breath while he sat without saying anything to either of us. Time lay heavy in the air while I waited.

"What do you want for your house, Julie?"

"Enough to make a profit, and more than I'd have earned if I'd invested the money in the stock market this past year."

"If you are sure this is what you want, and Molly says it is OK, you will go to your stories in Philadelphia and I will buy your house for what you say you want. But I'll deal with the Richardsons."

I knew he'd sell it for far more than he was going to pay me, but I didn't care. I'd be free to go and I wouldn't be losing money in the deal.

"And when could I get my share?"

"As soon as the Richardsons pay me. Molly will deposit the money in your bank when we have it."

She'd been depositing my paycheck in my bank all year, and I trusted her to do the same with the check from the sale. I wouldn't have to wait until the deal was finished with the Richardsons. I could go to Philadelphia whenever I was ready. I made a plane reservation for February first, knowing I'd hire a lawyer in the States if there was any problem collecting.

Every day after that until the day of my flight, I went to the office and made my rounds of the dining room every evening. The hotel filled up again with guests. Roo followed me everywhere, charming everyone. Having her to take care of grounded me, and I felt more wholly myself.

Judy, a friend from St. Louis, called to say she was planning to come to Torbellino with her husband for a vacation and would be there on Valentine's Day.

"Oh Judy, I'm so sorry, I'm not going to be here then. I'll be moving to Philadelphia on the first of February."

"Oh, I'm so disappointed. All the articles in the travel magazines rave about the place and I was looking forward to seeing you. How come you're leaving?"

"It's complicated. I'll explain it one day." I didn't want to spoil their vacation by telling her what she as a guest didn't need to know.

"We should have come sooner to visit, but I thought you were going to be there permanently."

"I thought so too. But I'll tell you what, the house I own on the property will still be mine when you get here. Why don't you come and stay at my house? You can still use all the facilities at the hotel, and it would save you a ton of money."

"That would be fantastic if we could! If I can do anything for you when we're there you can just let me know."

Over the next few weeks, I packed all of my personal belongings and bought a travel case for Roo. All the furniture and the fully stocked kitchen would stay with the house. I tried not to feel sad, but more like I was passing on a gift I had been given and loved but outgrown, one that I could never forget, even if I tried.

I didn't see Molly to tell her goodbye. I think she was avoiding me as much as I was avoiding her. Eliseo and Sebastiana knew I was leaving because they could see I was packing, but I hadn't had the heart to admit to them that it would be forever. When the cab pulled up, they were outside to hug me and wave goodbye. I could hardly look at them. Maybe one day I would send them a plane ticket and they could come to Philadelphia to visit or I'd come back to see them in Puerto Morelos where they had bought a plot of land. Little by little they were building a house with the money they saved from each month's salary. I was sure the Richardsons would be glad to have them continue taking care of the house once they owned it.

I never told the staff that I was going, although they probably had wind of it somehow. I just disappeared, which was a very Mexican way to leave.

When the plane broke through the clouds and the wheels touched down on the tarmac in Philadelphia, I wanted to leap over the other passengers and be the first one out of the plane. I felt like kissing the ground of Philadelphia, the City of Brotherly Love.

CHAPTER THIRTY

*I*t was a few days after Valentine's Day when I thought about calling my friend Judy on her vacation at El Torbellino.

"It's Julie Heifetz. I'm calling from Philadelphia to try to reach someone staying in my house," I said to the woman who answered the office phone.

"Oh, Julie," she said excitedly. "It's Abril. I'm so glad to hear from you. I never got to say goodbye to you before you left. I miss you."

"Oh, Abril. I'm sorry I didn't see you before I took off. I hope you're doing well. Listen, I'm calling now because my friend Judy is staying at my house this week. Could you please find her and ask her to call me back?"

"Judy? I think she and her husband are having lunch at the restaurant now. I saw a young American couple on the patio a few minutes ago when I walked by. Would you like me to call and see if she's there?"

"Yes, please."

"Just a minute. I'll transfer you."

She clicked off, and soon, Judy's voice was on the other end of the line.

"Julie? I'm so glad you called! Your house is amazing!" she raved. "I can't believe you're leaving this. It's paradise here. I'm so sad our vacation's over tomorrow."

"I meant to call sooner, but with my new job and getting settled here the time got away from me."

"Say, listen, I'm at the restaurant. Somebody here wants to say hello."

"Señora Julie?" He didn't need to say who he was. I would have recognized his voice anywhere. It was Eliseo, warm and bright as the sun in the Yucatan.

I tried to speak, but I started to cry instead, softly at first, but my tears gathered speed as the flood gates opened. I wanted to tell Eliseo how grateful I was to him for protecting me, for caring. I wanted him to know that. He waited patiently for me to say something, but all I could do was cry. The sorrow and disappointment that I'd never expressed had built up over the last year. Now, my frustration, anger, loneliness, and love came pouring out into the cellphone in helpless sobs. Only when I heard his voice did I realize that I would never see him again.

"Te amo, Señora," he whispered.

Te amo I wanted to say. I love you, too, but he was gone. I sat for a long time holding the phone in my hand, not ready to hang up, not ready to sever a connection with him or with that strange and complicated year, or with my house, or with my friendship with Molly. Some part of me still lived at Torbellino.

Work at the hospital was my salvation. The patients at MossRehab and their families fought so hard to climb their way back from brain trauma or spinal cord injury to reclaim their lives, and I loved working with them. Watching

311

someone come out of a month-long coma and learn to walk or speak again renewed my faith in possibilities and inspired me. Most of those that didn't recover somehow found the courage to continue on. Resilience was the watchword of their faith. At night, when the frogs in the woods behind my rented carriage house started their polyphonic song, I would forget where I was and think I was back in the jungle again.

It took a while for the check from the sale of my house to show up in my bank account. It was an enormous relief when it did. I thought my questions about Luis Felipe had ended. One evening after work, I was sitting in my carriage house when my cell phone rang.

"Hello, Julie," the woman's voice on the other end said when I answered. "This is Susan Picard. I own one of the houses on Luis Felipe's property. We met a few times when I was walking my poodles on the beach."

"Oh yes, I remember." I couldn't imagine why she was calling.

"I live in Philadelphia when I'm not at my house in Mexico. Molly said you were here now too, and she gave me your number."

"It's a surprise hearing from you."

"I know. Have you heard from Molly lately?"

"No, not for several months."

"I thought not. You might want to know what's happened there," Susan said, in her aristocratic Philadelphia accent.

"Tell me."

"Well, I happened to be at the hotel one day when some police came looking for Luis Felipe. He was in the restaurant where I was having lunch and they took him out in handcuffs. They put him in their patrol car and drove off with him. Everybody saw it happen. It was very upsetting, as you can imagine, especially for Molly. I thought you might want to give her a call. I know you've been friends for years."

"All right. Yes, I will. Thanks for letting me know, Susan."

I was shaking when we hung up. Luis Felipe was finally being held accountable for whatever he'd done and I felt some satisfaction in knowing my suspicions were justified. But I felt terrible for Molly. It must have been such a shock, seeing him taken away in handcuffs for crimes she probably knew nothing about. I emailed her without mentioning that Susan had called, hoping she'd tell me what had happened and why. I told her that the ceramic bowl she had given me had made the trip safely to my kitchen counter in Philadelphia and I used it every day, that Roo was fine, and that my job was going well. I asked how she and Luis Felipe were doing. I didn't know if she'd even answer. And then I got a message back.

> "Hi, Julie,
>
> I'm OK now, but we've had a little trouble here lately. One day, some bad men with guns took Luis Felipe to Guadalajara, where they kept him sequestered for six weeks. He's home now, and he's all right. We're starting to be able to put all that trouble behind us, but it was a very frightening time.
>
> Thanks for asking about us. I hope you're well. Do stay in touch.
>
> Love,
> Molly

I would have liked to believe Molly, that the men who came to take Luis Felipe away were "bad men" and that he

313

was innocent, perhaps the victim of a change in political leadership for the country. Maybe the jungle had distorted my ability to distinguish truth from chisme. Maybe he was simply a terrible manager and no criminal at all. Certainly he was no friend to me.

Molly and I stayed in touch by email every so often over the next few years until my email was hacked and I changed my email address and lost all of my contacts. She had no idea how to reach me. Through information on the web, I learned when they sold Torbellino, probably for muchos dineros. Over the years, I checked from time to time to see if I could find a phone number for her. People Search listed her as living in Miami, but by then, no one had landlines and cell numbers weren't given. I was sure they still owned their house in Mexico. Eventually I gave up trying to locate her. I was content, instead, just to think of her walking the beach at sunrise, barefoot with Lulu or a new beloved dog, just as we had walked together, with the sea breeze blowing through her fine hair.

EPILOGUE

*I*n May of 2020, when I had almost finished writing this book, Molly was so much in my thoughts that I tried again to find her. I put her name in People Search and a lovely pink page popped up on my computer screen. There was her name and the date of her birth and her death, April 17, 2020. The obituary was from a funeral home in Miami, but it gave no further information. It took hours for me to believe that this was the right Molly, my Molly. She was two years younger than me, which meant she was seventy-one, which seemed too young for her to have died. She had always looked youthful and vibrant and had no health issues that I knew of when we were last in touch. But that was fifteen years ago. Now, we were in the midst of a global pandemic, and coronavirus was the cause of death that occurred to me, but that seemed so unlikely. She had died only three weeks before I tried to find her phone number.

I called the hotel to ask if they knew what had happened to her, even though she and Luis Felipe no longer owned it. Torbellino was closed because of the pandemic. I searched my brain for anyone I might try to reach who might know her. Susan Picard had moved from Philadelphia to Florida and had no landline to call. After several days, I came up with her sister's name. She owned a newspaper in Missouri and I was able to reach her there. She told me Molly had died of cancer after many years of surgeries and a variety of treatments. She weighed seventy-nine pounds at the end.

I feel such a loss knowing she isn't here. I had counted her as my friend for more than thirty years when I moved to Mexico, but it turned out I didn't really know her at all. Our friends are the illusions we create of them, what we need them to be. Whatever Luis Felipe was or wasn't stopped mattering so much long ago.

Without Molly, there would have been no temple of unsurpassed beauty between sea and jungle, earth and sky. Luis Felipe was her Pygmalion. He gave her a life that she would never have known without him and he shaped the woman she became. I have to think she was happy with her choice.

I am grateful to them both for the experience they gave me; for my white stucco house with the bougainvillea tree blossoming outside my window; for the swarm of black butterflies that followed me down the path through the jungle like onyx snow falling from an azure sky; for exposure to the Mayan culture; for the chance to have met Eliseo and Sebastiana; for the hand-carved two-mile road I walked at midnight under the full moon and the starry Yucatecan sky. When I came back to the States after my year in what had once seemed like paradise, I no longer felt apologetic for the person I was or the life I had chosen to lead.

Dear reader,

We hope you enjoyed reading *As Far As the I Can See*. Please take a moment to leave a review, even if it's a short one. Your opinion is important to us.

Discover more books Julie Heifetz at
https://www.nextchapter.pub/authors/julie-heifetz

Want to know when one of our books is free or discounted? Join the newsletter at http://eepurl.com/bqqB3H

Best regards,
Julie Heifetz and the Next Chapter Team

Lightning Source UK Ltd.
Milton Keynes UK
UKHW021906230421
382536UK00010B/498/J